The Department for Lost Souls

By
Geezah Gobble

A bird sitting in a tree is not afraid of the branch breaking, because their trust is not in the branch, but in their own wings.

– Charlie Wardle

THANK YOU…

I want to thank the following people who created characters at different Departments within the Department for Lost Souls; you took my world and created something special.

Rayven - @Rayven_eclypse
Julia - @mysirensdream
Courtney - @Psychospear
Lawrence - @MannyP7565
Laura - @Laura_h440
Lisa - @FlyTheNerdFlag
Carolyn - @Porkbritches
Dakota - @Midnight_Belladonna
Tamlin - @they_them_their_grace
Megan - @massagepro2021

Thank you to Stormy. As my beta reader, this is ALL your fault…

And lastly, thank you to Jamie Blake, who without which, Gladys and their wonky brow truly wouldn't exist.

A NOTE FROM GEEZAH...

Hello my lovelies! What a journey it has been to get to this point. When I created Gladys in 2021 to bring some laughter into my own life, I never thought how much of a connection people would have with them. It truly boggles my mind.

Gladys was created to make me smile during a time when it was a struggle to do so. Through the scenarios and skits I made and posted onto TikTok, I found a little bit of comfort watching them back. And so, it appeared, did all of you! I always say that Gladys, first and foremost, is a comedy character. However, through all of your wonderful, touching and heartbreaking comments, messages and emails, Gladys became something bigger. Something I wasn't prepared for, but certainly adapted to. Gladys became a comfort character for a lot of you, and that is something I hold so beloved and close to my heart. I announced that I was writing a book in March of 2022, a whole year after the first ever Gladys video. Mainly because you all really wanted one and I kept putting off the idea because, cards on the table, I'm not a writer. I'm an avid reader, devouring fantasy books one after the other. I write every Gladys video myself, and I've written several stage productions. But a book? That is something for proper writers, right? Suzanne Collins and J. R. R. Tolkien for example! Not me.

So, here it is; The Department for Lost Souls. I've always strived to fight the right fight and give as many people a voice and representation as possible. The world is as beautiful and colorful as the people that cohabit it. I've tried to make that happen within the world of my story. You all deserve to be represented! And that is what I tried to do. If you recognize a small piece of yourself anywhere within these pages, then embrace that. Of course, I cannot fit every single walk of life in a single book. However, perhaps I can fit some more in a sequel! I will advise that there are some key pieces of information scattered throughout this book. Some things that might help you in your day-to-day life, or perhaps a bigger situation you find yourself in, or something personal and private. That is the wonderful thing about books, you can always find useful information in them somewhere, and I sincerely hope that if you find something you can apply to your life from these pages, that it helps you profusely. I wish nothing more than happiness and health for everyone who has connected in some way with Gladys, and to an extent, myself. As much as Gladys may have helped you, they did the same for me.

Something I'm told I do a lot is put others needs and wants ahead of my own. I'll never stop this. So, when I read comments, or get messages and emails, or I'm performing live, and someone walks up to me at an event and opens their heart to tell me their story, how I saved their life, I'm glad you're still here with us all. That you're living, surviving, thriving, being your authentic self. The world, as beautiful as it is, can be horrible and harsh. But you make it a little brighter by being here. Ironically, I created the very person to save me when I needed them, and in turn, it looks like a lot of people needed Gladys as well. I've written something that I am incredibly proud of, it took two years, genuine sleepless nights, a lot of thesaurus searches, even more days of putting it off out of my own fear and doubt of being bad. I even edited the book myself, so if you see a mitsake? No you didn't! And, between you and I, it might be bad. But I had so much fun creating and writing it! Developing an entire book from a character I created has been quite the experience! And if it is bad? Let it be! There are worse things in life than a bad book... Like having a cup of tea but no biscuits to dunk in it. Now THAT is bad!

Essentially what I'm trying to say is thank you. Thank you for embracing who you are, for supporting Gladys, for reading this book!

Gladys will always be here for you, whenever you need them. Be safe, keep on smiling, and be kind to yourself and those around you.

Love, Geezah Gobble x

~ Chapter One ~

GRACE

Grace burst through the front door and bound upstairs to her room, her safe haven. She threw her phone and a pair of jeans down on the bed in frustration and walked over to the mirror, trying to calm down. She pushed her curly hair out of her eyes and stared at her reflection.

"Why won't he answer?" She asked, eyes strained from tears which had long dried up. "Why didn't he tell me where he was going?"

She clenched her fists and looked around the room as if something would stand out to help. Posters of bands on the wall, remnants of her teenage years. Piles of clothes on the floor and bed. Stacks of plushies lined neatly on free floating shelves, staring back at her.

"Maybe he did tell me and I'm being stupid." She whispered to herself. She picked up her phone and scrolled through their message history.

5:31 pm

Grace: *You've been in the weirdest mood all day, what's going on?*

Gabe: *Oh, it's nothing...*

Grace: *See, you're already telling me... please!*

Gabe: *Alright, fine! Well, I've been talking to this guy for a few days and... We're meeting tonight!*

Grace: *Shut the front door! Gabe! That's amazing!*

Gabe: *I didn't say anything in case you didn't approve.*

Grace: *Approve of what?*

Gabe: *Well, talking online, and not telling you sooner.*

Grace: *You should always tell me sooner, but you know me better than anyone. I would support you in everything! If he isn't giving you any bad vibes, then I don't care! As long as he is making you happy!*

Knock-knock-knock.

Someone was at Grace's bedroom door.

"Sweetie, are you okay? You were back late, and you went straight upstairs after work."

"I'm fine mum, just a bad day." Grace sighed. "I just want some alone time. I'll be down in a bit." Annoyed that her train of thought was ruined, she listened to her mum's footsteps disappear downstairs and went back to Gabe's messages.

5:43 pm

Gabe: *Thank you so much, you're the actual best!*

Grace: *I know! So, where are you going? What's the plan?*

Gabe: *We're going to meet in the park (public place, y'know!), get some food, and just walk about, I guess.*

Grace: *Does he know how bad you are at conversation?*

Gabe: *No. But he will! Haha!*

Grace: *Will you let me know you're safe with him and keep me posted on stuff?*

Gabe: *Yeah, of course! If you don't hear from me... I've been kidnapped!*

Grace: *Omg, don't say that! No, you'll be fine. Just stay safe! I wish you had told me sooner! When we're done with work tomorrow, we'll go for a drive, and you can tell me all about it!*

Gabe: *I would love that. Love you! xx*

Grace: *Love you too! xx*

7:57 pm

Gabe: *I'm just waiting on him now! I'm so nervous, it's unreal.*

Grace: *You'll be fine. I hope it goes really well! Be yourself (the best bits anyway!)*

12:46 am

Grace: *Hey, how did the date go? xx*

9:07 am

Grace: *Are you coming into work today? x*

11:10 am

Grace: *Hey, I'm getting worried. You're not at work and Norma said you didn't call in sick today. Please answer asap!*

1:30 pm

Grace: *Gabe, I'm genuinely panicking for you, please let me know you're okay!*

2:28 pm

Grace: *No matter what has happened, I don't care! No questions asked, just let me know you're okay. I'll come get you.*

Why didn't Gabe show up for his shift when he's normally fifteen minutes early, with no sick call? Grace had annoyed her manager all day asking for updates, she even asked to leave early but there was no way they could let her leave, given how busy the restaurant was, so she kept a vigilant eye on the windows outside while she served people.

The park was the only clue she had, and she'd already spent an hour after work searching for him, checking the benches, vendors, and asking complete strangers if anyone had seen him. That's when she decided to check the local coffee shops, Gabe loved his coffee. The three local baristas Gabe was well acquainted with all confirmed that they hadn't seen him that day. There was only one other place he could be…

As Grace approached Gabe's house, she tried her best to not look panicked; if she did, she would have to reveal much more to Gabe's parents than he wanted, and Grace wouldn't do that to him. She straightened up and did her best to tidy her hair before knocking on the door. His mother answered with a whisk in her hand.

"Ah, Grace! You've caught me in the middle of making some coconut cake!" She chuckled. "It's not quite ready or I'd offer you some." Her eyes looked behind Grace, searching for someone. "Is Gabe not with you? He said he'd be at yours after work for a while and might stay the night."

4

Grace's heart sank as the words registered that Gabe wasn't there.

"Yeah, he's not with me, but he sent me over to get some new jeans. He spilt some coffee over them." Grace was shocked at how quickly she came up with the lie.

"Not his precious coffee, how will he survive?" His mum joked. "I'll go get them for you, just a minute."

Grace didn't like telling Gabe's mum a lie. She was a sweet woman with her head in the clouds, not really keeping up with the times, and set in her ways. There wasn't a bad bone in her body, but every time Grace looked at her, she was reminded of the story Gabe told her about a venomous rant she had about homosexuality.

"Against God and nature".

No wonder Gabe lied; Grace *had* to protect him because he wouldn't have a home to go back to if his mum found out.

Gabe's mum handed her a pair of jeans. "They're fresh out the dryer so they'll be perfect after his mishap! Tell him there's no rush home tomorrow, *but* coconut cake will be here!"

"Thank you, I will!" Grace shuffled from the doorstep.

As the door closed, Grace heard operatic singing echo from behind it. She stood still in the darkened doorstep, holding Gabe's clothes, her heart beating faster. None of this helped.

"Am I being stupid? Am I overreacting?" She thought to herself as she walked home, crying silently.

*   *   *

Grace hardly touched her food that night; worried sick for the disappearance of her best friend, and she could do nothing but sit and hope. It was pointless going to the police, they would turn her away since it was under forty-eight hours.

Gabe wasn't the type of person to purposefully find trouble or get himself into bad situations, and he certainly didn't avoid replying to Grace's messages.

When was it time to admit that something bad had happened?

"I'm ready to go. I'm so nervous! How do I look?" Grace's mum said, twirling in her new dress.

Grace rolled over on her bed, admired her mum's new dress, and smiled. "You look amazing!" She had to feign some excitement, enough not to bring the mood down.

Her mum never had a night out, so getting to have one with her workmates really meant more to her than it would anyone else. "Thank you!" She said primping her hair. "Oh, just my lipstick and then I'm out! I'll be home late. Will you be okay tonight?"

Grace wondered if it was a good time to mention the situation with Gabe. She knew her mum would drop absolutely everything and help look for him, but that would mean involving Gabe's mum and then revealing everything about him in general, and Grace couldn't do that in his absence. He trusted her with that information. Grace bit her lip. No, she wouldn't tell her mum until it was time to involve the police as well.

"I'll be fine! I've got some shows to catch up on, and I have snacks!" Grace said. Her mum smiled with excitement and went back to her room to finish up.

Grace put her phone on her bedside table and turned on the TV; a blonde anchor woman with a painful smile began talking about the weather. Grace lay on her back and let her mind go numb from the background noise, now realising how tired she was from all the stress of the day. As the anchor woman pointed at a map, mumbling about the temperature for the next few days, Grace's eyes got heavier and heavier, feeling the room drift away when-

BUZZ.

Grace's eyes bolted open instantly. She heard something but had no idea what it was. The TV was now showing an old action movie with lots of explosions in a city-
BUZZ.

Her phone! It was a message.

"Please, please, please be Gabe!" She begged.

It was.

00:21 am

Gabe: *GRACE WAREHOUSE LOCATION ON HELP!*

*   *   *

Grace was instantly wide awake, filled with adrenaline. Finally, she'd heard back from Gabe. Tears began to fill her eyes, but she had to focus; there was no time for relief. This was a loaded message and she needed to act fast.

She checked the location app on her phone and searched for Gabe. She'd tried earlier but it only told her where he was last seen, which was at the park. This time his profile picture pinged and shot the map over to an old warehouse on the pier.

Why? How?

She dismissed the questions; she truly couldn't care less about ever getting an answer to them, she just wanted Gabe to be safe.

"Mum!" She shouted urgently. There was no reply, but as she got out of bed, she noticed the time. She grabbed an oversized brown jumper from the floor and put on her white running shoes. Somehow, she'd managed to sleep for hours, and it was past midnight. That meant her mum was still out, and she was drinking with workmates…which meant the car was still here with the keys! Grace's eyes widened in realisation as she said out loud "I can get him!"

As she ran downstairs, she noticed the note on the kitchen worktop from her mum.

"You were out for the count. I've left money for food if you want a treat. I'll be back late. Love you, darling!"

Grace grabbed the money and the car keys and ran out of the house to the car. She brought the location app back up on her phone and sat it on the passenger seat.

As Grace took off, speeding down the road, she thought about the words in the message Gabe had sent. He likely only had time for one message, and he chose her. It didn't matter what he got himself into, or what situation someone put him in, he was in trouble, and she was coming to help.

"Help…" She mouthed to herself while driving down the darkened streets. She'd only ever heard the word when it was at work, or from her mum around the house. This was a different kind of help. Its heaviness really weighed on her shoulders; she was responsible for someone else's life. As the orange streetlights flashed overhead in rhythm, her stomach turned over trying to imagine what sort of danger he was in, and before tears clouded her vision, she arrived at the pier.

As she parked outside the entry gates, she felt the bitter cold among the dark emptiness in front of her. Despite being near the sea, it was surprisingly quiet this late at night. She grabbed her phone and closed the car door. She needed to work out which one of these warehouses Gabe was in, or at least, which one his phone was in.

As Grace crept around the pier, she kept her wits about her, tiptoeing over puddles and keeping her phone brightness to a minimum. She peered at the screen gently and noticed Gabe's location was coming from warehouse three.

As she got to the large door, she noticed it was slightly ajar. She pulled on it and let its heavy weight swing open the rest of the way, and tentatively stepped inside.

The air was thick, surprisingly dry, and stale, as if it hadn't been used in centuries. The space was filled with wooden boxes and crates of varying shapes and sizes, stacked as far as Grace could see. It felt like a maze. She stayed close to the wall, keeping as quiet as possible. A dim moonbeam appeared through an overhead window and illuminated a decorated container at the back of the warehouse. In her gut it felt like the right place to check, better than going through countless boxes. As she approached the container door, it came into focus and revealed itself to be a makeshift control room.

Grace wrapped her palm and fingers around the handle and took a moment to survey the room. She felt eyes stalking her in the dark, burning their gaze through her skull. She couldn't see much, but she was sure *something* was there.

There was a slight noise! Her ears sharpened as she homed in, hoping it would repeat itself.

It happened again! This time, she could make out gentle sobs.

Grace opened the door brazenly, ready to see Gabe, but he wasn't there.

"Gabe?" She whispered, and instantly the sobbing stopped, followed by shuffling. Grace's eyes adjusted to the darkness and made out a doorframe at the opposite end of the control room. As she walked through, she had to use her phone screen for light, careful not to trip on the upturned floorboards. As the phone light pierced through the dust and darkness, Grace's heart stopped as she saw Gabe lying on his side, his hands and legs tied up with purple leathery rope. His face was dirtied with scratches and bruises all over, his clothes ripped in several places.

They locked eyes in the dim artificial light, and both flooded with tears.

"Grace!" Gabe muffled from behind his gag, overwhelmed to see his friend again.

"I'll get you out!" She whispered urgently as she started to detangle the ropes around his legs. She couldn't tell if the feel of the leather was wet or cold. "Don't worry, you don't need to explain. I'm just so happy I found you!" The knots were intricately woven, as if great care had been taken so Gabe couldn't move an inch. She found a joining section keeping his ankles bound together and got them free.

"I didn't tell your mum, don't worry! I didn't tell anyone!" As she started to work on the rope around his legs, her heart sank as she heard asynchronous footsteps approach, and she realised every single mistake she made getting to Gabe.

"Good." A voiced slithered from behind.

Gabe let out a veiled yell from behind his gag. Breathing quickly, Grace turned and pointed her phone light towards the voice. Her legs froze to the ground, trying to believe what she was seeing. A murky dark shadow of a man stood six feet from Grace, cloaked in thick smoke, with no face.

"Not telling anyone might have just saved your life." He spoke slowly, enjoying the moment of fear. "Might have."

Grace turned the phone's flashlight on and shone it at the Shadow Man. He yelped in anger at the blinding light and tried to knock the phone out of her hand, but she took the chance and darted to his side, pushed him against the wall with all her might, and ran.

"I'll get you, Gabe!" She shouted as she ran for the large warehouse door, making sure Gabe heard and had hope she'd come back. And she would. She had to.

As Grace sprinted through the warehouse door, she heard bounding footsteps behind. She didn't care how close they were, she had to keep moving.

The car came into view and she slammed into the driver's door; quickly got the keys out, got inside, and within seconds locked the doors. Grace took a single moment to breathe. This was too much. After a few deep breaths, her brain kicked back in, and she started the car. As the engine started, the Shadow Man rammed his full body weight against Grace's door, cracking the window. Grace screamed loudly and took off as he tried the door.

"What do I do?" She yelled to herself as the warehouse slowly disappeared behind her. She couldn't go home, if the Shadow Man followed her, then he would know where she lives! Nowhere would be open at this time of night except…

She picked up her phone, and while trying to keep her eyes on the road, she typed, 'Police Station Near Me'. She checked the rear-view and side mirrors. Nothing. She was safe, for now.

Five miles away.

"I can do that." She tried to convince herself.

Grace sped down the road, the streets were quiet, and nobody was out at this time of night driving, but she didn't want to take any chances. As Grace made a sharp turn down a single-track path, her phone slipped out of her hand. She tried to lean down on the passenger's seat to feel for it, but it was gone. She had to worry about it later. She knew roughly where she was going to get to the police station for safety. As Grace got back up, she looked in the rear-view mirror again and noticed the reflection was blackened. Her eyes darted to the road for a millisecond hoping she was imagining it, then dared to look back at the mirror again. It was gone.

"Thank God." she said to herself.

In Grace's periphery a bright light rapidly approached. Before she had time to take in a full breath, Grace felt immense pressure coming from her legs and felt weightlessness as the world outside the window tumbled, instantly going dark.

*   *   *

Grace felt weird.

Something wasn't right.

It was like she was swimming.

She could feel the air around her, like an invisible silk.

How long had she felt like this? A minute? An hour? A day?

Grace suddenly felt a sense of gravity as solid ground came into sensation underneath her feet.

The rest of her senses came back into focus. She could hear a gentle hum, a smell of printer ink, and taste the sweetness in the air.

Then, a fractured memory.

A car? Lights? A truck…?

"Oh…" She said breathlessly, as she opened her eyes to soft white sunbeams, shining down and surrounding her. It wasn't irritating and there was no need to squint. Grace bravely stepped forwards, her legs shaking as each gentle step came down one after the other. As she walked, the gentle hum became less quiet, the smell of ink got stronger, and in the distance, she saw an ivory wall with a square space burrowed through it. When she approached it, the sunbeams stopped casting around her and as she made her way through, the atmosphere felt different. An odd familiar warmth washed over her and chained itself around Grace's ankles, forcing her feet to continue walking, but she stopped as she felt the wave of temptation leave her body, stunned at her new surroundings.

It was an office.

Old wooden furniture with a varnished shine, stacks of papers and filing cabinets in every nook and cranny, doors labelled with room titles that didn't make any sense to Grace… and then she saw another person. They were behind a desk, typing on a computer.

Grace couldn't feel her voice, but she was ready to ask for help. She found the courage to unstick her feet from the ground and tentatively approached the desk. As she got closer and could make out the person behind it, she immediately noticed blue and gold eyeshadow, bold eyebrows, short dark hair, a pair of thick black rimmed glasses balancing on the end of their nose and a black shirt adorned with white daises. They looked up and locked eyes with Grace, and it was then she noticed one eyebrow was painted on much higher than the other.

"Oh, my apologies, my lovely! You caught me typing about pie. That won't be the first and last time that happens!" They chuckled.

Grace froze, looking deep into the person's eyes. Their voice was welcoming, homely, but it had an eeriness about it too.

The person behind the desk leaned forward. "You alright, my lovely? You're looking awfully tense and scratched up. What's yer name?"

Grace wasn't taking in what they were saying. Her brain was just racing to understand what happened before getting here. The car. The phone. The truck. Why did her stomach drop every time she thought of the truck?

"Not to worry if you're not ready to talk. It happens. I can only imagine it was a wee bit sudden for ye, and I totally understand. Sometimes people never talk again. But you don't seem the type." They winked at Grace. "Do you have a name at all, my lovely, and I can help get you where you need to be?"

Grace tried to open her mouth, but her lips trembled. She looked at the person behind the desk and told them with her eyes she was trying to say something.

They nodded and smiled. Grace took her time.

"I'm," she said softly, wanting to start with her name, but there was so much going on in her brain — memories, questions — she just didn't know where to start.

"I'm... what... I wasn't here."

The stranger behind the desk nodded and Grace grew frustrated and blurted out "Where am I?" A good question to start with, she thought.

Grace had seen offices before, but not something like this. The person behind the desk was friendly enough but didn't look like anyone she'd seen in movies or on TV. So, where was she?

The person behind the desk chuckled. "Oh, my apologies again. I should've welcomed ye officially. What am a like? Heed like a sieve!" They adjusted the glasses on the end of their nose and smiled.

"Welcome to the Department for Lost Souls."

~ Chapter Two ~

THE DEPARTMENT FOR LOST SOULS

"The... what?" Grace whispered.

"The Department for Lost Souls, my lovely."

Grace stared back at them in confusion. "What? What is that? That's not real!"

"Oh, I assure ye it is. Otherwise, I'd be out of a job!" They chuckled. "I can only imagine it was a wee bit sudden for ye, and ye're a bit confused at what's happening. So let me fill ye in officially, my lovely!"

"What was sudden?" Grace asked but was ignored by the jolly stranger as they shuffled around their desk trying to find something.

"Ah, there it is! It's always in the last place ye look. Although, why would ye keep looking after ye found it? There's one for a fortune cookie!" They winked at Grace and continued as if it didn't happen. "Right, you watch this wee video, and you'll be up to speed!" They handed Grace a rectangular metal slab, it was thin and light with a brightly lit screen coating the surface. On the screen was the word "PLAY". Grace tapped the glass and it buzzed into action. A man with orange hair, polished makeup, and long white robes fastened around them in a fashionable way appeared and proceeded to talk.

"Hello and welcome to you, our new Soul! You have arrived at the offices of the Department for Lost Souls. As a new Soul here, I'm sure you have plenty of questions, but if you give us time, we have full confidence that all will be answered.

Here at the Department for Lost Souls you'll be greeted by our friendly staff who will get you to where you need to be. After all, you are a Lost Soul, but no one wants to be lost forever, right? From here, there are many roads that you can take. But of course, that depends on your deeds from your time of living.

There is no clear path for any one Soul that comes here, everyone is different. With that in mind, it is important to understand that you will belong to one of three places: Paradise, Purgatory, and Inferno.

Although you will ultimately join one of these places, you will be able to visit any number of other Departments we have (Inferno Souls come with limitations).

Your time of living may have ended, but that isn't the end of it all. We hope that when you find where you belong, you will be happy and make the most of it. After all, you did choose it!

We sincerely wish you a wonderful rest of your day."

As the orientation ended and the credits quickly rolled up, Grace noticed Virgil was the name of the man in the video. She handed back the device, left with more questions than answers. The person behind the desk rolled their eyes at the video. "I know, darling. I know! It's a slap in the face of business etiquette, and wee Virgil did his best to look professional, but between you, me, and the rest of Paradise, that video took fifteen days to shoot. He couldn't remember a word!"

"STOP!" Grace yelled, shocking herself. "I know you're being friendly, but please... stop all of this. Where am I? Who are you? What's going on?"

The nameless stranger sat upright and straightened their shoulders. "I understand. Okay, let me explain it for ye, my lovely. Nothing's helped ye so far to understand, so this is gonna be a wee bit of a shock."

"Please..." Grace whispered, tears filling her eyes. Deep down she knew already but needed to hear the words out loud.

"Ye've passed on." They leaned forward and kept their voice low. "Ye're no longer living, and what remains is your Soul. Souls usually arrive in the Afterlife where they need to be, but there's times when a Soul is taken when they were unprepared for it, and they arrive here at the Department for Lost Souls. I came through here myself and I can assure ye it truly isn't as scary as it sounds, my lovely." They lifted a box of tissues for Grace, watching the tears fall from her eyes and down her cheeks. "Take a wee tissue, it's absolutely justified to cry, my lovely."

Grace took a tissue and dabbed it in her eyes. "Thank you..."

"-Gladys." They blurted out unexpectedly.

"Gladys?"

"Aye, that's the one. You can count on me, my lovely. I'll make sure ye get where ye need to be, safe and sound." They said trying to brighten the mood.

"Thank you... Gladys. But I can't be... I can't be dead." Grace said, scrunching up the tissue. A pinch of glitter echoed from her hand catching Gladys' eye.

"What was that?" They said.

"I said-" Grace stuttered.

17

"No, no, I heard what ye said. Did ye see that from your hand?" They asked.

Grace raised her hands and showed them to Gladys in confusion, turning them front to back. "What did you see?"

Gladys adjusted their glasses. "Oh, it was just something I don't see too often I'm afraid. But it's not there, so not to worry!" Gladys clapped their hands. "So, what's your name and I'll check where ye're going, my lovely?"

"Grace."

Gladys promptly typed on their keyboard, and scanned the monitor, tongue sticking out to the side in deep concentration. "Ah yes, here we go! Well, the good news is, you're going to our Paradise Department!"

Grace felt a small wave of relief. She knew of the three places Virgil talked about in the video from her school days, too nervous to imagine what it meant if she was going to the Inferno.

"So, what ye're gonna do is go down this hallway," Gladys pointed right, "go all the way to the end, you'll see an elevator, take it all the way to the top, and ye're gonna ask for Agnes."

"Agnes?" Grace confirmed.

"Aye that's the one, ye can't miss her. She's the one with her desk completely covered in tropical plants. 'Agnes the Rainforest' we call her." Gladys smiled.

Grace peered down the hallway and back to Gladys. "I can't be dead." She said.

"I know it feels that way my lovely, but when it's time, it's time." Gladys said, smiling back at her.

"No, you don't understand. I can't be dead. I just can't. I was doing something. It was important. I just... can't remember." Grace clenched her fists to her temples, trying to pry the memory out.

Gladys nodded. "A little bit of memory loss is completely normal, my lovely. There is nothing to worry about. Think of it as a gift, not all people want to immediately remember how they passed." Gladys smiled with empathy. "But it does come back, it's not gone forever. Whatever it was you were doing, you'll remember it soon enough! And if it's anything we can help with, you just let us know."

Grace looked up from her hands. "But if it's something from when I was living, how can you help?"

"Well, it depends on what it is my lovely, but we've got lots of departments that'll help ye out." Gladys said reassuringly.

Grace didn't know what to make of her situation. She'd just been told she was dead, going to Paradise, had memory loss, and was going to meet a woman who loves tropical plants. This absolutely could not be happening.

"Okay." Grace said, going with the flow. There were so many more questions she wanted to ask but didn't know how to word them. "The elevator and straight up?"

Gladys smiled. "That's right, my lovely! And remember, you're going to ask for-"

"Agnes, I remember. Thanks, Gladys." Grace started to walk down the hallway when Gladys shouted gently from behind her.

"Grace, hen! If there's anything I can help with, you just come back to me, ye hear? I'm always happy to help."

Grace looked back and smiled the best she could.

*　　　*　　　*

As Grace numbly glided down the hall, she noticed pictures hanging up of employees, work nights out, and annual conferences. Cheery faces captured by grainy cameras, as if they'd forgotten they were dead. Her mind refocused on what Gladys told her. They were nice and friendly, but the news wasn't easy to fathom, and even with a strong head on her shoulders, she was really trying to keep it together until she felt safe and let her emotions out.

"Keep it in." She quietly told herself.

Grace arrived at the elevator. Two ordinary silver doors with stained glass above the frame; a relaxing sky scene of white clouds with the sun peeking through them. Faceless figures with wings stood on the clouds, clad in ruby and emerald cloth. Mesmerised at the depiction, she pressed an art-deco button at the side and the doors opened smoothly. Grace stepped inside and turned, noticing the buttons were pastel coloured, cascading within each other but never mixing. She looked at the highest one first, it had the word 'Top' above it.

"All the way to the top." Grace whispered and pressed the button.

The elevator whirled into action. Grace watched as the walls and floor inside slid from view and revealed an opaque glass. She could see outside! Grace was stunned at the different-sized copper cogs and gears, discoloured due to time, clicking and spinning, fitting into each other seamlessly and moving the elevator along. She felt like she was inside a giant mechanical clock.

Hypnotised, Grace jumped when a loud doorbell rang, the walls and floor came back into view, and the doors opened.

"Welcome to the Paradise Department." A friendly voice was heard over the intercom.

As Grace stepped out, she was immediately met by a jungle of plants. Stems and vines decorated the walls, cut clean and well maintained. As she walked around pots of lilies and chrysanthemums, she saw a woman sat at a large desk. She had large round glasses, a thin gaunt face, and a huge head of frizzy brown hair with the odd twig and leaf poking out of it. Grace noticed her earthy cardigan had a peace symbol on the lapel and it made her smile.

"Welcome to the Paradise Department." A politely spoken voice piped up. "My name is Agnes and if you sniff it, you buy it. How can I help you?" Agnes looked at Grace, blinking impatiently.

"Oh, you're Agnes?" Grace tried to confirm.

Agnes rolled her eyes. "I don't have time to repeat myself. I am Agnes: I have one hundred and eighty-seven plants to tend to, a new all-nut diet that's driving me up the wall, and a filing system I'm having to learn while teaching the rest of the Paradise staff." She took a deep breath. "So, apologies if I'm not in my best moment with you... How can I help you?"

Grace looked back to the elevator and wanted to speak with Gladys again, at least they were nice. Shouldn't Paradise be filled with happiness and sunshine?

"Well, I was speaking with Gladys and she—"

"— They." Agnes interrupted and raised an eyebrow. "You get told only once."

"— they told me to speak to you because apparently I belong here?"

Agnes turned to the monitor on her desk. "Alright angel, what's your name?"

"Grace."

"Okay yes, perfect. I have you here, your accommodation is ready for you." Agnes said, tapping a pencil on the table. "However, given your personal circumstances and how you passed on, you have the choice to go to your personal accommodation now *or* you can go to the Meditation and Self-Care Halls to heal first. What would you like to do?"

Grace was too scared to ask questions, but she had to. "What's the Meditation and Self-Care—"

"The Meditation and Self-Care Halls are where you go to mentally, spiritually, and physically heal yourself from any trauma. In a nutshell — oh there I go talking about nuts again, this diet is becoming a personality — the Halls do a lot more than that of course, but that's just a brief for you."

Agnes' head titled and stared wide-eyed through her glasses at Grace for an answer.

"Oh, well…" Grace's mind was a little muddy and forgetful right now, but Gladys said that would clear soon. "I think I'll just go straight to my accommodation, if that's alright?"

Agnes rolled her eyes again. "Why are you asking me? It's your decision!"

She pressed a blue button on her desk, and a door to her right opened. A tall man walked in, the hair on his head was more unkept and wild than Agnes', but his beard was styled proudly. He wore a pristine white suit with flared trouser legs, and jet-black dress shoes, buffed like a mirror.

"Hairy Harry, can you escort Grace to her accommodation? Here's the key!"

Harry took the key with a sweet smile. "Of course, I can. It'd be a great pleasure." Grace instantly recognised the molasses charm behind his accent. "If you'll follow me Grace, I'll take you to your new home." He turned to face her and gestured out his arm to walk with him.

"Thanks, Agnes!" Grace said as she walked by the desk. Agnes was already deep in a 'Nuts for Nuts' monthly magazine, ignoring Grace.

As the pair left Paradise's reception, they entered a corridor built from frosted glass and Harry giggled. "She's not usually like that. Really, she's a sweet person, but this new craze of a nut diet is driving her-"

"-Nuts?" Grace joked.

Harry let out a huge laugh. "Yes, exactly! Shame you caught her on a day like today, hopefully next time you see her she's more welcoming. Speaking of which…" Harry slowed down, spun on his heels, and gestured his hands above his head. "Welcome to Paradise, Grace! It's amazing here, there's so much to do, places to see, and people to talk to!"

"It does sound like… well, paradise." Grace felt at ease around Harry. "I'm sorry if this is a blunt question but-"

Harry put his hand on Grace's shoulder as they walked. "I'll give you the benefit of the doubt Grace, it's your first day here. Ask anything you want."

Grace sighed with relief. "Okay, well… are you an Angel?"

"Interesting. Why do you ask?"

"Well, you're dressed in a white suit, you're really friendly, and you're gliding as you walk." Grace said, imitating his walk.

Harry laughed. "That's brilliant. I like that! First, this is my uniform, and second, I'm just happy. I 'glide' when I'm happy, I guess! And to answer your question; no, I'm not an Angel. They're a very different kind of being."

"That's crazy." Said Grace.

"What's crazy?" Asked Harry, a little puzzled.

"*They* exist. The Angels! We take the idea of them for granted, but just knowing they exist? It's crazy!"

"Oh yes, I understand. When I was alive, I was quite the Christian. I went to church in my finest every single Sunday, prayed at every meal, and volunteered at as many charity events I could do. So, I knew all about my faith and Angels. But nothing prepared me for when I first saw one." His eyes misted over with a shine of tears.

"What did they look like?" Grace asked, putting her hand on his arm, stopping them both.

Harry smiled and wiped a tear from his eye. "She was the most beautiful woman I'd ever seen. At the State County Fair, dressed up in a clean gingham gown, light blue, with the most sensational hair down to her shoulders. She was a masterpiece." He took out a navy handkerchief hidden in his jacket pocket and wiped at his welling-up eyes. "Of course, I know what you meant. I just miss my darling Betty so much."

Grace stared in confusion. "Wait, what happened to her?"

"Nothing, that's the thing. It's bittersweet. I died well before my time, a year into our marriage. But she continues to live such a wonderfully long life." He sniffed, and tucked the handkerchief back into his pocket. "Look at me, talking away about my Betty, and I didn't even answer your question. I swear, I try to find any excuse to talk about her."

"She sounds like a wonderful person." Grace said softly.

"She is. She truly is." Harry nodded and continued to escort Grace down the corridor until they found themselves at an iridescent glass staircase, with long shallow steps going on for an eternity. They both looked up the long flight and Harry beamed. "Ah, here we are! Grace, if you'll follow me your humble abode awaits!" He climbed ahead of Grace, bouncing up each step. Grace followed, hoping the stairs would end quickly but before she could finish the thought, she was at the peak and was met with a landscape of architecture.

A reflective shine came from every high-rise building in the distance, immaculately polished with wonderfully sleek curved edges. Pastel apartment blocks towered over the metallic paved streets. Single sized cottages with neat and tidy front gardens busied the remaining space, closest to the pearlescent gated entrance.

Grace audibly gasped at the grand size of it all. She tentatively joined Harry who'd walked ahead and was waiting for her at the entrance gates.

Harry took her hand and smiled. "And now, officially welcome to Paradise."

*　　　　*　　　　*

As Grace and Harry strode passed suburbia, she couldn't believe how busy Paradise was. The atmosphere was tranquil, but everyone had somewhere to be. Hurried faces graciously tipping their hat for someone to go in front of them, the constant bright smiles at Grace as they passed by, it creeped her out. Stalls and shops lined the streets with well-kept grass bordering the pathways, ornate flowers tastefully decorating the streetlamps. Everything was so clean; she had never seen a road sparkle before.

Harry stayed close to Grace, making sure she wasn't feeling uncomfortable. "When I arrived here, I was truly overwhelmed. I'm not ashamed to tell you this because I think it's healing, but when I got to my home here, I sat looking out the window and I cried. I don't mean a little tear either, I really let go." He watched as Grace was silent, taking everything in. "It's something else, isn't it?"

Grace couldn't find her voice and just nodded as they walked.

Finally, they reached a humble apartment building around the corner from a fish market, its blue pastel stood out from everything on the street. Harry stopped and called to Grace who'd walked on in a daze. "Well, here we are!"

Grace spun around and scanned the building. "*This* is my house?"

"Certainly is." Harry chuckled back. "Allow me to give you the tour, but fair warning you won't like the décor! It'll feel empty as you walk in, there's no personal touch or homeliness. Give it time though and you'll feel at home here." Trying his best to reassure her.

Grace could never call this place home. Everyone else could, but it was just a house to her. They went inside and took an elevator to the fourth floor, stepped out, and immediately met a door with her name on it. A balloon archway around the frame decorated the entrance, with a large hamper sitting on the floor filled with an abundance of multi-coloured envelopes addressed to Grace. Gifts, snacks, and an extra fluffy teddy lay underneath.

"My, my… it looks like you've got quite the welcome wagon!" Harry said, smiling at the hamper and balloons.

"This is for me? But who — how did they know I'd be here?" Grace asked.

Harry chuckled as he picked up the hamper. "Neighbours to a new Soul arriving are always informed of them coming. It's not mandatory, but it's advised you help make their welcome a little easier. Looks like you hit the jackpot with your neighbours!" He reached into his pocket with his free hand and pulled out a golden key. "This is yours. I think it's only right that you open the door for the first time."

Grace reached out slowly and took the key, her hand trembling. She looked to Harry who winked back at her reassuringly, she smiled and slid the key into the lock, rotated it, and gently pushed the door open.

It shouldn't have come as a surprise, given how nice everything had been walking through Paradise, but Grace was stunned at the décor that met her eyes.

A continuous flush of varnished oak ran across the floor of the entire house. Ornaments and furniture carved from the same hardwood thoughtfully placed throughout. An earthy green paint on the wall made it feel friendly and comfortable.

Grace took short steps inside and peered into the other rooms. There was a large bedroom with a queen-sized bed and walk in wardrobe, an open plan living room connecting to the kitchen, and a fully tiled bathroom with a separate bath and shower. She didn't like to admit it, but she enjoyed saying to herself she could live here.

"May I?" Harry asked from the door. Grace looked over her shoulder and nodded with a smile. "Now remember what I said about the décor? It might not be up to scratch now, but the decorating team will be around in the next few days, and they'll help you out making this place well and truly yours. They're wonderful people, you'll really like them!"

"Thank you." Grace blurted out more suddenly than she intended. "I don't know where I am in my own head; I've not really had time to think or come to terms with anything. But thank you for making me forget for a little while."

"You don't need to thank me, Grace. I enjoy meeting new people, and I could tell you had gone through something quite sudden."

"I don't remember anything."

"Now don't you worry about that, it's in the past now. Nothing to be done to change it, unfortunately. Otherwise, I'd be sitting on my front porch with a large cup of coffee, with Betty humming her favourite tune beside me. You just focus on what's happening ahead of you." Harry put his hand on her shoulder and smiled gently. "You're very sweet, and I hope to run into you again. You ask the most interesting questions!"

"You're going?" Grace asked.

"My job is to escort you to your new home. I've done so, and if I do say so myself, impeccably!" He laughed, stroking his beard proudly.

Grace twirled her thumbs anxiously. "I'm not sure — I don't... I don't know if I can be alone right now." Harry tilted his head, silently asking her why. Grace gave into the emotions building up and let go of a whimper as she spoke. "I'm scared..." was all she could manage to begin with. She took a deep breath and tried again. "I don't know what to do."

Harry let out a small sigh through his nostrils. "Grace, it's natural to feel like this. If you'd like, I'm happy to stay a little longer and order some food. I can reach out to some of the other departments who can check in on you or even introduce you to some of your neighbours." He wrapped his arms around Grace, giving her the warmest embrace. "I can only give you an old man's help, it's up to you if you take it." He felt a nod of Grace's head from his shoulder and let go of the hug, wiping a few tears from her face.

"When I arrived at my home, I felt the same as you. I was lost, confused, and alone... but I embraced that sadness. I'd sit at my window and watch this beautiful place buzz throughout the day, and hum at night. All I wanted was my

Betty to be here with me. I embraced the sadness because it's healthy to cry. I believe our tears carry that pain, and we cannot heal if we don't let go of what's causing us pain."

He smiled at Grace, eyes welling up, and waited for her to look back at him. "But the trick to embracing your sadness? Don't let it consume you. It's easier said than done I'll tell you that! But that's the trick. I cannot tell you what to do, but I can only advise you based on my *many* years of experience. Look at me now! Handsome as I ever was, smiling from sunshine to sundown and just between us," he lowered his voice to a whisper, "I *still* embrace that sadness, because it gets easier every time you do. It doesn't go away; you just learn how to live with it."

Grace threw her arms around Harry and thanked him through tears. He squeezed back tightly. "Would you like me to check in on you tomorrow?" He asked.

"Yes please!" She said wiping away her tears.

"I'll be round tomorrow afternoon, and maybe we can go out for coffee and a chat, if you're up for it of course?"

"I'd really appreciate that. Thank you, Harry." Grace said, smiling.

"The pleasure was all mine, Grace! It was sincerely a treat to meet you today, and if you need anything at all, the phone in the kitchen has all the important people you can contact on speed dial. Of course, my name will be in there too!"

Harry put his hand on Grace's shoulder, winked, and glided out the front door, quietly whistling an unfamiliar tune. Grace closed the door and locked it slowly with the golden key Harry gave her. She walked into the living room, taking in the apartment again.

Alone.

She wanted nothing more than her mum to walk out of the bathroom and give her a hug, she needed a friendly face she recognised. She walked into the bedroom and sat on the edge of the bed. It didn't feel like her bed at home, this felt like a stranger's bed.

She thought about Harry's advice. She lay down at the foot of the bed, closed her eyes and listened to the slight bustle of noise from the street outside. A single tear fell down the side of her cheek, and within seconds she was curled up and letting her emotions out, telling herself through the tears and loud sobs: "Don't let it consume you."

~ Chapter Three ~

THE MEDITATION AND SELF-CARE HALLS

Grace woke slowly. Keeping her eyes closed, she felt the bed and the comforting warmth it gave her as she stretched. There was a peculiar scent of vanilla creeping its way into Grace's lungs as she breathed in. Her mum had always preferred florals, she was used to that being the natural smell of a space lived in.

As she opened her eyes and lifted her head from the pillow to observe the room, her stomach dropped. A flicker of happiness left the warmth of the bed as it got colder, and the vanilla scent became stale and bitter.

"It really happened?" She questioned out loud, noticing she was still wearing her clothes.

She crept out of the bed and squinted passed the sunlight through the window; it looked like a new day was just beginning. Market stalls and shops below were opening, the busy bodies darting between each other were so few, and birds were tweeting songs to each other across the lampposts. The sun here was so different, it felt safer and friendlier, as if you could stand in it all day and not be burned by its domineering presence.

Her stomach growled; she hadn't eaten at all yesterday. Noticing the phone on the wall in her periphery, Grace made her way to the kitchen. Raiding the cupboards and the fridge, Grace made a coffee and found some cereal, and had three bowls full, eyeing the phone the whole time. Satisfying the ravenous hunger, she cleaned up and picked up the phone receiver; noticing a piece of paper taped to the side with a list of names and speed dial numbers. She only recognised three of them: Harry, Agnes, and Gladys.

She didn't want to annoy Harry; he was good for comfort, and she was supposed to be seeing him later.

Agnes was a no go until she was off the nut diet.

Gladys!

"Come back and see me! I'm always happy to help!" Grace remembered.

"Number forty-two." Grace mouthed to herself. She went to dial in the number as she noticed a small note beside the name:

"During working hours, you can always pop by my desk!"

Grace hung up the receiver immediately, she just wanted to be in Gladys' company again. There was something so reassuring about the way they spoke to her; it made Grace feel like everything was going to be okay. She needed that.

Grace slipped her shoes on, grabbed her key and flew out the door, locking it behind her. As Grace waited for the elevator, she thought she should speak to Agnes first just to get permission to see Gladys, she didn't want to just barge in. As she left the apartment building, the streets had busied with so many friendly faces smiling, tipping their hats, and giving her the thumbs up, commenting on how beautiful the day was.

She felt so out of place, everyone here was the best version of themselves, she couldn't be further from that.

Grace made her way through suburbia, passed the pearly entrance gates, and down the staircase. She slowed her pace walking through the corridor out of respect, and as she approached Agnes' desk, she noticed her hair was more of a mess than yesterday.

"Hi Agnes, I was wondering—" Agnes raised a finger to stop Grace from speaking.

"I still have forty-two seconds of my break, and breaks are all the time I get to graze." Agnes blinked. "...I mean eat."

Grace stepped back, wide-eyed. It turns out it wasn't just yesterday; Agnes was always a little frustrated.

She looked around in silence while Agnes chewed on a bag of mixed nuts and slurped a drink of cloudy liquid.

Agnes swallowed hard and smacked her lips. "Ah, lime juice and nuts. A flawless combination!" She said trying to hold back the sheer disgust. Grace half expected a fledgling to fall out of her hair from the full body shiver Agnes ungraciously tried to hide. "So, you were wondering?" Agnes urged.

"I was wondering if I could go speak to Gladys?" She asked, stepping forward.

"Oh, you don't need to ask permission, just go see them. The elevator is behind you, just press the button marked 'DLS'." Agnes said in a tone to indicate this was the end of the conversation.

Grace smiled. "Thanks, Agne—" Agnes coughed loudly, cutting her off. Grace nodded firmly, secretly hoping she wouldn't need to speak to Agnes much in the future.

Grace navigated her way through potted plants, called the elevator, and pressed 'DLS' inside. The carriage whirled into action once again and within a moment, the doors pinged and glided open. Grace stepped out and was met with bodies pushing their way passed each other, stacks of paperwork with folders being carried by little legs and hugged by weak arms, reems of paper on wheeled carts being pushed between doorways. It was the same hallway, but Grace couldn't have imagined it being this busy during the working day. As she carefully made her way down the corridor to Gladys, not bumping into anyone carrying more than they should have, she glanced at occupied chairs filled with people in a hurry to be seen. How could everyone be so busy and impatient? Grace wondered.

Grace got to the end of the corridor and could see Gladys was already talking to someone. She felt instant relief seeing their daisy print shirt, blue eye shadow, and quizzical eyebrow, eternally judging. Grace smiled and stood at the doorway, waiting until they had a free moment. She couldn't help overhearing the conversation.

"Ye understand, my lovely?" Gladys said, holding onto the person's hand. "Ye're not to blame for a thing. *You* are a wondrous Soul, and in my opinion, ye were taken too early. Looking at yer file here, ye were a shining example of how Souls should be." Gladys smiled gently. "Now, you listen to me, and you listen well; I can guarantee there's a wonderful thing called Karma, and an even more wonderful person that works in the Karma Department called Kandice. I'll be having a conversation about you and yer... I won't call them partner, cause a partner wouldn't lay a finger on the love of their life. They'll get exactly what's coming to them, Kandice always finds a way. And if she doesn't, I will!" Gladys laughed and let go of the person's hand.

"Oh, I nearly forgot. I'm babblin' away while there's some good news to tell you! I know what I've told you is a lot to digest, but listen, you've been gifted a Celestial Ticket Pass. Isn't that wonderful?" Gladys leaned down under their desk, opened a long drawer, and pulled out a white ticket with a golden lace design over it. "Now, a Celestial Ticket Pass means that someone on this side has gifted this to make your passing a lot easier and more calming. It's a lot to go through, and we don't take it lightly. But whoever it was, they were looking out for ye! They must have seen what ye were going through and wanted to help in the only way they could." Gladys handed over the Celestial Ticket Pass to the teary eyed stranger and smiled.

"Now, you take that ticket pass to the elevator like I told ye and speak to Agnes, alright? You take care, and if there's anything I can help ye with, ye come see me!" They said and waved them off down the corridor that Grace was standing in. Grace smiled as they locked eyes with Gladys. "Oh! It's yerself! How are you, my lovely?" They asked, gesturing for her to come over to their desk.

Grace skipped over. "I'm doing okay. I still can't remember anything, but I'm hoping what you said was true and it'll come back to me."

"Oh yes, indeedy it will!" Gladys nodded. "Took me eight weeks to recover my memory, never did remember that Bolognese recipe though." They said, furrowing their brow.

Grace laughed, looked down and fixed the hair in front of her face. Gladys noticed glitter fall from her hand and disappear. "Are you feeling okay, my lovely?"

She looked up quickly. "I mean, apart from everything that's happened, I'm just overwhelmed a little, but yeah. I guess in general, I'm okay. Why?" Grace asked.

"Oh, no reason. I just wanted to make sure. Ye just seemed to have a look in your eye, is all." Gladys said, taking their glasses off to give them a good clean. They were clearly seeing things.

"Well, I guess I wanted to apologise for yesterday, for the way I acted." Grace said. "I mean, I lashed out at you, and you were nothing but kind to me. I cannot thank you enough for that!"

Gladys smiled at her. "You don't need to thank me at all, my lovely!" They said, putting their glasses back on the end of their nose.

"I had a good cry and sleep, and I feel a lot better. Not amazing. Just better. And I'm meeting Harry later as well!"

Gladys laughed out loud, "Oh my days, Hairy Harry! We all love him here. He's such a character and a gen-u-ine gentleman. One of a kind!"

"He is a character. You could have given me more warning about Agnes though." Grace said, the corner of her mouth curling into a smile.

Gladys' eyes rolled. "Agnes is one of those people who tries anything, and it sticks or it doesn't, most of the time not. Let me guess... it was a new diet."

Grace raised her eyebrows, amused. "It was! All about nuts."

"A diet has never been more apt, my lovely. She's harmless, really, but my word, does she love a fad!" Gladys said, giggling.

"Agnes said there was a department that could help me get better. Like, heal me and stuff? The uh... the Department for Self-Healing or something?" Grace asked, hoping Gladys would know.

"Almost there, my lovely. The Meditation and Self-Care Halls." Gladys confirmed.

Grace slapped the desk lightly. "That's it!"

"Here, I'm due a wee break, I'll take you there myself, my lovely. So much easier than telling you all the directions!" They said as they got up from behind their desk and waved for Grace to follow them.

"What's it like, the Medication Halls?" Grace asked, still unsure of the name.

Gladys chuckled as they escorted Grace through several doorways into a corridor she didn't recognise. "It's a wee bit of a mouthful, especially since most of the other departments begin with 'the Department of...'. It's *the Meditation and Self-Care Halls*, and they're incredible." They made a left turn down another corridor. "You just feel this overwhelming sense of peace about you, it's quite bizarre. And the staff are so kind, especially Rhiannon. She's covered head to toe in tattoos, and you'll want to stay in the Halls to hear the story behind each one." They made a final turn to the right, and Grace saw an amber glow at the end of the long corridor, coming from a marble archway.

"That's… That's so pretty." Was all she could muster.

"That's the glow of the Halls! I do like walking this way sometimes just to feel that light on me. You'll feel its wonders as we get closer." Gladys took a deep breath, taking in the warm light.

As they got closer, Grace felt the tense muscles around her neck relaxing. Her shoulders dropped slowly, and her mind became still and empty. "Do you live here permanently?" Grace asked, feeling the words leave her mouth before her brain could catch up to the sensation.

"Oh aye, I do. I have a place in Paradise, but I've often wondered about moving here just for convenience. I'm hardly at home these days. I spend most of my time in Purgatory, what with work and general life. By the time I get home, I just use it to sleep. But it's nice enough, ma wee flat."

"What's your place like? Is everyone's the same?" Grace asked.

"No, no, much like before, it depends on who built them. Most blocks are the same, but unless we're in the same building, they'll be different, my lovely. My place is just a wee flat, nothing fancy. Except, I have a wee hatch in the wall between my kitchen and living room. I felt like I was in a celebrity mansion, I've always wanted one of them!"

Grace had never met someone like Gladys before. She wanted to say that having a hatch in the wall was nothing special and it's normal in many houses, but it was Gladys' slice of heaven. She was slowly understanding who they were, and appreciating that Gladys praised the smaller things in life.

"I do hope you remember that thing ye forgot, my lovely" Gladys cheered, as they approached the archway of the Meditation and Self-Care Halls.

"Me too." Grace said.

"It's nothing to worry about. It'll come to ye in time, it always does. Well... most of the time!" Gladys laughed in pain at the lost Bolognese recipe. They stroked the smooth surface of the archway, closed their eyes, and took another deep breath. "There's something about this moment before passing through here that just makes me so happy." They opened their eyes, smiled, and gestured for Grace to walk through the archway. "After you, my lovely."

*　　　*　　　*

With the amber glow and archway now behind her, Grace felt the gravity in the room lift as if she was on the moon, able to bounce around effortlessly. There was no path ahead, just shallow footprints in a vastness of silver sand. On either side in the distance, golden waves gently splashed against the sandbar, coming to a calm as they approached the shore. A synthetic sun at twilight sat hidden behind the horizon, emanating the source of the amber glow Grace had witnessed outside.

"It's like magic walking through that archway, works every single time." Gladys said, standing beside Grace. "Sometimes I just stand here for five minutes and leave."

Grace tuned her ears to hear calming woodwind playing from afar. "Where is that music coming from? It's so nice." She asked.

"Nobody knows, it's just here. I couldn't even tell you what instrument it is!" Gladys chuckled, guiding Grace forward. "There are some places in all Three Realms that are a whole creation of their own. The Meditation and Self-Care Halls are one of them." Grace nodded in agreement as she walked slowly beside Gladys, stunned at her surroundings. "I came here when I first arrived. I was a little worse for wear myself, and it was Big Barbara who was in my seat at the time, she never believed in any of the options that this place offered, so I had to find it myself." Gladys pointed ahead of them. "That's exactly who we're looking for."

Grace finally took her eyes off the world around her and concentrated on the person slowly approaching them.

He had buttery smooth skin, no blemishes or freckles anywhere, a bald head and clean-shaven face with a faint musk of sandalwood gracing the air around him. He was short and thin with his burgundy robe trailing behind every step he took. Slung across his neck were more necklaces than Grace had ever seen on a single person. Layers upon layers, all different shapes, sizes, materials, and colours. Each with its own signature of gems and runic symbols.

"Gladys you absolute vision. I'm glad to see you take more than two steps through here." The man smiled warmly.

Gladys fixed the glasses on the end of their nose. "Oh, you know me too well Tony. I'm always in here just for a quick buzz of relaxation and then I'm away. Busy, busy!"

"You need to make a full-day appointment with us soon, look after yourself!" Tony said. His eyes and then body slowly turned to Grace. "And who is this you've brought to our Halls?"

"This is Grace, she's a new Soul who arrived with us yesterday. She's just struggling a little with the adjustment. Do ye reckon you'd be able to help her?" Gladys asked, their piercing eyes shining.

"Grace." Tony breathed, letting the name float in the air. "Anything for a new Soul! And of course…anything for Gladys."

Gladys smiled and clapped their hands together. "Perfect! Grace hen, I'll leave you in the very capable hands of Tony-with-the-necklaces. I've had my dose of relaxation, so I'm ready to head back to work. Don't want Mr Morgan flappin' cause I'm not there!" They held Grace's hand and smiled. "Ye're in good hands here, my lovely. I cannot recommend it enough."

Grace smiled back. "Thank you so much, Gladys. What do I do once I'm done?"

"Tony-with-the-necklaces will let you know everything, my lovely." Gladys leaned into Grace for a hug, and it took her by surprise, she felt safe in their arms. Gladys adjusted their shirt and slicked their hair back behind their ears. "Right, I'm away! Grace, look after yerself, hen. Tony, we need a wee coffee soon." Tony and Grace nodded gently and waved Gladys goodbye as they walked back the way they came, disappearing through the marble arch.

"Isn't Gladys just wonderful? I've known them since they arrived. They've never changed." Tony turned and walked deeper into the Halls, leaving Grace standing on the spot. "This way Grace, and we'll find out exactly what you need." Grace jumped to catch up.

"What I need? What do you mean?" She asked.

"The Meditation and Self-Care Halls are here for everyone who needs help mentally, physically, and spiritually. Even for those who have gone through trauma or have arrived with diseases that are affecting the brain, like Alzheimer's. Although not everything is completely curable, the Halls and its plethora of treatments minimise the damage that's been done and allow healing to begin."

"That's incredible, and all of that is done here?" Grace asked.

"Yes, it is indeed." Tony replied proudly. "The first step comes from within the Souls themselves. We can't help them if they don't want it to begin with." He shrugged. "But we do everything to support every being that comes through the Halls."

Grace realised they had been walking with no destination in mind. "Um, Tony, where is it that I'm going in the Halls?"

"I don't know."

39

"What do you mean?" Grace asked, puzzled.

"You've not told me what's ailing you, Grace. I find it rude to ask, and I think it's better if someone opens up naturally. You'd find it quite surprising how much people reveal while walking."

"Oh, well… What do you want me to say?" She said feeling put on the spot.

"Whatever you'd like. I'll be able to get you to the right place as soon as I know what troubles you. Why did Gladys bring you here? Why don't we start with that." He said calmly.

"Gladys said it might help me remember things I'd forgotten. Is that something you're able to-"

"Here we are!" Tony boomed, stopping them both from walking. "The Healing Pools of Anamnesis."

Tony smiled and pointed behind her. Grace turned back and witnessed the final moments of the silver sand she had been walking on build a large Grecian bathhouse. Grace's jaw slacked watching steps appear from the ground as Tony encouraged her forward. They climbed the steps together, passed some lockers and a cubicle, and came to the pool's edge. The water was so clear and still, it looked empty.

Tony gestured around him. "You'll find a bathing outfit, towels, and a secure area to change in your own time. We find the Pool's water heals best when it's in contact with as much of the body as possible. It is very shallow so if you're not comfortable around water, please say and we can explore alternatives."

Grace nodded and smiled back. "No, this is perfect. I just walk over, get changed, and lie back in the pool?"

"It's as simple as that." Tony confirmed. "If you want to soak for longer, we have lotions and aromas to combine to add to the water. My favourite's caramel and mint, odd combination but it works for me!" Tony gently elbowed one of the pillars and four red velvet cords unfurled from the ceiling, dangling at each corner of the pool. "If you need me at all, pull on these and I'll come to assist immediately."

"Thank you so much. I'll probably use it when I think I'm done... how do I know when I'm done?" Grace asked, excited to know what would happen next.

"You'll know. Just open and relax your mind when you're in the water." He smiled and began to glide away with his long strides, his necklaces barely making a sound.

Left alone surrounded by a woodwind soundtrack, Grace took a moment to breathe in the therapeutic energy the Halls were filling her with. As she let go of her breath slowly, she made her way to the cubicle, got changed into a burgundy bathing suit, packed her curly hair tightly into a swimming cap, and grabbed a large towel. She stood at a pillar and couldn't help but chuckle at the amount of different coloured bottles occupying the surrounding edge of the pool.

Grace found the corner steps and waded into the water. It remained still and enveloped around Grace's skin as she took each step. The water was just above her own body temperature, exactly the way she liked baths. It wasn't as deep as she thought, coming to just above her hip.

Grace eyed a dark brown bottle from the edge labelled *Morning Vanilla Latte*. It's the only good part of waking up, so why not? She thought.

As she unscrewed the lid and poured the scented liquid into the water, a wave of comfort fell over her as the aroma began to occupy the room. The brown liquid didn't dirty the pool water, it just vanished leaving no trace but the deep scent of vanilla and coffee beans lightly in the air.

Grace put the bottle back, waded to the centre of the pool, and looked around her to make sure no one was there. She took a deep breath, slowly relaxed her body, and lay on her back, letting the water keep her afloat. Letting it tingle on her skin — the concoction of heat, sensation, and aroma — it felt like she was home in a much larger version of her bath.

Home.

Grace let her mind wander. She didn't know why there was a tear sliding down the side of her face, connecting to the water in the pool. She would give anything to open her eyes right now and see her own bathroom. Going downstairs to watch her mum making a pasta dish in the kitchen. Grace furrowed her brow and let out a small gasp as she realised, she hadn't properly said goodbye to her mum. Do a lot of people go through the same thing? They must.

But… this was *her* mum. Why didn't she say goodbye to her? Grace missed her so much. She was always there to help her when she needed it. Never judgemental, and always caring without question. She had brought up Grace alone with no husband or other children to fall back on, she was her only family. Now Grace was gone, she must be so alone.

Grace couldn't bear to think about that. It only caused her to be more upset and her mum wasn't what she'd forgotten, she would *never* forget her.

She had to leave the painful memories of her mum aside and refocus on what she'd forgotten. Her memory was foggy and scattered, snippets playing in the wrong order and out of sync. "Open and relax your mind." She remembered what Tony said.

Grace tried to stop thinking and just let the moment take her. Her mind stayed in her room. She was on her bed. Her TV was playing with a blonde anchor-woman on it. Did something happen worldwide and that's why she's here?

No. It was simpler than that. Something was missing from the memory right in front of her.

Not something.

Someone.

Was there a missing person on TV?

Someone *was* missing.

Grace felt her blood run cold through her neck down to her chest. Everything rushed back. She saw the texts on her phone, the drive to a warehouse, someone tied up, being chased in her car, a bright light—

She splashed in the water, trying to find her feet. She stood up and couldn't stop the tears sliding down her face.

"GABE!"

~ Chapter Four ~

THE SHIMMER

Grace jumped out of the pool and sat at the edge, pushing the bottles aside, trying to catch her breath. It didn't feel real, it was like she was dreaming in some sort of trance. But this was absolutely a memory.

She could remember it all. Gabe, her best friend, was probably gone now, and she couldn't save him. Her mum will never know the full story either; robbed of the chance to say 'I love you' one last time. Grace wiped the tears from her cheeks and tried to stop choking up as she focused on something in her memory of Gabe. A faceless shadowy figure was chasing her. *It* was the reason she's here now.

She stood up as her memory pushed something else forward.

Her last moment. She remembered it now.

Grace let the silence of the pool do the talking, even the music around her had stopped, as if the Halls itself knew what just happened.

She remembered the car; the bright lights were rushing towards her. The quick and heavy pressure... and then... walking towards Gladys.

She clasped her hands over her mouth, unsure of what to do next.

Grace took a moment and silently mouthed 'Gladys'.

She dashed for the changing room to get out of the wet bathing suit as fast as she could. Fully dressed and towel-dried, she promptly walked for the dangling cord and pulled it firmly, making sure to rearrange the mess she'd made of the bottles. Tony appeared out of nowhere, striding towards her.

"Grace, I do hope everything worked out well for—"

"I remember everything, Tony." Grace interrupted. "I remember everything. I need to get back to Gladys. Can you take me, please?"

"I can get you back to the entrance, certainly. I can't take you any further however, but I'm sure it's simple enough to find them." Tony said reassuringly.

Grace nodded and walked with Tony down the bathhouse steps. The entire structure crumbled before them into the ground, the water of the pool receding to the shore surrounding them. Once the sand had settled and dried, they continued their way to the entrance. They walked back in silence, neither pressing the other for answers to questions they were desperate to ask. As they got to the marble arched entrance, Tony placed his hand on Grace's shoulder and nodded, smiling.

She closed her eyes and smiled back. "Thank you, Tony."

Grace passed through the arch and began to recall all the twists and turns Gladys led her through earlier. She did get lost at one point but was put back on course by a messy haired boy named Myles who had mistaken Grace for an astral projection. Before long, Grace was turning a final corner and could hear the familiar and friendly voice of Gladys not too far away.

"Have ye ever heard of such a thing as an ice-cream sandwich?" Gladys asked.

"Please tell me this isn't you just hearing about them? I grew up on them!" Another voice chimed in, this one Grace hadn't heard before.

"Oh, I was feeling experimental last night and got myself something new for after my dinner, and let me tell you... I've never run to get another packet of something faster in all my life!" Gladys said, and the other voice laughed.

"I've got a box of biscuitses here if anyone is wanting any." A deeper voice spoke up after their laughter calmed down.

"Wit? Did you just say biscuits-es?" Gladys asked.

"Yes." The deeper voice replied.

"Biscuitses is not the plural for biscuits, Mr Morgan; I don't know where you're getting that from!" Gladys piped up.

"No, no, now I'm sure I've heard a few people say that in my time." Said the other voice.

Grace turned the corner and approached the front desk of DLS.

"Brenda, don't you be encouraging him!" Gladys said as they turned around and spotted Grace standing in front of their desk. "Oh, my lovely, are you alright? Your hair's all wet!"

"I remember." Grace said, her eyes glossy from tears.

"Oh..."

"Yeah... It's bad. But I remembered what I forgot. I can't believe I forgot... My friend, they're in danger!" Grace blurted out.

Gladys turned to the woman beside them and said, "This is who I was telling you about, Brenda; this is Grace." Brenda looked over to Grace from another desk and smiled. She was a dumpy older woman, wearing a smart-casual brown suit just a little small for her, with a tonne of pockets all over the jacket. Her hair was curly and black, tied up into a messy bun. "Now, you tell me what's going on, my lovely." Gladys said, turning back to Grace.

Grace took a deep breath. "My friend is in danger. I was helping him out of a situation, he was kidnapped and tied up. I got him loose a little bit, but the person who did that to him started chasing me. That's how I ended up here. But I don't know if my friend is okay. I need help. I need to help him, please! What can I do?"

"You need to breathe, my lovely. You're working yourself up, just take a moment. I know it's a lot to take in." Gladys said with a gentle smile.

Brenda stood up from their desk, walked around, and put her arm around Grace. "Oh, sweetie, you listen to Gladys."

"I don't have time. I've wasted so much of it already! I need to help my friend! What can I do?" Grace asked in desperation.

"My lovely…" Gladys breathed, "there is nothing to be done. We cannot interfere with the Land of the Living. It simply cannot be done."

Grace's heart sank. "No, there must be something. He needs to be saved!"

"Well… that's not entirely true, Gladys." Brenda said. "We can interfere in slight ways, you know that."

"Yes, but they're miniscule most of the time."

"But, why not?" Brenda raised her eyebrows at Gladys. They stared at each other for several seconds, having a telepathic conversation with their eyes. Gladys slowly blinked, their long eyelashes brushing the rim of their glasses, and Brenda turned back to Grace. "The Department of Tokens and Mementos could send something meaningful to help aid your friend."

"It needs to be me; I need to go back and help him. Sending a little token or whatever won't do anything!" Grace was getting more frustrated every minute that they couldn't just open a door and go back. "I don't..." Grace caught her next sentence before it left her mouth.

"What was it ye were going to say, my lovely?" Gladys asked.

"I... don't even know if he's still alive." Grace closed her eyes and bit her lip, holding back the tears.

"Have you checked sweetheart?" Brenda asked.

"What?" Grace choked.

"Have you checked if they're with us in any of the Three Realms?" She continued.

"I didn't know — I didn't know I could check!" Grace said shocked.

"Of course you can. You can go to the Historical and Biographical Library; they have a book for everything there!"

"Brenda, why make it that difficult? We can check here." Gladys beamed.

"We're not allowed to search for a Soul's name who isn't directly in front of us Gladys, you know that!" Brenda said defensively as she sat back at her desk. "That's one of the first things you learn here."

With a twinkle in their eye, Gladys winked at Grace and swung their chair in Brenda's direction. "Oh, my word. I had no idea we weren't allowed to do that, Brenda hen. I'm shocked, I truly am." Gladys swivelled to face Mr Morgan who was finishing a chocolate-covered biscuit with one hand and filing paperwork with the other.

He was a short, hunched man who was missing every follicle of hair on his head, which congregated around his upper lip into a massive bushy moustache. His Hawaiian shirt obnoxiously stood out from the rest of his clothing, proud to look different from the boring trousers and tie to match.

"Mr Morgan, are we not allowed to use our systems to search for a Soul to see if they've passed onto our side yet?" They asked loudly.

Mr Morgan cleared his throat and answered without turning around. "Well, you see, this goes back years. There was a time that there was a functionality to be able to do so; it was put there for certain procedures, of course. I can't quite remember what they were now that I think about it. Anyway, the functionality of being able to do so was indeed there and could be used as intended, but—"

Gladys turned back to Grace and leaned over the desk. "What's your friend's name, my lovely?" They asked in a hushed whisper.

"Oh… eh, Gabriel." Grace whispered back.

Gladys typed quietly on their keyboard as Brenda watched on in horror, listening to Mr Morgan's spiel. "That name isn't coming up with anyone related to you, my lovely. Did they go by a nickname, or a chosen name?" Gladys urged.

"Gabe." Grace whispered back.

Gladys typed again, scanning the monitor quickly and nodded. "Gabe's not with us, my lovely. He's still very much alive."

Grace let out a sigh of relief, and a silent tear fell down her cheek.

"— So, I guess what I'm getting at here is that morally and professionally, it is severely frowned upon to do so... So, no, we cannot use the system to find out if a Soul has passed." Mr Morgan finished and took another biscuit.

"Right well, that's good to know, Mr Morgan! From this moment onwards, I *will not* be using the system to do so." Gladys said, smiling at Brenda who rolled her eyes. "So, there you are, my lovely. Gabe is still alive!"

Grace wrapped her hand in her sleeve and wiped away the tears. As she did, Gladys noticed again golden glitter falling from Grace's hand.

"Did anyone else see that?" Gladys asked, their painted eyebrow raised higher than usual.

"See what?" Brenda asked.

"What I was talking to you about earlier..." Gladys mouthed a word to Brenda that Grace couldn't make out.

Brenda scanned Grace up and down. "Well, it isn't there so it can't be." She sniffed matter-of-factly. "Like I said Gladys, you either have it or you don't. There is no in-between."

Grace furrowed her brow, confused at what they were talking about. "Have what?"

"Nothing for you to get your hopes up about, sweetheart." Brenda affirmed. "You don't have it, and so there's no point getting worked up to be let down."

Grace was still confused, what could be so bad they wouldn't tell her. "I understand I don't have it, so... just tell me."

Gladys peered over the rim of their glasses at Grace, weighed up the decision, and opened their mouth slowly. "Listen, I'm the type of person who believes it's in everyone's interest to be transparent. I think she should know, Brenda hen."

Brenda shook her head. "I said what I said, and I don't think you should."

Grace sighed frustratedly. "I've had a rough couple of days, I've gone through a lot. Please, just tell me and don't mess me around. What do or don't I have?"

Gladys put their elbows on their desk and leaned in towards Grace.

"The Shimmer."

*   *   *

"The Shimmer?" Grace asked.

"The Shimmer." Gladys confirmed.

"Yeah, the Shimmer." Brenda chimed in.

"And what is a... 'Shimmer'?"

Gladys looked over to Brenda, and they locked eyes once again.

"Well, isn't this the conversation I tried to avoid?" Brenda said, smirking. "So please tell us, enlighten us all what the Shimmer is, Gladys."

Gladys furrowed their un-arched brow at Brenda. Perhaps Brenda was right for once, maybe they shouldn't have spoken so openly about it. Gladys couldn't help feeling somewhere in their gut that it was the right thing to do.

"The Shimmer, my lovely," Gladys began, choosing their words carefully, "is something that glitters around you."

"Going great!" Brenda scoffed, giving a small thumbs up.

"It's actually more difficult to explain than I first thought." Gladys licked their lips and continued. "When a Soul comes through to us, they look just like the every-day-type person that we're all used to. However, there are some rare moments where someone comes through to us with the Shimmer. Now, the Shimmer is like a glittering aura around them that can only be seen here, not in the Land of the Living. It's almost like a life force. Each person's Shimmer is individual in its colour and shape it can take around them. When we see a person come through with the Shimmer, we must urge them to go back." Gladys looked down at their hands for a moment and looked back up at Grace. "You see, when a person has the Shimmer, it means they have not fully passed on, it is not their time."

Grace blinked, her mind whirling with questions.

"Regardless of the reason why they ended up in front of our desks, they must go back. If they stay here too long, then they're taken to another place which isn't in the Three Realms, which I don't agree with. So, we urge them to go back."

Grace opened their mouth very slowly. "And by 'go back' you mean..."

"Go back to the Land of the Living, aye."

"So, it *is* possible?" Grace exclaimed.

"Well yes, to a degree, my lovely, but like I said *only* if you have the Shimmer."

Grace stood in shock. She can go back, there is a way; she just needs to get the Shimmer. Grace's mind was in such a blur of questions, she didn't notice Brenda offering her a chocolate doughnut.

"I have an emergency stash. They help with shock." Brenda said.

Grace looked down at the doughnut, glistening with a ludicrous amount of chocolate sprinkles. She didn't even have a response.

"So, I can go back?" She asked again.

Gladys sighed. "Only if you had the Shimmer, my lovely. Unfortunately, you don't."

"Then what are you seeing?" Grace asked puzzled. It was important for her to know as much as possible about the Shimmer, she needed to find the flaw to get back and save Gabe.

Gladys was visibly confused. They looked Grace up and down and tried to remember exactly what they saw. A bright gold glitter falling from Grace's sleeve, they had seen it previously when Grace first arrived.

"I don't know. Hands up! I don't know what it is I saw. My eyes are playing tricks on me, these glasses aren't what they used to be."

"No, what is it you're seeing? I can't see it; you have to tell me." Grace said.

"I don't... Well, it was this bright golden... I don't know — glitter! This bright golden glitter, which to me does look like—"

"Gladys, don't say it." Brenda interrupted.

"— It does look like the Shimmer." Gladys shrugged.

Grace stood completely still; her eyes widened.

"But... the issue is that the Shimmer is a constant thing. It stays around you the entire time, like an aura. Whereas... I'm looking at you right now, and well, it's not there at all."

"But you *did* see it?" Grace pressed.

"...Potentially."

Grace bit her lip while Brenda watched the conversation unfold between mouthfuls of doughnut, chocolate sprinkles peppering her desk.

"Okay, so to make sure I understand... the *only* way for me to go back is if I have the Shimmer? Full stop, that's it. Right?" Grace asked.

"Unless you want to go through the Reincarnation Department's lengthy process? Yes." Brenda said through a mouthful.

Grace felt like going home was within her grasp, and as quickly as the hope came, it disappeared.

"I told you it was going to give her false hope, Gladys. I tried to stop it. But the good news is, your friend is alive!" Brenda said sympathetically, licking chocolate smudges from her fingers.

Grace didn't know what to do but find a spot on Gladys' desk to zone out on with her mind. She was so close to being able to return, letting herself get worked up and hopeful, and now with that excitement gone, she felt empty.

Gladys could see the light leaving Grace's hopeful eyes. "Brenda is right, my lovely. Your friend is alive and well."

Grace scoffed. "He's just alive. You don't know if he's well or safe! You don't know how I left him." She said, raising her voice slightly. "What do I do now to help him?"

"You can't." Brenda said bluntly. Gladys gave her a light push and made a gesture towards Grace. Brenda took the hint. "Sorry, I mean, you can't, my lovely." She said in her best Gladys voice.

Gladys rolled their eyes.

Grace raised her head sharply. "Wait. I remember untying him. He was on the ground; I think I got his legs free." Grace was using her hands to try and remember what happened. "And then I heard the Shadow Man's voice, and he chased me to my car."

"Oh, that sounds horrifying, my lovely." Gladys shivered.

Grace nodded. "So maybe... maybe I got him untied and distracted the Shadow Man long enough for Gabe to get away safely. Right?" She looked to Gladys and Brenda for reassurance.

"There's every chance of that, my lovely. Every chance." Gladys said with a genuine and cheerful tone.

"What about the Viewing Platforms?" Mr Morgan said, placing a pile of papers down on Brenda's desk.

Gladys gasped. "Oh, I'm such a tool. The Viewing Platforms!"

Brenda smacked her forehead. "Of course!"

"What are they?" Grace asked.

"The Viewing Platforms allow ye to see people or places in the Land of the Living. Mostly for sentimental reasons but I think you should go check on Gabe." Gladys said, turning to type on their keyboard.

"I'll... be able to see him?" Grace questioned, careful not to get her hopes up this time.

"Oh yes. It might not be everything you're hoping for, but it's something." Gladys assured. After they finished typing, a small white ticket printed from under the desk. Gladys tore it off and handed it over to Grace. "Now, this is a Viewing Platform Priority Entry. Which means you'll get first access to any available Platform for your use, my lovely."

"Thank you!" Grace said smiling.

Knowing Gladys gave her a ticket that said 'Priority' on it made her feel special and that maybe there was still something that could be done to help.

"Where are the Platforms?" She asked.

"The Viewing Platforms are in Paradise, my lovely." Gladys said, adjusting their glasses at the end of their nose. "You go back to the elevator and show your ticket to Agnes, she'll get Kenneth, and he'll take you to the Viewing Platforms. You'll know which one Kenneth is, he's the one with the massive pigtails." Gladys winked.

Grace smiled, thanked them all, and started the long walk back to the elevator. She may not have the Shimmer like Gladys and Brenda said, but at least she had a plan to see her best friend. Grace missed him so much and felt ashamed she had forgotten him earlier. But once she got to the Viewing Platforms and saved him, and she *will* save him, she would make it up to him.

~ Chapter Five ~

THE VIEWING PLATFORMS

Grace pushed by the large plants blocking the doorway leading to the Viewing Platforms. Agnes had told her to go the opposite way she'd walked with Hairy Harry to Paradise. She told her to stop and wait for Kenneth when she reached the giant sculpture of 'a-face-that-was-made-by-someone-famous.' Agnes couldn't remember their name. "How famous could they've been?" She moaned to Grace before pointing her in the right direction.

Grace had only just stood next to the statue when she heard a "Yoo-hoo!" from a jolly voice behind her. She turned to see someone she could only assume was Kenneth.

"Are you Grace?" The man asked.

"Yeah, I am, and I'm guessing you're… Kenneth?"

"The very same!" He said with an abundance of laughter. He was a short, plump man whose face beamed with the brightest and cheekiest smile. He wore a white shirt accompanied by a tweed waistcoat and trousers, and polished black dress shoes with leather laces tied tight. As he laughed his pigtails bounced around his torso. Gladys wasn't lying when she said Kenneth had massive pigtails. They were thick and long, each securely tied with hairbands, one bright yellow and the other pink.

"I'll show you the way to the Viewing Platforms. They're just along here, if you'd follow me!" He turned with a bounce in his step and walked a few paces before he swivelled on his heel to face Grace again. "Sweetie?" He asked with such loud enthusiasm that Grace saw others around them look annoyed.

Grace hadn't even had time to begin walking behind him, his steps were so small. "What?"

"Would you like a sweetie? I always carry a sweetie. They make the day a little brighter I find!" He picked two out of his tight tweed waistcoat pockets. "This one is a strawberry-flavoured chewy one. And this one is a boiled sweet that tastes like custard. That's my favourite sweetie! Would you like a little sweetie?" He said with his large, friendly smile and rosy cheeks.

Grace couldn't help but let out a little giggle. He was so different from everyone else she had met so far, so full of energy compared to the gentle warmth of Hairy Harry. "Oh, I'll try your favourite one, I think." She said, trying to match his energy.

"Smart girl. Yes, you are!" He handed over the boiled sweet and walked briskly again. "Come now, keep up! Lots to plenty, see to do!" He stopped and let out a large wheeze of laughter. "I should really think about doing comedy one day!" He chuckled and continued walking. For a small and stout man, he walked quite fast Grace thought. At least she would get to the Viewing Platforms faster.

As they walked, Grace noticed the walls were emblazoned with stars and constellations, as well as golden-tinted clouds that followed them as they moved, as if she were in the sky herself.

"Beautiful, isn't it?" Kenneth boomed, still walking ahead of her, pigtails bouncing.

"It really is. It's like a moving painting." Grace said bewildered.

"A moving painting?" Kenneth laughed. "What an absurd and hilarious idea! You're quite filled with wit, I dare say."

Grace understood Kenneth was the type of person who found absolute joy in everything. She knew what she said wasn't in the slightest bit funny, but his nature was too kind to be mocking her in front of her face.

"And right around the corner," Kenneth said as he twirled around it, "is the Viewing Platforms Gateway!"

As Grace turned the corner she saw a large cast iron gate, it's bars and spikes on the top were disjointed and misshapen, like one she had seen in horror movies to keep people out of the derelict mansion. Except this one wasn't rusted, it was shining and pristine, with a plaque in the centre that read:

'Viewing Platforms
Please keep your arms and legs close at all times'

Grace couldn't see beyond the gate itself. A celestial veil hung high from the ceiling, hiding whatever was beyond. It made her feel uneasy.

"Kenneth?" Grace quizzed.

"Yeeeees?" He said picking another sweetie to eat.

"How do the Viewing Platforms work? The sign says to keep my arms and legs to myself. Is that right?" She asked.

Kenneth's cheery smile squinted. He looked at the sign, took a moment to read it and chuckled. "Oh. Now that you mention it, I've never actually read it before. Fool, I am!" He dug around in his tweed jacket pocket, trying to find another sweetie. "Well, they work in quite an odd way I won't lie to you, Grace. We go through these gates, and we'll be on a Platform, and it'll have a little station on it that you simply lay your hand on and..." Kenneth stopped digging around for the sweetie, and his expression changed to genuine confusion. "You know, I don't actually know what happens next." He looked at Grace, who joined in with a confused face. "That is to say, I don't know how it works!" He laughed once again.

"I know what happens next; I just don't know how it works! But you place your hand on the station, and before you know it, you're viewing something on a platform!" He waved Grace closer with his hand, as if he had a secret to tell her. Grace leaned in. "That's why they call them the Viewing Platforms." He whispered and let out another wheezing howl of laughter. "Oh, I need to write that one down!" he said as he approached the large gates. "Are you ready?"

"I'm ready!" She called back, her ears still ringing from his laughter.

Kenneth revealed a platinum key card that was loosely hanging around his neck and waved it in front of the gates hinges. The mechanisms sprung into life from inside the padlock, whirring and ticking like being inside a grandfather clock. With a stop and a sudden twang, the gate slowly swung open towards Grace. She nervously stepped forward passed the gate and through the veil, it brushed on her skin like satin and smelled of artificial flowers. On the other side was a dark room with a long narrow walkway dimly lit by the grouting in the tiled floor to guide the way, accompanied by a single handrail. At the end of the walkway was a large shallow bowl with a cut-out at the front to step inside, a panel with lights and buttons blinking around the circumference, and a safety rail at the surrounding edge.

Kenneth bounded along the walkway, onto the platform and offered his hand for Grace to come aboard. "Come on now, this is the whole reason we're here!"

Grace took a deep breath, gripped the handrail and shuffled along the walkway. When she reached the end she took his hand, climbed aboard, and studied the surrounding panel. Every dial and doodad had unrecognisable symbols carved into its face, nothing Grace could understand.

"So, my dear Grace, now is the time!" Kenneth smiled, and with his hand gestured towards a section of buttons and gadgets in front of her.

She looked down at it and then back at him quickly. "Oh, what? I don't have a clue what to do. This is my first time."

"Ah, I knew I was forgetting something. Not to worry!" He said as he popped a round sweetie in his mouth. "All you have to do, and it's very simple; you'll laugh at how simple it is. All you have to do... is listen. Are you listening, dear girl? All you have to do is — oh it's lemon and lime — all you have to do is, and frankly, I don't know why they make a big deal out of it; it's so simple." Grace raised her eyebrows, both bemused and fascinated by what Kenneth was saying in the most indirect way.

"All you have to do, is simply place your hand in that box there." He said after swallowing the sweetie and clearing his throat. He gestured to a teal-coloured cut-out on the panel to his left. "And then you think of a particular person or place that picks your plight." Kenneth smiled and then chuckled gently. "Oh my, that was some alliteration!"

"That's it? I just think?" Grace asked.

"Yes, that's all." Kenneth said unwrapping an orange sweetie.

Grace shrugged and placed her hand inside the box and felt an odd cooling sensation. A gritty gel inside swirled around her fingers, connecting to every nerve ending in her hand. She felt a pull as if he was one with the console, grateful she didn't have to put her face into it instead. The platform began to hum gently and vibrate beneath her feet, feeling like it had lifted itself from the ground below.

"And now you think. Don't get caught up in details, just the name of the person or place." Kenneth gently reminded her.

"A person. Gabe." Grace said smiling, feeling slightly nervous.

"You don't need to tell me sweet girl, no. Just in your mind. Think. Some people find it helpful if they close their eyes. Think of their name, their face." Kenneth continued, but Grace began to tune them out to concentrate.

She did as he said, closed her eyes and thought of Gabe's innocent face and dark eyes. As she did, she felt a slight breeze around her, it flowed around her neck and down her back, making her shiver. She opened her eyes and glanced at Kenneth, who smiled reassuringly.

"It's fine, it just means you're doing it right. Give it one more moment and you'll see." He said.

As she kept Gabe in her thoughts she slowly blinked. As her eyelids opened, everything surrounding her disappeared, even the floor below her. She was standing in a jet-black room with a singular spotlight highlighting a figure on the ground in front of her.

Grace gasped.

There he was.

Grace smiled and let her eyes fill with tears, she was just so happy to see him. He was still tied up, but it was loosening as he moved his body incredibly slowly. Grace looked for Kenneth through her glossy eyes, desperate to tell him the good news. A gentle and calm voice filled the void around Grace.

"I can't see what you're seeing, Grace." Kenneth said. "It's connected to you. Whatever you are seeing, it's exactly what's happening now. It can really help people to see those they've left behind, but sometimes it can hurt as well. It's awfully bittersweet, I think. There is no denying however, it's an absolute wonder."

Grace nodded and watched Gabe move slowly.

"I've seen people spend years of their time here watching their loved ones like this. We can list the words to describe the bond we have to one another, but if I've learned anything, it's emotion that solidifies that bond more than gesture. It's simply a wonder."

Grace swallowed her tears. Just knowing he was still okay was the weight off her shoulders she needed. "Thank you so much, Kenneth."

"I didn't do this, you did!" He said.

Grace felt the grip from her hand loosen, the void around her fade from existence, and the warmness of air come back to the room. She turned to face Kenneth and smiled, but a question formed in her mind.

"Why was he moving so slowly?" She asked. "I've been here for over a day, and he was still tied up like when I found him."

"Ah yes, another oversight on my part." Kenneth said shaking his head. "Time moves differently from our world to theirs. No one's sure of the time difference."

"But why? Surely there's a reason why?" Grace asked, confused.

"No one knows, unfortunately. It's one of times big mysteries, I suppose." Kenneth opened his palm to reveal a toffee he was softening and popped it into his mouth. "No one is meant to know everything." A question formed on Grace's tongue before her brain had a chance to hear it.

"How can I talk to him? Is that possible?" She asked.

"Not from up here, we only *view*, we can't communicate. Have you ever heard of genuine communication from the 'other side'?" He said chuckling.

"All the time, actually." Grace said, thinking of the TV shows claiming they'd contacted ghosts. "Well, it's hard to tell if it's real or not."

"Most of it isn't, my dear. It's also not my department, so I can't tell you the ins and outs of it. However…" He took a dramatic pause to shovel in a few multicoloured sweeties into his mouth and spoke between each chew. "… the Department for Domestic Hauntings might be able to help you." He said, smiling cheekily at her.

Grace nodded, knowing her next move, she was going to talk to Gabe.

She felt the hum of the platform gradually come to a still, strolled with Kenneth along the walkway through the veil, and brushed her hand along the gate's bars, thanking it for its help.

~ Chapter Six ~

THE DEPARTMENT FOR DOMESTIC HAUNTINGS

After several wrong turns and an unprovoked chat about fabric softener, Grace tentatively approached a large oak door with a gold plaque in the centre that read:

'Domestic Hauntings'

Now that Grace had seen Gabe with her own eyes, her determination was stronger than ever. She knocked on the door three times, and with each knock she felt more confident she'd be able to help him, especially since learning time was moving slower for Gabe.

The door creaked open, ajar enough for a large face to peer around the corner and startle her.

"Hi." They said quickly.

"Oh, hey!" Grace cheered back.

Their eyes looked through Grace and blinked.

"Okay." They said and closed the door slowly.

"Wait! I'm looking to speak to someone here. Can you help?" Grace hurriedly yelled through the closing gap.

The door creaked open further this time and a hand grabbed Grace and yanked her inside. As the door was barricaded shut, Grace heard a quiet voice from behind her, "I sure can help, because here at Domestic Hauntings, we believe that helping is the key to helping."

Grace turned to meet the quirky stranger that graciously invited her in and was met by the overpowering smell of cotton candy. Towering over Grace was a tall and rotund woman with an oversized dark green knitted jumper on, with a single daisy embroidered in the middle. She wore small black pump shoes over fishnet tights and had straight blonde hair in a bob down to her chin.

Grace stepped back a few paces and smiled awkwardly. She could feel heat on her neck and turned her attention to the room she was in. It was reasonably small and had a single desk, overcrowded with unorganised folders, reems of paper, and stationary. An office chair hid behind the desk, bent out of shape and unbearably low to the floor. A fireplace lit the dank and gloomy atmosphere, accompanied by two chairs facing opposite each other. Grace mentally picked out which one was comfier but was nudged out the way and beaten to the chair by her host.

A hand waved at Grace to sit down.

"I'm Amanda. Everyone just calls me 'Big Mandy'. It's *my* nickname, so get your own. I'm always trendsetting here." They said in a quiet but monotonous voice.

"Do you want me to call you Amanda or Big Mandy? Or just... Mandy?" Grace asked innocently as she sat on a very flat cushion.

"Never Mandy." She said, as soon as the question left Grace's lips. "And never 'Big'. Always 'Big Mandy.'"

Grace swallowed hard, unsure how to handle Big Mandy.

"Let's start with your name."

"Oh, I'm Grace."

"Grace. Can I help you?" She said and reached for papers on her desk, remembering what she was doing before Grace interrupted.

Grace took a confident breath in. "I was up on the Viewing Platforms, and I saw that my friend was in danger, and I wanted to help them."

Big Mandy stopped shuffling the papers and looked at Grace. "And you're wanting me to do *what* with your friend?"

"I don't know. This is my first proper day here, and I'm not sure what this place even does." Grace said, less confident this time.

"The Department for Domestic Hauntings doesn't allow you, or any Soul, to go back to the Land of the Living and save them. You'd have to become a Guardian Angel to be able to do that." Big Mandy scoffed insensitively. "I *can* get in touch with the Guardian Angel Bureau and set up a meeting to see if you're—"

"No, I don't need any of that!" Grace interrupted, suddenly feeling overwhelmed that the conversation was not going where she wanted it to. "I want to help my friend, it's literally life or death for him. I just want to go back and do something. Whisper something or give them a sign — anything!"

Big Mandy tilted her head slightly. "When you decide to return to the Land of the Living as a Spirit, there is no returning."

"What do you mean?"

"I couldn't say it any clearer." Big Mandy said staring blankly at Grace.

"I'm still new around here..." She said, hoping Big Mandy could read between the lines.

It took a few seconds but Big Mandy's eyes refocused. "If you go back to the Land of the Living you'll return as a

Spirit, but you can't come back to any of the Three Realms on this side. It would be until the end of time."

Grace listened to every word said, not realising she had been gazing at the daisy on Big Mandy's jumper.

"It was a gift." Big Mandy affirmed.

Grace just smiled, hoping she wasn't being a nuisance.

"Oh. Who from?"

"You don't know them."

Trying to be nice around Big Mandy was difficult Grace thought. They were so direct and curt; she'd have preferred to be talking with Rainforest Agnes.

She didn't want to get bogged down annoying department heads, so Grace refocused on what Big Mandy had just told her. It would explain why there were sightings of Spirits always haunting the same location, they were stuck there and couldn't go back. If she could save Gabe, then she would remain trapped in the Land of the Living and couldn't reunite when it was his time to pass over.

"Even if I saved my friend, I wouldn't be able see him again?" Grace asked slowly.

"That's a loose *if*." Big Mandy said.

"But he'd be alive though." Grace said, weighing up the choice.

"I cannot confirm nor deny what will happen when you return, as these are your choices, and I am not able to help in your own personal circumstances, reasons, or methods going forward." Big Mandy read off a card she'd picked up from the desk.

Grace didn't want Gabe to miss out on the rest of his life. But who knew where the Shadow Man was now? They could be miles away, leaving Gabe alone to escape, or on the way back to finish the job. Grace had a moment of clarity, realising how much she knew her friend. His life would be wonderful; she would save him, and shortly afterwards he would learn of what happened in the car crash. Heartbroken,

The Department for Lost Souls

he'd have to tell her mum of the news, but they would have each other. Her mum would take Gabe in as her own if he was ever abandoned by his family, and they would honour Grace and live fulfilling lives. And when it was their time to come over to the other side, they'd learn entirely of what she'd done for Gabe.

Seconds went by in total silence, nothing but the fire crackling in Grace's ears.

"Well? What will it be? Should I start the paperwork on your Domestic Haunting?" Big Mandy asked, one hand hovering over a ghoulishly green folder.

Grace opened her mouth and took a breath to speak when another voice filled the room, making them both jump.

"There is another option." Slithered the voice coming from behind Grace. She whisked around in her chair to see who was speaking and noticed movement in the corner next to the door. There was no shape of a human body, just a conglomeration of mass forming into existence.

"Who is that?" Big Mandy demanded, raising their voice and standing up out of her chair.

The unnamed form slid forward and glared at Big Mandy, its eyes caught sight of Grace and a wide smile appeared. Grace had never seen so many sets of teeth in a mouth before. It was made of a dark purple goo, glossy and sticky, like congealed wine that had gone off and smelt exactly like it looked. Its eyes protruded from the rest of the body, coated in a milky substance that made Grace wince.

Eventually a shape became recognisable and Big Mandy sighed and sat back down. "Ooze. What are you doing here? You're not supposed to be near this department."

"Ooze?" Grace asked, still in disgust.

"Yes, that's me." Ooze confirmed, its slimy voice surrounding Grace, sending shivers across her body.

"Answer me, Ooze." Big Mandy pressed, growing annoyed.

68

Ooze's mouth moved around its body before relaxing near its shoulder. "I'm here to help little Grace."

"Oh. No, Ooze. None of this nonsense." Big Mandy rolled her eyes.

"Not nonsense, no. I'm just here to help." Its mouth pushed out of its body to reach closer to Grace. "There may be another way to help get you back to the Land of the Living." Ooze said seductively in a greasy voice.

Big Mandy stood up and pointed at the door. "Get out of this department at once. I demand it! If you don't, I'll talk to Satan about you overstepping your perimeter!"

Grace pulled her eyes away from Ooze and turned to Big Mandy. "They're real?!"

"Yes. That's not important though."

She leaned heavily on the desk, trying to intimidate Ooze, and the wood began to moan. "NOW!"

Gooey arms appeared, hands up in defeat. "Very well, so be it. You win, *Mandy*. If you want my help, I'll be at the Hole."

It said, smirking at Grace as it slid through the cracks of the door and disappeared.

"Sorry you ever had to meet that creature." Big Mandy said, sitting down. "Now, your Domestic Haunting—"

"— It just said there may be another way…" Grace butted in, confused.

"— If it's the Guardian Angel Bureau its talking about, there isn't a way to return. If you did go through the Bureau, it's a four hundred and seventy-three step programme with no guarantee at the end." Big Mandy sighed. "I won't tell you what to do but trust me that the only ways back to the Land of the Living are through Domestic Hauntings and the Guardian Angel Bureau."

"… And the Shimmer." Grace whispered.

"I haven't heard about one of them for a long time."

"Yeah." Grace said, defeated.

No one wanted to talk to her about the Shimmer. She only knew because she'd pressed Gladys about it, and they didn't even tell her about going back as a Spirit through Domestic Hauntings. Maybe Gladys already knew there was no guarantee of helping Gabe. But here was someone else — some*thing* else — offering another option. She would be crazy not to find out more about it. If it was more unreasonable than a Domestic Haunting, then she could just turn away.

"What do you say? Any further thoughts, Grace?" Big Mandy asked.

Grace took a breath. "I have to think about it. I didn't know about any of this stuff until you told me. I just need to let my mind sit with it for a while. Is that okay?"

"You know where I am whenever you want to sign the papers." Big Mandy nodded. "I'm sorry if I've been difficult, Grace."

Grace smiled and shook her head. "Not at all, you've been really helpful, thank you. I really do love your daisy print jumper by the way, it's just like Gladys' shirt."

Big Mandy beamed and stood up with Grace, escorting her to the door. The door handle unlocked, and the hinges creaked as the door swung open. Grace left Domestic Hauntings and rested against the cool wall next to the door, it shutting and locking behind her, trying to work out what to do next.

"The Hole." She said to herself quietly.

Ooze said something about finding them at the Hole. Where, and more importantly *what* was the Hole?

~ Chapter Seven ~

TOKENS AND MEMENTOS

With a burning question on her mind, Grace was on her way back to the Department for Lost Souls, hoping to find Gladys still at their desk. She was prepared to do what Big Mandy offered but couldn't help feeling that Ooze's invitation was more lucrative. She turned the corner and saw Gladys at their desk with another Soul. Grace kept her distance to give them the time they needed with Gladys.

"Oh, my lovely. Here, take a wee tissue." They said, handing over a box of tissues to the Soul who had their head in their hands. "Listen my lovely, they cannot hurt you anymore. Those awful people? No matter who they are, they did this to ye. Ye didn't do this to yersel'. Ye were just living yer most authentic life, and for some reason — the incorrect reason — they thought that was wrong." Gladys leaned in and whispered something to the Soul, but Grace couldn't hear.

"Now, let's get ye where you need to be. What's yer name?" Grace couldn't hear the response from the Soul. "No no, my lovely. Yer chosen name, the name *you* go by. I can assure ye, it's the only name ye'll ever be called here." Gladys assured, smiling warmly. The Soul whispered their name out of earshot, and Gladys typed away, scanning the monitor for the results. "Ah, there we are! You're going to our Paradise Department." Gladys cheered. "You'll be well looked after. All you have to do is —" Gladys spotted Grace in their periphery and smiled at her. "— sorry my lovely, I just saw someone I know. Right, ye're gonna go straight down this hallway, and at the end, you'll see an elevator. Take that elevator all the way to the top and ask for Agnes. She'll help ye from there, my lovely. And please, look after yourself. More importantly, don't be so hard on yersel'." Gladys said and squeezed the Soul's hand gently.

A quiet thank you was heard, and the Soul walked passed Grace looking shaken up and numb. She wanted to offer a kind word, but they looked so lost in thought, and Grace remembered how she was when she arrived, so decided against it.

"Grace hen, are ye alright?" Gladys called over, snapping her out of her thoughts.

"Yeah, I'm doing a lot better." She said, approaching the desk. "I went to the Viewing Platforms and found my friend!"

Gladys clasped their hands and smiled brightly. "Oh, I'm so made up to hear that, my lovely! How were they?"

"Well, they might still be in danger, but I didn't realise time moves differently." She said.

"I know, my lovely, it's bizarre, isn't it? I told them that we needed to look at the way we introduce Souls here. We need to give them a wee folder or something, explaining all the jargon and whatnot." Gladys said, leaning their elbows on the desk.

"Yeah. I mean, I'm not going to pretend to understand it." Grace said with a hint of sarcasm.

Gladys eyed her.

"Ooh, look at you being funny, that makes a nice change. Right, my lovely, what can I do for ye?" They asked, tailing off the end of a chuckle.

"Well, I was wondering... do you know what or where the Hole is?" Grace asked innocently.

Gladys' eyes widened in shock, and their painted brows furrowed in confusion. "How... how do you know about that?"

"When I saw Big Mandy earlier, this creature appeared, a slimy thing called Ooze—"

"It's always Ooze." Gladys rolled their eyes. "Listen to me, my lovely, and you listen well. Don't you go looking for the Hole, and don't be talking to Ooze or listening to any word it says." Gladys took a little breath and leaned in closer to Grace. "Ooze is one of Satan's Familiars. They'll say and do anything to cause all sorts of hassle to kind Souls. They've clearly seen you and thought you'd be a good target... Haud on a wee minute. *When* did you meet Ooze?"

Grace was taken aback by the sudden severity of Gladys' tone. "Before I came here, like half an hour ago, I think? I was only speaking to Big Mandy about —"

"— Big Mandy?" Gladys interrupted. "Big Mandy introduced ye to Ooze?" Gladys couldn't believe what they were hearing. Brenda's ears pricked up at the commotion, she nosily watched, wiping down her hands and locking a drawer in her desk.

"No, Big Mandy didn't *introduce* me to Ooze." Grace clambered to find her words.

"What were ye even doing in Domestic Hauntings, Grace?" Gladys interrogated.

"Kenneth told me there may be a way to communicate with Gabe. But when I got there, Ooze crept in and told me to meet it at the Hole." Grace blurted out.

Gladys leaned back, soaking in the story. "Right. Well, I'm glad you didn't listen to Ooze and go straight there, and on top of that, you didn't sign any paperwork with Big Mandy. She drives Mr Morgan wild with her filing system."

"Yeah, I thought about it though." Grace admitted.

"Of course you did, my lovely. Of course, you did. The reason I didn't tell ye about Domestic Hauntings is because I know what the offer is. And truly, I never have, and probably never will, recommend it to anyone. Of course, there are still many who do sign those papers. Poor Souls." Gladys explained, looking mournfully passed Grace.

"So…" Grace said, bringing Gladys back from their thoughts, "… where is the Hole?"

"Grace, my lovely—" They started.

"— It's the entrance to the Inferno Department, just down that way." Brenda butted in, biting into a sandwich and pointing left. Gladys rolled their head back in frustration while Grace peered down the corridor where Brenda gestured.

The Inferno Department was in the opposite direction of the Paradise Department, which made sense Grace thought. The corridor looked relatively the same as the one to Paradise, but there was a touch of melancholy in the air. Grace couldn't see the end, as if the lights had burnt out, leaving an ominous void to be explored. She felt uneasy; transfixed by the darkness, as if unseen eyes were matching her gaze.

"Down there? That's the entrance to the Inferno?" Grace gulped.

"It is indeed, sweetheart. And trust me when I say, none of us like to look over that way. I bet you hadn't even noticed it before now?" Brenda said.

"I - I didn't." Grace realised.

"It's that much of a void, we don't usually engage unless necessary. Right, Gladys?" Brenda confirmed at Gladys who was glaring at her. She locked eyes with Gladys, confused, and started to raise her sandwich slowly up to her mouth.

"The entrance to the Inferno is a hole?" Grace asked.

Brenda pulled away from Gladys' glare. "Yes! Well, there are stairs, but sometimes we forget to tell those who truly deserve to jump down the Hole how to switch them on." She chuckled while taking another bite of her sandwich.

"Don't you be getting any ideas about going there, my lovely!" Gladys warned. "The Inferno is for Inferno Souls only. For those who have done wrong with no remorse."

Grace looked down the uninviting corridor to the Hole and back to Gladys. "I mean, if it means I don't need to walk down that hallway... Why does it give me a feeling of—"

"Regret?" Gladys finished.

"Fear?" Brenda added.

"Loneliness. It just makes me feel lonely." She said, with a shiver. "I won't go to the Hole, but I still need to help Gabe. Is there anything you can think of? If I can return as a Spirit and haunt somewhere till the end of time, surely I can do something smaller than that?"

Brenda snapped her fingers, and a small bit of mayonnaise from her now-finished sandwich flew across the table and landed on Gladys' computer screen. "I've got it! Now that we know where he is, why don't we get Mary involved?" She asked, looking over to Gladys.

"Mary? As in Scary-Mary-With-The-Hail-Marys in Tokens and Mementos?" Gladys asked, bemused.

"Yes!"

Grace chuckled at the nickname. "Sorry, what? Scary-Mary-What?" She asked.

"Scary-Mary-With-The-Hail-Marys." Gladys said. "She gives me the creeps." Grace stared at Gladys expectantly. "Oh, the 'Hail-Mary' part. Well, she finds any reason for ye to do a Hail-Mary prayer when ye talk to her. I needed a favour from her once and couldn't get her on the phone, so I marched all the way there, even stopped in for a coffee as a wee gesture. She said she only drank decaf and got me to do forty Hail-Mary's."

"And she makes you say them too. You can't leave till you do." Brenda added.

"If you look past that though, it's not the worst idea, my lovely." Gladys said, nodding to Grace. "Ahh, No. Now hold on a wee minute. Why am I remembering a situation that you were involved in Brenda, with Mary?"

Brenda blinked. "Me? Oh, I don't remember."

"Aye, it's coming back to me now… The white dove feather!"

"The white dove feather!" Brenda said with a tone suggesting there was a bigger story to be told. She leant in towards Grace. "Before I first arrived here, about thirty or forty years ago, I'd saved up quite a lot of money in my life, which wasn't easy given what I was going through. I scrimped and saved to get me out, and the beauty of it was? No one knew about it. I never even put it in the bank!"

"How much did you save?" Grace asked.

"Twenty-three and a half thousand." Brenda answered proudly.

"You had that much and didn't put it in a bank?" Grace said, bewildered.

"Hindsight's a wonderful thing… I just saved it in my house, under the floorboards. If you knew, you knew!"

"C'mon hen, get to the good bit." Gladys encouraged.

"Well, when I passed on, I wanted to give the money to someone I loved. I couldn't bring it with me! So, I go down to speak to Scary-Mary—"

"— With-The-Hail-Marys." Grace and Gladys finished together.

"Yeah! And so, she explains after I've signed all the papers without reading them, that I can't use words. Bear in mind that I just told her my plan was to leave a *note* hidden somewhere my sister would look. And she turns around after I've signed and says *I can't use words!*"

Gladys rolled her eyes. "Aye, she's a right piece of work, that Mary."

"I'm at a loss trying to think what I can do. Well, I remember that my sister is obsessed with doves. Little trinkets, broches, hairclips — everything was about them. I told Mary to lay a single white dove feather on top of where the money was hidden. I felt like that was fool proof!"

"Well, did she see it?" Grace asked intently.

"Yes!" Brenda said, smiling. "I was overjoyed watching from the Viewing Platforms as she picked it up and smiled to herself. I was teary-eyed and everything, it was a wonderful moment."

"The money — did she see the money? Did she ever find it?" Grace asked.

"… No. After she was done with the feather, she adjusted her bra strap and left." Brenda shrugged. "I gave up after that. I've got no idea what happened to the money. Whoever moved in after me either got lucky or has no idea."

Gladys sighed. "That means Mary's out of the equation altogether. Grace, I hate to be the one to say it, but I don't think there is anything we can do. I wasn't lying to you when I said that without the Shimmer there really isn't a way back. I didn't tell you about Domestic Hauntings because I never recommend anyone do that. And Tokens and Mementos are fickle unless you have a watertight idea they can do. Divine Intervention is left for apocalyptic times, not just for one Soul."

Grace nodded slowly in agreement, there really was nothing to be done. The more she thought about it, the less she wanted to pursue a Domestic Haunting, regardless of how dedicated she felt at the time. It truly was worse than a last resort. But, despite Gladys warning Grace about Ooze, she couldn't help but feel this was still something to be explored…

"It's alright. You did what you could." She said, as Gladys blinked through the glasses on the end of their nose.

"You probably deal with a hundred people like me a day, and I'm probably the most stubborn. I'm sorry."

"Don't you be apologising at all, my lovely." Gladys reassured. "It's perfectly normal what you're going through. I just wish there was something more I could do, besides the Viewing Platforms and the Historical and Biographical Library, there's frustratingly nothing."

A spark in Grace's brain ignited and set off a plan of action. "Yeah, I might just need to keep an eye on him slowly, I guess, with the Platforms and the Library. I think I'll head there now; the walk can clear my head and maybe a new place will distract me a little."

Brenda smiled. "That-a girl. Do you know where you're going to get to the Library?" Grace shook her head. "You head for Paradise, but you'll take the first left. All the way down at the end, there are glass doors. Go straight through them, and you'll be at the reception."

"Perfect, thanks Brenda." Grace said, hurriedly leaving their company, waving them goodbye. Gladys smiled back in silence; it was unusual for them to be so quiet. Gossiping started the instant Grace was out of view. She found the first left Brenda had instructed her to take, turned the corner, and stopped, resting against the wall.

She had no intention of going to the Library.

She had to make her way to the Hole.

She had to speak to Ooze.

~ Chapter Eight ~

THE HOLE

Grace stood with her back against the cool wall, her eyes transfixed on her shoes, trying to think how she was going to get passed Gladys and Brenda at their desks. There wasn't a clear route around them.

"That's fourteen Souls needing a Guidance Pass, and don't forget to—" A tall woman with long brunette hair, tied tight in a ponytail, turned the corner and walked straight into Grace, dropping the files in her hands.

"I'm so sorry!" Grace said, instantly bending down to pick up the scattered documents.

Towering over Grace, the woman stood still, holding her fingers at her temples. "Just leave them, it's fine." Her alto voice moaned. "It's not like I spent thirty minutes putting these in order for the next two weeks of intake. I'm sure I'll find another half an hour somewhere, because I'm *really* not busy at all." Grace felt the hostility from the woman and kept her eyes on the floor.

"This is a lot of paperwork." She said, scuffling the sheets neatly and putting them back into one pile.

"I know!" The woman said curtly. "That's what you get when you work day and night in Complaints. I'm Eileen."

"I'm Grace." She said, standing up and handing the folders back to Eileen, who struggled to keep them balanced.

She was very slender with a razor-sharp chin. The ponytail keeping her thick brunette hair was tied so tight, Grace could see the strain in her face. Wrapping her pencil thin body was a cerulean pinstripe suit, with a polka dot handkerchief in the breast pocket. Matching coloured heels fashionably accented the entire look, as if she was a runway model from the designer magazines Grace read growing up.

"What do people have to complain about in the Afterlife?" Asked Grace.

Eileen sighed. "Remember everything you wanted to complain about when you were alive?"

Grace shrugged. "I guess."

"Triple it! People are never happy."

Eileen screwed her face and made a mocking voice. "*My bedroom isn't the right shade of cream. The queue for Astral Replication is too long. The response time for complaints says fourteen days but I was contacted in three...*" She let out an even heavier sigh. "It's never ending."

"When I was in Paradise——" Grace began.

"A Paradise Soul? Makes sense. You don't have that look in your eyes made for the Inferno." Eileen interrupted.

"W-What look?" Grace asked, confused.

"Regret." Eileen said widening her eyes at Grace. "Sorry, you were saying something."

"Y-yeah. When I was in Paradise——"

"Walk with me." Eileen interrupted again, and briskly started to stride down the corridor. Grace jumped into motion and followed.

"— Well, everyone seemed to be happy and content. I got a huge welcome basket from my neighbours." Grace said to Eileen's back, struggling to keep up with her pace.

"Paradise is filled with complaints. I mean, who complains about the colour of cream?" Eileen scoffed as she tilted her head. Grace gave no response, unsure if it was rhetorical. "Exactly. Naturally, Inferno has a *huge* number of complaints but there's not much we can do there when a Soul has no remorse."

An awkward silence occurred for a few moments before Grace realised she had to break the stillness of the conversation. "Where gives you the most complaints?"

Eileen tutted and shook her head. "The SOUL BLNDR."

"The what?" Grace asked, imagining a torture chamber.

"You've never been? Count your lucky stars!" Eileen chuckled. "It's the Department for Lost Souls cafe on the third floor. Thanks to Maggie, Margaret, Magz, and Marge; DLS has the highest rates of complaints. Unless you're wanting a melancholy cheese toastie? Avoid."

Eileen stopped as she approached a wooden door with a frosted glass window in the centre. Etched in black lettering across the glass read *Complaints*. A large queue was formed outside and twisted around the corner, stretching as far as Grace could see. "This is me. It was good to talk to you. Where was it you were heading?"

Grace realised she'd blindly followed Eileen without thinking, the run in must have done a number on her memory she thought. "I was making my way to the Inferno hallway."

Eileen raised a curious eyebrow to Grace, not too dissimilar to the way Gladys would. "I won't ask. It's back the way we came." Grace gave a panicked look and Eileen nodded. "I get it. Gladys interrogation?"

"Maybe?" Grace said, not sure if Eileen was going to help her or tell Gladys.

She shuffled the weight of the folders around, allowing a pinkie finger to escape, and pointed down another corridor. "Go *that* way until you reach the Department for Reincarnation. Turn left and you'll see the darker halls, keep going and you'll know when you're in the Inferno hallways, sugar." Eileen smiled and pushed the door open with her behind, throwing down the folders into an unseen filing cabinet.

"Thank you!" Grace said relieved and turned away from the grumpy faces watching on as she was helped, and not them.

"Hang on!" Eileen called after Grace. "Which department are you... actually, if you're not telling Gladys, the less I know, the better." She affirmed. Grace nodded in thanks; grateful she didn't have to elaborate.

Eileen adjusted her suit jacket, put on a fake smile, and breathed out sharply. "Okay, who's first?"

"I can't tie these shoes!" An older lady at the front of the queue whined in disgust.

"They're Velcro, Mrs. Taylor." Eileen sighed as she escorted the elderly lady inside and closed the door, leaving the disgruntled queuers to grunt and mumble amongst themselves.

Grace chuckled to herself, took a moment to memorise Eileen's instructions, and followed the path until she reached The Department for Reincarnation. The lighting shifted from a warm glow to an ice-cold chill, emanating from the fluorescent tubing embedded into the ceiling. At an alcove in the corridor, Grace noticed a large stone sculpture. It had three individual spirals twist amongst themselves, coming to a point at the top, carved with interlocking spirals within. At the base of the sculpture there was a bronze plaque that read:

"Rebirth is an overflowing adventure!"

Grace noted to discuss the option of Reincarnation with Gladys. She could already hear the reasons why it wouldn't be a plausible solution. *"Ye wouldn't have yer memories; it'd be a new life!"* There was always a catch.

Grace continued down the twists and turns of Reincarnation's corridors until she felt the air get thicker and the light get darker around her. She hadn't noticed the aesthetic change again to a mixture of wood and brickwork; however, she did notice things looked less maintained. Dying plants looking uncatered for, crooked pictures with most of the frames rotted and chipped, and a strong damp smell. None of it made her feel uneasy, until she made the final step into the Inferno hallway.

It wasn't the easiest place to see in, except with the help of badly spaced candles hanging on the walls, but it wasn't as dark as Gladys made out from their desk. Grace squinted down the opposite end of the corridor and could make out DLS' reception in the faint light. She had managed to give Gladys and Brenda the slip, completely unnoticed.

Grace took in a difficult breath and lightly treaded in the direction of the Hole, not knowing if there would be a warning or just a sudden lack of ground at her feet as she fell. She kept her hand against the wall as she tiptoed through the corridor, feeling the grainy brickwork against her fingertips as they slid along the wall. The dull candlelight barely lit the wall she was being guided by, its colour drained of any life, crumbling and mouldy between the mortices. Suddenly her wrist bumped into a large offset arch, spanning the entire hallway width. Cruelly scratched into the brick-and-mortar thousands of times across the arch, were the words:

'The Hole'

Grace's stomach churned in unease, wondering who, or what, etched such a careless and unforgiving name. She crept forward under the arch and was approached by more candlelight illuminating from the other end. Stepping out into the room she was met with a large pit in the centre, devoid of light. Candles shoddily placed into the mortice holes, the wax dripping onto the floor. Black veins leaked from the Hole's stone perimeter into the floor surrounding it, as if something evil was trying to escape.

She had made it.

Grace swallowed hard and placed her hand over the space above the Hole, careful to keep her bodyweight from shifting. It was strange, Grace thought. No heat. This was supposed to be the entrance to the Inferno, a place of fire and flames. She edged forward gently and peered down the Hole carefully. Debris around her foot fell in, clattering off the sides, echoing all the way down. Grace jumped back in fear and planted her body firmly against the cold wall. The Hole was simply a void, sucking any feelings of hope or happiness out of her, leaving her empty inside.

As Grace calmed, she felt her hands were wet, slimy and dirty from the wall she'd just touched. She tried to wipe it off, but it never transferred. As she glanced at her palms to get a better look, Grace heard a steady dripping sound crescendo and increase in speed around her feet. As she looked up slowly, she noticed the liquid was coming from inside the wall itself. Her hands buzzed in vibration from the goo as it shifted in form around her fingers, leaping off and joining the puddle below. A greasy voice came from above Grace's eye level.

"Hello."

Grace's stomach dropped as she turned her attention up to see a forming mouth grinning at her, rows of teeth misshapen and crooked. She couldn't scream out of fear and alerting the entirety of DLS.

Breathing heavily, Grace leapt back, avoiding the Hole, and pushed her body as close to the brickwork as possible, her gaze fixed on the terrifying sight in front of her. She stared as the puddle took on a humanoid shape, sifting between hues of purple. All evidence of the creature was gone from the wall and floor, now pulsing in rhythm with Grace's heartbeat. Two white eyes appeared from behind the goo, off centre to the creature's mouth.

Grace stammered her next question. "Oo... Ooze?"

"Yes." It said, the smile exposing its barbaric bridgework.

Grace shuddered through her panicked breathing. "You said... there was another way... to get to Gabe... What is it?"

Ooze spat out in laughter. "There are many ways to get back to the Land of the Living... to your friend." Its mouth shifted place, sliding to the centre of its form. "But most think it's too dangerous."

"I'm not most. I'm already..." Grace choked on saying the next word. But after a small breath and a moment to collect herself, she firmed her voice. "Dead. What is it?"

"Not what, but *who*." Ooze said, slithering across the Hole's perimeter. "Have you heard of the Sleeping Lord?" It asked with a watery purr.

Grace took a moment to think. She was beginning to calm, becoming hypnotised by Ooze's slippery tongue. "No. But I imagine they have something to do with...?" She asked, tilting her head towards the Hole.

"*He* is the one that can take you back to your friend." Ooze smiled while its milky eyes widened. "The Sleeping Lord can break that delicate line between the Living and the Dead... If you can wake him up."

Ooze had slowly made it halfway around to Grace at this point. "That means he can get you back to your friend. To help them."

"You didn't answer me." Grace commanded.

Ooze stopped moving. "What?"

"I asked you if he had something to do with the Inferno, and you didn't answer." She confirmed.

Ooze sputtered another laugh. "He *is* the Inferno."

Grace furrowed her brow and eyed Ooze, its hypnosis broken. "I doubt he'll do something like this for free though, right?" Grace chuckled to herself. "The Sleeping Lord... I mean, when he wakes up, won't he just cause chaos? He *is* the Inferno after all."

Ooze's eyes receded into the shape and reappeared at the top.

"No." It said firmly.

"The Sleeping Lord of the Inferno? Not going to cause chaos? I know I'm new here, but even I know that sounds unbelievable!" Grace said. "If you're not going to tell me the truth, then I don't know why you even bothered."

"He would just want... a little revenge." Ooze blurted out.

Grace slowly nodded. "Mhm. Revenge on who?"

"On his brothers. They betrayed him. *They* deserve it."

"And he just lets me go back to help my friend and live my life?"

She repeated the same sentence in her head again. It was a simple question, given the circumstances.

"Yes. *You* just need to wake him up." Ooze menacingly purred.

Grace laughed. "Why can't you do it?"

"Because it requires something I cannot touch." It said sharply.

"Your weird talking-in-riddles-and-being-mysterious stuff isn't making sense. Just tell me from the beginning, exactly what it is I have to do?"

Grace felt hurried, as if Gladys knew where she was, ready to storm through the archway and drag her out by the ear.

Ooze deformed its humanoid shape as it backed against the wall, sticking to the brickwork and coating it entirely. The candles glowed more intensely while the slime shifted, as Ooze began to tell a story.

"There was a time when the Sleeping Lord ruled the Inferno. He was the voice inside every Inferno Soul, commanding legions of Demons with a wave of his hand, unchallenged and free to rain destruction. His brothers — Satan and Lucifer — felt that his decisions were harsh and illogical, causing an imbalance between the Three Realms. They worked together, tricking their brother into believing there was a way they could move up and rule the Inferno, Purgatory, and in time… Paradise. They all went forward with the plan. However, just before the Sleeping Lord made his final command to attack the other Realms, Satan and Lucifer broke off his horns. Without them, he was powerless. They placed him in the coldest depths of the Inferno in a timeless sleep, and he's been that way ever since."

Ooze's shape returned to its original form as the candlelight dimmed. "*That's* why he wants revenge on them, that's what you must do to wake him up."

Grace blinked; mouth wide open. Satan? Lucifer? Demons? It all seemed like a nightmare.

"You… want me to wake up the Devil?" She asked.

"No!" Ooze spat. "The Devil is not the Sleeping Lord. It is their pet."

Grace tilted her head in confusion. "So… who is the Sleeping Lord?"

"Beelzebub." Ooze said with a haunting smile. Grace could see the glee in its milky eyes. "It's been too long since I said his name out loud."

Grace swallowed hard, trying to remember everything she just heard. Ooze hadn't explicitly said it, but reading between the lines, she had to find the horns and return them to Beelzebub, placing them on his head. After he'd had revenge on his brothers, he could send her back to be with Gabe and her mum.

"I have to wake up…" Grace muttered.

"Beelzebub." Ooze finished for her with a lick of its mouth.

As difficult as it was, Grace looked at Ooze intently, trying to find any signs that it was lying.

"No catches?" She pried.

"No catches." It promised.

Despite Gladys' warnings, there might be some truth to its words somewhere, Grace thought. She knew she had to keep her trust at arm's length. Even if Beelzebub tricked her and sent her back as a mouse, she'd still find a way to make that work and save Gabe. She'd make anything work.

"Okay." She said after a final breath. "Where are the horns?"

Ooze's milky eyes widened; its gaping mouth almost split in two with such a wide grin.

"To retrieve them, you're going to have to first find Pandora's Box."

~ Chapter Nine ~

PANDORA'S BOX

"Thirty-seven... Thirty-eight... Thirty-nine..."

"Gladys. I swear, I would never touch them!" Brenda pleaded.

"Barry the Baker is awfully precise with the number of sprinkles he puts on his doughnuts. If I find one missing? It's your heed!" Gladys accused.

"You're not listening to me, Gladys." Brenda sighed. "I have no reason to touch your doughnuts. I have a drawer filled with—"

Gladys raised a finger at Brenda. "I'm trying to count hundreds and thousands here. You know what I'm getting from you? Hundreds and thousands of excuses! Barry made these doughnuts, they're nothing to be sneezed at."

Gladys turned their head to see a Soul standing in front of their desk. A young girl in a pale blue dress with yellow flowers on it, wearing red rubber boots made for large puddles. "Oh hello, my lovely!" Gladys said, raising their voice cheerfully. "What's your name?"

The little girl bit her lip, tilted her head down, and twirled her hands together. "Um... O-Olivia."

"That's a beautiful name." Gladys said, beaming at her.

Olivia looked around, her bottom lip trembling. "I can't find my mummy... I don't... Where's mummy?" Tears began to form in Olivia's eyes.

"Don't you worry, my lovely. You're in Auntie Gladys' hands now!" Gladys said cheerfully, trying to keep Olivia's spirits up. "Let's see if we can find your mummy together, how does that sound?"

Olivia nodded, looking up to Gladys.

"Brenda?" Gladys called, raising both eyebrows at her. Brenda got the hint and dropped her custard cream, quickly typing on the crumb covered keyboard. Gladys reached their hand across the desk and signalled for Olivia to hold it.

"That's a very pretty dress!" They said squeezing her hand gently.

The little girl nodded again and looked down at it, holding the seam at the bottom out so Gladys could see all the flowers. "My mummy got it for me."

"Your mummy got it for you? She must love you very much!" Gladys beamed.

Olivia giggled as tears soaked her cheeks. She twirled on the spot, spinning the dress.

"Wow! What flower is that on your dress?" Gladys asked.

"A sunflower?" Olivia guessed.

"A sunflower? Is that your favourite flower?" Gladys continued, looking to Brenda for a result.

"Yeah." Olivia said, through an embarrassed smile.

"Do you want to know a secret?" Gladys leaned in as they whispered.

Olivia nodded quickly.

"My favourite's a daisy." They said, pointing to their shirt, making Olivia giggle.

Brenda took in a deep breath and grinned. "It looks like your mummy is waiting for you in Gladys' favourite place."

Gladys' eyes lit up in genuine delight. "Oh my goodness, the Sunshine Department!"

Olivia smiled; her water-filled eyes drying. Brenda cleared her throat, and Gladys looked over.

"She's tiny. Take her!" Brenda mouthed.

Gladys subtly nodded. "Y'know what? I'm having so much fun talking to you, I'm going to take you there myself. Is that okay, my lovely?" Olivia laughed and bounced on the spot. "That's settled then. Follow me, my lovely." Gladys got up from their desk, placed their hand on Olivia's shoulder, and walked them down the Paradise corridor. Brenda could still hear Gladys chatting away to Olivia in the distance. "Ye know, we could both wear the same size of dress."

Brenda smiled to herself and continued typing away at her keyboard until she realised something important; Gladys hadn't eaten their doughnut. Brenda glanced down both corridors and couldn't see them, the coast was clear. She wheeled her chair across to Gladys' desk and eyed the delicious doughnut sat on top of some stacked folders. Golden baked dough, glistening with pink and white icing, covered in thousands of multicoloured sugary sprinkles. The sickening aroma of sweetness was too much for her to resist; she had to have a bite. Like a royal crown, Brenda lifted the grand prize off its plinth with every finger from both hands and coveted it, holding it high above her head, ready to dethrone Gladys of their lineage. Brenda opened her mouth wide and closed her eyes, moving the doughnut closer until—

"You'll regret that." Mr Morgan's wispy voice came from behind.

Brenda sharply opened their eyes, doughnut still suspended in the air.

"Gladys'll go right through you." He warned.

"It's just a doughnut. You're acting like this is the greatest thing to ever exist!" Brenda said, dismissing his warning.

"It's not just *any* doughnut, that's a doughnut made by Barry the Baker." Mr Morgan laughed.

Brenda looked at him, simultaneously confused and uncaring.

"You've never had one, have you?"

"I'm about to!" Brenda scoffed and took a large bite out of the doughnut.

Her mouth exploded with flavour as her eyes rolled back and she gasped, thankful she was sitting down, or she would have fainted. Swirls of real strawberry jam laced throughout the dough, clashing with the hint of vanilla. The crunch of the individual sprinkles could be felt against Brenda's fillings. And that glaze, like a sugary waterfall cascading across her gums. "For all that is right and mighty in the world, that is worth every single Soul on God's green Earth, and then some!" She said through salivating chews of the doughnut.

"I ran into Five-Dog-Margaret on the way to the Sunshine Department, she said she would take wee Olivia there since she was about to start her shift — MY EYES BETTER BE DECIEVING ME!" Gladys thundered, witnessing Brenda shovelling the last piece of the doughnut into her mouth.

Brenda locked eyes with Gladys, rogue sprinkles stuck to the side of her mouth.

Gladys adjusted the glasses on the end of their nose.

Mr Morgan slowly hid behind a filing cabinet. He knew this wasn't going to be pretty.

"I can explain!" Brenda said, quickly.

"Can you? Aye?" Gladys said, speeding over to their desk. "Well, that's fabulous, isn't it? You can explain. Well, you know what? You can explain it to me, and then you can explain it to Big Red!" Gladys scrambled in their pocket to find their mobile phone, pressed a few buttons, and put the receiver to their ear, staring down Brenda.

"Gladys hen, I'll get you another one, I promise! Wait, you have Big Red on speed dial?"

"Never mind who I do and don't have on speed dial." Gladys barked, flustering with their phone as they realised the call didn't go through. "And no, you can't just 'get me another one'. There's a seven month waiting list! Each day a heartbreak."

"Is this a bad time?" Grace asked.

Gladys and Brenda jumped; they had been caught up in their own argument and hadn't seen Grace come into the room.

"Grace, my lovely! Oh, ye gave me a wee fright there." Gladys said, throwing the phone back into their pocket. "How are you doing, my lovely? Did you make it to the Historical and Biographical Library?"

"Yeah, it wasn't what I expected." Grace lied.

"No, it never is here. Everyone's full of surprises." Gladys joked as they glared back to Brenda, still brimming with rage.

"Did you speak to P?" Brenda chimed in.

"Who?" Grace asked.

Gladys butted back in. "P, the Librarian. Surely ye would have spoken to—"

"Oh, yes! I just spoke to them, sorry! There're so many people I've met recently, it's hard to keep track of names." Grace smiled, trying hard to be as convincing as possible.

"Oh here, that reminds me." Gladys said, walking back around to their desk chair and sitting down. "Ye might want to see some friendly faces, now that you've settled in a little. Tasha in Reconnections is fabulous at reuniting passed on Souls to their loved ones. Do you want me to help you get in touch with any family on this side?" Gladys had their fingers poised, ready to start typing to make the arrangements.

Grace wasn't too sure. Why did Gladys offer this now and not earlier? Did they suspect she was lying? She couldn't get paranoid. On the plus side, she would be able to see Granny Ethel again. Her heart swelled at the memories of her Granny's false teeth falling out during a comedy show. Adventures in the park, feeding the swans every Sunday. And sharing ice cream during movie night, clashing spoons for the last scoopful.

Grace took a moment to collect her thoughts. She wasn't going to be here much longer, and if she were to meet Granny again, she wouldn't be able to leave. Saying goodbye once was already difficult enough, she couldn't do it again so soon.

"No. I'm all good for now but thank you." Grace decided. "I probably will in the future. It's just too much for me right now."

Gladys nodded. "Don't you explain yourself to me, my lovely. You do what's right for you."

Grace repeated that last sentence back to herself. That's exactly what she was trying to do. But first, she needed to find Pandora's Box. According to Ooze it was lost to time, which was no help. She needed to find out more about the Box but couldn't just blurt it out. It would seem too random, and she had a feeling that Gladys would catch onto something, their brain was switched on when it needed to be. But Gladys did love to talk…

"How do you get used to this place?" Grace asked, needing to lead the conversation in a certain direction. "It feels unbelievable. Some of it's like magic."

Brenda laughed. "You haven't even seen half of it. The things you'll learn, sweetheart, it's unreal!"

Grace nodded, feeling like she was getting somewhere. "When I was alive, some people said there was an Afterlife. Most didn't believe in it, and yet, here I am, a Ghost!"

"Oh, no, ye're not a Ghost, my lovely. You're a Soul. Ghosts are Earthbound entities; they have chosen to return and remain there." Gladys corrected.

"I thought that was a Spirit?" Grace asked, confused.

"Poh-tay-to, po-tah-to." Gladys slowly blinked and shrugged.

"Well, you know what I mean. I'm a Soul. It's so weird!" Grace said, hoping Gladys would move the conversation forward, but they didn't.

"I know what you mean, sweetheart." Brenda jumped in. "There is a magic-like quality to some of it. The Meditation and Self-Care Halls are a perfect example of that. I still don't know how they work. Thankfully, not my department, not my problem!" She chuckled. "But y'know, after a while, you eventually stop questioning and just accept it."

"That makes sense. But it makes me wonder, with all the weird and wonderful things that I've seen so far, what else is true. Like zombies!" Grace asked, continuing to steer the conversation.

"Zombies?" Gladys asked, bemused, looking heavily over the glasses on the end of their nose.

"Yeah, zombies! Stuff like that."

"Made up. A fantasy. They don't exist, sweetheart. They're just for the movies." Brenda said.

"I cannae imagine how things on this side would change if they *were* real!" Gladys shivered, having flashbacks of a 'Code Red' situation from years back.

This clearly wasn't working. She needed to push the conversation more.

"Well, what about historical things?" Grace asked.

"They're mostly in the Land of the Living, unless there's explicit instruction, we keep an eye on them." Gladys said.

Grace's eyes widened; she was getting closer. "Like what?" She asked.

"Oh, you're going to need to be specific. The only thing bigger than my appetite is history." Brenda said.

It couldn't be the first thing, that'd be too obvious. "Like Excalibur?" She asked.

Gladys and Brenda both looked at each other.

"Well, there is a version of Excalibur in the Land of the Living, if memory serves me right... but I think everything that was attributed to it — the magic powers and all that — was 'legend'. Y'know, when things get passed down over time." Brenda explained.

"That makes sense. Well, what about..." Grace tried to rack her brain for anything. "The Ten Commandments? They were written on stone tablets, right?"

"Now, ye see, that's an interesting one because time really screwed them up." Gladys said.

"In what way?" Grace quizzed.

"They definitely existed, but no one can confirm what was officially written on them." Gladys affirmed.

Grace looked to Brenda for confirmation.

"It's true! They—"

"— I'll be the one to say it though; there were some important commandments left out." Gladys interrupted.

"No one ever denies that, Gladys!" Brenda said, tutting.

"See, if it'd been me, I'd've chiselled one or *eight* extra commandments. The world would be in much better shape than the shambles it's in now!" Gladys puffed.

Brenda sighed, waiting for Gladys to calm down from their outburst. "— They did exist, but there was one fine detail that was overlooked... No one made a copy."

Grace furrowed her brow. "What do you mean?"

"Over time they got worn down. They crumbled and broke, just became useless pieces of stone…"

"Oh… That's—"

"Crazy is what it is!" Mr Morgan jumped out from behind a filing cabinet. "Who doesn't make a copy? It's absurd!"

"Calm down, Mr Morgan. You'll go into a frenzy!" Gladys said, turning around to him.

"Well, what about Pandora's Box?" Grace finally asked.

Gladys whirled their chair around to face Grace, their painted brow raised higher than usual.

"It's made up." Brenda laughed.

Gladys kept her eyes on Grace longer than usual then turned to Brenda to laugh with her. "Aye, it's one of those ancient stories, but it's been changed so many times I can't tell if it's the original anymore. It's like that ship thing, what's it called?" Gladys asked, distracting from the topic.

Grace shook her head, no idea what Gladys meant.

"The Ship of Theseus!" Brenda piped up, the pair laughing amongst themselves. "I'll need to be careful. I almost sounded intelligent there!"

"Huh. Yeah…" Grace said, feigning a smile but sounding defeated.

"You know, you could probably find more about it in the Historical and Biographical Library." Brenda said innocently.

Gladys turned and scowled at Brenda. "Aye, but why bother? Why waste your time? It's made up. It's as real as the Loch Ness Monster!" They laughed.

Grace caught that Gladys had been keeping an eye on her ever since she brought up Pandora's Box, it wasn't a coincidence. They hadn't asked her any follow-up questions so maybe she didn't cause too much suspicion.

"Well, I'm going to head back to my place for a bit and just chill, I think." Grace said, after the laughter had gone down. "I still haven't properly looked through the hamper I got from my neighbours." She said as an excuse.

"You're lucky you got a hamper!" Brenda chuckled. "All I got was a box of candles and some toothpicks."

Gladys put their elbows on their desk and leaned forward, pointing a cheeky and yet oddly serious finger towards Grace. "Straight home, mind. And stay safe!"

"I will. See you later!" Grace nodded and got on her way, feeling a portentous stare burn a hole into the back of her head.

~ Chapter Ten ~

THE HISTORICAL AND BIOGRAPHICAL LIBRARY

Grace waited at a pair of large opaque doors, checking behind her every so often to see if Gladys or Brenda had followed her, trying not to think what would have been said if she got caught. Carved into the glass in swirling typography was her destination:

'The Historical and Biographical Library'

She pushed lightly on a cut-out groove and both doors swung open lightly, a smell of mint escaped and invaded her nostrils. Grace stepped through and entered a small semi-circular room decorated in teal wallpaper, with small golden flowers hidden throughout. Shelves haphazardly screwed into the walls, balancing books and magazines, some falling off and piling up below. In front of her was a titanium brushed desk, stacked with multicoloured books and a dusty chrome bell.

"Not much of a library." Grace said to herself.

"Not much of a what?" A voice called out from behind the stacks of books on the desk.

"Hello?" She called.

"Please keep your voice down, this is a library!" The voice snapped as they wheeled themselves out from behind the stack of books. "I'm only joking, there's no one here but me." They rolled their wheelchair from the side of the desk for a better look at Grace.

They had long black hair with green tips, half of it close shaved to the side of their head. Purple lipstick and eyeshadow with a red lip piercing of a devil's tail. A black netted vest under a grey professional suit jacket and skirt with deliberate torn out patches, cruelly stitched together with different coloured plaid. On their feet were ballet slippers, punked up with punched in spikes and lace meant for another type of shoe.

"Not seen you around here before. I'm P, I'm the librarian here at the Historical and Biographical Library." They stopped their chair and grabbed Grace's hand to shake it.

"I'm Grace." She said startled, fighting off a violent handshake. "I'm here to find a book on... well, I don't even know if there will be books about it."

"We have *every* book here. I'll help you find what you're looking for." P said, spinning their chair around and heading behind the desk. They typed painfully slow on their keyboard; a shock compared to the records set by Gladys. "Cards on the table before this blasted computer 'outs' me. My real name is Paige, but I had to shorten it cause people found it ironic, working in a library y'know? So, it's just 'P' regardless of what *it* says." They scowled at their monitor as Grace chuckled at their sense of humour.

"Welcome, *Paige*; we hope you have a lovely day." An electronic voice came from the speakers next to the monitor.

P rolled their eyes. "Anyway, that's enough about me. How long will your stay be?" They asked.

Grace got confused. "My stay? Um, I'm not sure..."

P took a deep breath and smiled. "That's all good, let me just give you a little rundown on how it all works here then. Behind me is the actual Historical and Biographical Library, and it's big. I mean it. *Big*. In there will be a literal sea of books and documents; just ignore them and go straight to a computer, they can be tricky to find if you've not been here before. When you find one, type in what you're looking for and it'll do the legwork for you. If you're unsure when something was written, you can pinpoint an event around the time to help. Unless you want to browse, in which case I'd suggest a six-hour pass. However, if you're wanting something longer, then you'll need to join the Library Hotel System, which'll only take moments to do. There are themed rooms you can also stay in and get lost in a good book, which can be a lot of fun if you're an avid reader like me."

Grace was nodding along at the not-so-little rundown and smiled at the thought of having themed rooms for some of the books she'd read in her youth.

"I think I just need the computer because I sort-of-know what I'm looking for." She hesitated.

"Great, easy work for me. If you just give me your SRN, I'll get you your first HABL card. I say first because you'll lose it, everyone does." P said, chuckling.

"HABL card?" Grace asked, confused.

"Historical and Biographical Library Card." P confirmed.

"SRN?"

"Soul Reference Number. Do you not know what yours is?" P asked.

"No." Grace was concerned. "I only got here recently; I didn't know I had one."

P smacked their forehead. "That explains it. When you get home, your SRN should have been mailed to you, but

I can get that HABL card for you and you can go right through."

Grace nodded, agonising minutes passing as P typed on their keyboard. A small black cube slowly lifted itself from the surface of the desk, with a thin slit on the top. A white card shot out from the gap and P caught it mid-air.

"Go on... take it." P said, holding out the card with two fingers. Grace took it and mouthed a "thank you" while inspecting the reflective ivory card.

"Your SRN is on there as well as in the mail. To be honest, you could also ask the receptionists in any of the departments, as long as they're one of the nice ones..."

"Like Gladys?" Grace said, smiling.

P slammed the table in joy. "Yes! Exactly like Gladys. Your HABL number is printed on the back, and it's been scanned for a six-hour pass. I think you're all set so whenever you're ready, just head in behind me and enjoy your visit." P smiled innocently.

Grace peered behind P. "There's no door..."

P slowly turned their chair to the wall behind them, glanced for a few moments, and turned back to their desk. They typed on their keyboard and turned again to the wall.

Grace didn't know what she was waiting for, then suddenly, the wallpaper parted, and two halves of the wall swung open on interlocking hinges, perfectly disguising the illusion from the other side. P winked at the grandiosity of the moment and beckoned Grace to go in.

"One more thing before you go," P said, shaking Grace's hand again. "the Library is a big place, so the floor will illuminate your steps until you leave, so you don't get lost. Just try not to cross paths with some of the more *regular* visitors, their prints are everywhere!"

Grace nodded, thanking P for their help, breaking free from the never-ending handshake. She stepped into the Library and was met with smell of old paper mixed with a hint of ink; she could taste it on her tongue. She looked back and saw P waving frantically as the wall receded shut and left Grace standing alone in the vast cavern of knowledge and history.

There were columns of bookshelves in every direction. They twisted and turned, diagonally aligning themselves with the angles of other shelves, stacked with books of different shapes, sizes, and colours. Grace looked high above her to see a pale blue sky with light wisps of clouds, as if there was no ceiling. It must have reflected the time of day it was in the Afterlife, she thought. She scrunched up her eyes and opened them again to get another intake of the Library. Masses of books melded with the floor as she looked further afield, the floor awash with bioluminescent footprints, careful not to cross step with each other.

There were people everywhere: browsing, reading, laying down, having snacks, laughing and talking, debating, and crying; each of them had a book in their hand. Grace thought back to the handful of books she'd read in her life, and in this moment, seeing the emotions these people felt, she regretted not reading more. The infinite knowledge, the endless adventures — she suddenly had a lust to read every single one.

But she couldn't, she had to focus on what she was here for. Grace started her journey through the encyclopaedic ocean and wondered aimlessly for what felt like hours. She tripped several times on glossy magazine covers that had been left out in the open, and had to stop at one point because too many footprints started overlapping each other and she couldn't tell hers apart. This was a lot more difficult than she expected, but with some luck and a singular flickering light bulb guiding her curiosity, Grace stumbled on a dingey monitor and keyboard in the crevice of a column. She noticed the section she was in read:

'Wooden Spoons Directory: History, Recipes, Arts and Crafts, Funerals, and Juggling'

Grace ignored the ridiculousness of the section and vied for the keyboard. Some of the letters were missing and there was no mouse, so she clicked the enter button and a search bar appeared for her to type.

'*Pandora*' she typed and hit the enter key.

A large hourglass appeared on the monitor and spun for several seconds before disappearing and displaying a large list of results. Grace glanced over it and saw the search result totalling to sixty-two thousand, seven-hundred and eighty-seven entries. Grace swallowed and scanned the names of the authors, books, publishers, and illustrators. But halfway through the third page, nothing was jumping out to her. She couldn't stand here and click through every single search result.

Grace bit her lip in thought and decided to go back to the beginning and add the word '*box*' to the search bar.

Forty-eight thousand and twelve results came up.

"It's an improvement." Grace shrugged.

She noticed on the bottom right of the screen a flashing page that read '*Original file available.*' She used the arrow keys to navigate her way to the file and pressed enter and a single image of a cartoon book with the word '*Theogony*' written on it popped up.

"The-oh-gone-ey." Grace tried to pronounce it. She had no idea what it meant, but she figured if it was an original file, then it might be of some use.

Grace clicked enter again on the image of the book and large text appeared on the screen in front reading:

'*Please be patient.*
Your book will be here momentarily.'

Behind the monitor Grace could hear a cluttering of mechanisms crunch and click, the noise stopped then a bell pinged, making Grace jump. A puffing sound could be heard above coming from behind her, but Grace couldn't see what it was until the book made its presence known; being carried by a mechanical hook on a steam powered cart. It was wooden; adorned in golden panels, with screws holding it neatly together. The railway appeared and disappeared behind it as it travelled, as if the carriage's presence disturbed the invisibility of the tracks. Grace was mesmerised watching this tiny train carry her book across the entire Library, she'd ignored the idea that the entire rail system must have been connected to each section, spanning across a complex network like a huge industrial brain.

The cart reached the column and followed a circular path spiralling around to the bottom where Grace stood. It slowed to a stop and mechanically unhooked the book from its grasp. It was large with a dusty brown leather cover, discoloured and frayed. On the front in black letters engraved into the leather was the title: '*Theogony*'.

Grace opened the book and was hit with a powerful mist of dust. Coughing and waving it away, she picked up half the pages and began to flip through them quickly, trying not to damage them further.

"Into the theatrics yourself?" A woman's voice boomed through an open bookshelf, their face peering through the gap.

Grace got such a fright she nearly dropped the book on the floor but scrambled to catch it. She looked up quickly to identify the voice and see the face, but it had disappeared. She turned around to see a tall, pale-faced woman with white hair styled into a coiffed updo standing in front of her. Grace backed off, clutching the book to her chest, still breathing heavily from the fright she got before.

The woman was wearing an asymmetrical white suit and a pencil skirt. Her makeup was bold with purple lips, black smoky eyes, powerfully pencilled eyebrows, and a well-defined nose.

"… Is it a play or something?" Grace asked nervously, holding the book away from her chest.

"Some say it's fact." The woman said. "Some say it's fiction. But then, most things people write about tend to come from some sort of truth, don't they?" She asked, concerned with a small piece of dust about to land on the sleeve of her suit.

Grace felt uneasy. This woman just appeared out of nowhere, spoke with a smooth, smoky voice, and didn't completely answer Grace's question. Or maybe she just confused Grace with her answer? They were clearly well-read and intelligent.

Grace had been lost in her own thoughts; she didn't realise she'd been asked a question. "Sorry, I'm Grace." She blurted out, trying not to be rude. "I'm new here."

"Lucy." The woman replied, her lips curling into a gentle smile. "Enjoy the read." She said, nodding to the book Grace had picked. "I often find that once I'm done reading the piece, I want to find out more. And who knows more than the writers themselves? They give you more insight into the inspiration and how the work translates from thought to page."

"I'm not actually that big on reading. I've not read a book in a long time." Grace admitted, embarrassingly.

Lucy let out a low laugh. "Then you've picked a heavy piece to start off your reading habit, but it's theatrical and fun to follow." She tapped the red book she had tucked under her arm and pivoted on her heel. "I've got what I came for. I hope you find what you're after."

Lucy glided passed Grace and turned the corner of the section and disappeared, their footprints glowing behind their path.

Trying to shake the whole interaction off her shoulders, she turned her attention to the book in her hands and flipped through the pages again to find anything on Pandora's Box. She would need to quickly read each page from start to finish to find it, but she was growing impatient. Grace buried her eyes into the pages and read as quickly as she could. *Pandora.*

She'd found it!

Her eyes widened as she leaned in to read what it said. Lucy was right; it was a difficult read. It was set up like a Greek poem, names being mentioned like: Zeus, Hermes, Epimetheus...

And then Grace let her fingers fall slowly over a sentence that jumped out to her the most:

"But the woman took the lid off the big jar with her hands
And scattered all the miseries that spell sorrow for men."

There was no mention of a box.

But Pandora was a woman, and she opened a big jar? Maybe this was some sort of clue? Grace needed more time with the book.

She made her way back to the entrance of the Library, noticing Lucy's prints were gone. She carefully retraced her footsteps; grateful she didn't make the mistake of crossing her prints with others. Her mind was still whirling over excitement that she found something to do with Pandora's Box, but she was confused that it wasn't a plain answer to where or what it was. Quickly she found her way back and was met with P putting some books back onto the lower shelves near the opened wall.

"There she is!" P said, smiling from their chair. "Did you find what you were after?"

"Yeah! I think so. I hope so!" She said. "Do I need to check the book out?"

"Yes, you do. Give it to me and I'll put it into the system."

Grace handed it over and P whipped out a device from a hidden pocket in their wheelchair and flicked through the pages of the book. They scanned a barcode near the middle, closed it, and eyed the title before looking back up to Grace, who just smiled sweetly. P nodded, grinning back.

Grace was deep in thought about what Lucy had told her. "Is it possible to speak to the author of a book?" She asked.

"Yes! It depends on the author to be honest; some never want to speak to fans, and some have given up writing altogether." P flipped the book and read the back, finding the author's name. "Hesiod. Right? I take it you want to speak to Hesiod?"

"Did he write—"

"— Theogony." P finished for her. "Thee-O-Juh-Nee. Hesiod wrote this a *long* time ago. Last I heard, he was holding dramatic readings of his work, pretty much every day. I think he's one of those old-fashioned theatrics, you know? Let's find out together." They grabbed Grace's hand again and yanked her back to their desk, typed on their keyboard, and waited for the screen to ping with information. "Yeah, he's theatrical alright. He's writing new pieces based on, and I quote, '*Modern vs. History*'. Revolutionary..." P smirked. "Do you still want to take this out?"

"No. Thank you so much, you've been amazing!" Grace said.

"It's what I'm here for!" P said running their fingers through half of their hair. "Listen, if you're going to speak to Hesiod, he's residing in Paradise near Olympus."

"Olympus?!" Grace exclaimed, reaching a tone in her voice she hadn't reached before.

"Yeah. Just ask Agnes at Paradise Reception, she'll lead you right."

"Oh... thank you." Grace sighed, unhappy at the thought of going to Agnes again.

"You'll be alright. Good luck!" P waved and smiled.

~ Chapter Eleven ~

A TRUSTED FRIEND

Gladys sat down at their desk with a fresh mug of tea and placed five biscuits down beside it. "Four is a nice even number, but you always crave one more." Brenda's confectionary wisdom rung in Gladys' ear. They logged back into the computer and started scrolling through the countless emails.

"I see Betsy D'evosha is up to her usual chaos. It's always fascinated me that a poltergeist managed to land a whole department to look after." Gladys tutted loudly.

"Oh, no..." Brenda moaned, looking at her own screen.

Gladys ignored her, she probably just wanted a gab.

Brenda cleared her throat and moaned again. "OH, NO..."

Gladys rolled their eyes. "What is it Brenda, hen?"

"Remember Kelly sent that mass email out about her birthday buffet? She's just confirmed who's catering the whole thing... and it isn't pretty."

Gladys slowly swivelled their chair to face Brenda and leaned back, giving her full attention. "That tells me it's not pizza."

"It's not pizza, Gladys."

"That tells me she booked the buffet too late to get the pizza from 'D'Angelo's', and we all know that Kelly's next go-to place is the one-that-shan't-be-named!" Both Gladys and Brenda gave a visible shudder. "So, she would've gone into a panic and went for that lovely wee Greek place we went for lunch one day, the one who gave us our drinks for free."

"As soon as you heard that, you went bottoms up and had to be dragged home!" Brenda laughed.

"Indeed I did not! You and your nonsense. I know that Kelly had a bit of a spat with the owner in there a few months back, probably tried to get it catered by them and got told exactly where to stuff her buffet... But where would she go next?"

Brenda looked at the email and back to Gladys. "I could just tell you —"

"'VERONICAS!'" Gladys shouted, startling Brenda. "She's gonna do a full 'doughnuts-for-dinner' vibe and get 'Veronicas' to cater the buffet with its desserts and — Oh, no... now hang on... she got a cake from there for her niece and she said it was *absolutely* rotten, you would have preferred a shoe!"

Brenda opened her drawer and took out a packet of custard cream biscuits. Something told her Gladys may be here for some time.

"If I were Kelly, where would I go? ... 'The Pie in a Pot' gave her food poisoning, she found a hair in 'The White Rabbit', she's barred from 'La BoCréme'..."

"Remember she went full 'Karen' mode when a chef refused to serve her anything other than soup?" Brenda chimed in, crumbs falling in-between her keyboard.

"Oh, I don't remember that happening. Where was that?" Gladys asked.

"'Soups, Soups 'n' Soups'." Brenda said with a straight face.

Gladys blinked slowly. "Kelly's lucky she managed to get anywhere at this point. Who is it? I give up. Put me out my misery, what did she settle for?"

Brenda opened her mouth to answer, and a small gasp came out, she tried again and winced as the words hit the air. "The 'SOUL BLNDR'…"

Gladys stood up and sat down again quickly in anger. "The 'SOUL BLNDR?' The. SOUL. BLNDR. The food'll show up a month late with Maggie, Margaret, Magz, and Marge floating about like tomorrow doesn't exist! The guests are gonna show up and chow down on tablecloth. Happy birthday Kelly hen here's your cake, it's arriving by pigeon! The pigeon would at least arrive within a week. And what is she serving? What did the *wonderful* chefs of the 'SOUL BLNDR' whip up for a birthday buffet? Dry croissants and a baked potato you don't know if you should smother in butter to give it a morsel of flavour or give CPR!"

Gladys spun their chair to face the desk and took a few deep breaths. "Now, I apologise Brenda, but you know what I'm like around Kelly, she drives me up the wall."

"Oh, I know, but you hide it well…" Brenda said, scrunching up the finished packet of biscuits. Gladys started typing between furious slurps of tea.

"Brenda, you need to change the subject and fast because I'm seconds away from phoning her extension." Gladys said, eyes darting all over their screen to distract them.

"… How are you and Hot Stuff? Have you cinched the deal?" Brenda nodded, hoping the tactic worked.

Gladys' chair gave out an ominous squeak.

"That's none of yer business!" Gladys said flustered.

"It'll be my business after a few cocktails." Brenda giggled as Gladys gave a cheeky smile.

Gladys found Kelly's email and re-read the devastating news multiple times before typing a three paragraphed reply, declining the invitation, trying to be as polite as possible.

"There! I've replied, and I've added you in Brenda, hen." Gladys said, lifting their glasses and rubbing the bridge of their nose.

"I take it we're not go—"

"No we are not! I'll order in from anywhere of your choice. Anywhere but the 'SOUL BLNDR.'" They said, sounding exhausted.

Brenda turned to Gladys and examined their face. "Are you okay, sweetheart?"

"Aye, why?"

"You seem a little off, even before Kelly's email. You just don't seem a hundred percent there, and now you look exhausted." Brenda said empathetically.

Gladys waved her away. "Oh, don't be silly, I'm absolutely fine."

"Gladys, in all the time I've known you, you have only rubbed the bridge of your nose out of stress."

"I'm fine!" Gladys said rolling their eyes, doing a double take looking over at Brenda who was staring at them with pursed lips. "Fine… I just… here's the truth of it; I've got some concerns with that Grace."

"Big Grace, Tall Grace, or Grace-the-Face?" Brenda asked.

"No, no… Grace." Gladys urged.

"Greasy Grace, Gassy Grace, or No-grace-Grace?" Brenda continued.

"Grace!" Gladys said, bewildered at how many Graces' they knew. "The one we were speaking to earlier. I just… have concerns with her in general."

Brenda thought about it and furrowed her brow. "But why? I can't think of anything."

Gladys held their half empty mug close to their chest, turned to face Brenda, and sat leaning back in prime gossip position. "In all the years that we've worked here, how many people have mentioned something crazy like Pandora's Box? Or came back to see us so many times this early in their Soul Journey? Let's not even get started on that whole Shimmer thing." Gladys took a sip and swallowed hard in thought. "Pandora's Box was just the final thing, y'know? Who says things like that?"

"There was that one guy who thought there was a highway to hell." Mr Morgan piped up from behind a large tower of folders.

"Jesus H Chri—" Brenda yelled, clutching her chest. "You really do just blend into the background there Mr Morgan!"

"It's a gift and a curse." He chuckled.

Brenda breathed out heavily. "I don't think there's anything to worry about, she's a smart girl. Respectful, a bit bold when she needs to be, but she's got a good head on her shoulders. You get like this every now and again, but it's just your nature."

"I'm a worrier, that's what it is, hen." Gladys nodded their head, looking away from Brenda.

"You are. You're overthinking. Have another cup of tea and take a good fifteen minutes to yourself." Brenda suggested. "I'll even make it for you."

"No no, you're right. I'll take my mind off Grace with another cup of tea. I might just *accidentally* get another couple of biscuits..." Gladys winked at Brenda as they stood up and made their way to the DLS staff break room. They closed the door and leaned against it, trying to let their mind empty.

There was more concerning them than what they let on to Brenda. Grace *might* have spoken to Ooze, and *maybe* a conversation happened between them, and *perhaps* something about Pandora's Box was brought up? But how would Grace have got to the Hole or anywhere near the Inferno without getting lost and asking for directions? Any logical person would have told her to avoid the Hole at all costs.

Gladys opened the top shelf cupboard marked '*Phyllis back off!*', found a yellow cup, and clicked the kettle to boil.

"My gut is telling me something…" Gladys said to themselves as they readied the tea bags and sugar. They took out their phone, tapped, and scrolled until they found who they were looking for.

The phone rang.

Twice.

It kept ringing.

An automated voice said the person they were trying to reach couldn't come to the phone, and to leave a voicemail after the beep.

"Who leaves a voicemail these days— Hiya Hot Stuff, it's me, G-Doll! Aye… So, listen… It's just playing on my mind a little, it's probably nothing to worry about, but you know me." Gladys took a breath. "There's a Soul talking about Pandora's Box and—"

"I thought I'd come in and check up on you, Gladys." Mr Morgan said, suddenly appearing and closing the door behind him. Gladys jumped, turned around, and hung up the phone, fumbling to get it back into their pocket. "Are you sure you're okay? You're acting awfully on edge ever since Grace arrived." Mr Morgan asked, quietly playing with his moustache.

"Since she arrived? Oh no, not that long." Gladys said, pouring the boiled water from the kettle into the cup.

"Fair. But I've noticed you being on edge as of late. I *do* notice these things. I can't help but overhear your chats with Brenda." Mr Morgan said, watching Gladys get him his cup out of the cupboard.

"You heard what I said to Brenda, just Grace making me overthink things. I'm a worrier!" Gladys confirmed with a smile and stirred their tea.

"Gladys." Mr Morgan faced them directly, and grabbed their arms gently so they were now looking directly at each other. "For decades I've known you. This is the most bizarre I've seen you be. You're uneasy at your desk, you're over-drinking tea and scoffing biscuits, coming in here to make phone calls—"

"No, I wasn't—"

"Gladys. I'm not just a colleague, I'm a trusted friend. At least, that's how I view us." He said fixing his glasses awkwardly. Gladys did always appreciate his wise and friendly face. "I may not have the same relationship with you like Brenda does — we've never gone for cocktails — but just know you can speak to me confidentially. You speak your mind and you're a very open person and yet... this just doesn't seem like you." Mr Morgan ended their turn of speaking with an inflection which meant Gladys had to respond.

Gladys opened their mouth, but nothing came out. Mr Morgan only smiled back showing he'd be patient. Gladys thought about the words to say but didn't know how to tell him.

"Okay, why don't I try some conversational questions?" Mr Morgan suggested. Gladys nodded their head and hoped for the best. "Good... Is it about that Grace who has been coming to see you a lot recently?"

Gladys nodded.

"I figured as much. Is it about those questions they were asking last time?"

Gladys nodded, this time feeling stupid for letting Mr Morgan corner them in this way.

"Gladys." Mr Morgan chuckled, his gentle laughter making Gladys smile. "There's no such thing as Pandora's Box. There's nothing to worry about."

Gladys' smile left their face. "Well..."

Mr Morgan stopped laughing and his moustache twitched.

"What do you mean *well...*?"

~ Chapter Twelve ~

OLYMPUS

"Agnes?" Grace asked, reaching her desk.

Agnes looked up from her magazine while throwing a handful of nuts into her mouth. "Hold on." She said, chewing the nuts slowly. She swallowed hard and forced a smile, showing how nice they tasted. Her twitching eye told Grace quite the opposite though.

"Hairy Harry was looking for you." She scowled at Grace.

Grace immediately felt horrendous, she'd completely forgotten about her get-together with him. She got caught up with the Meditation and Self-Care Halls, the Viewing Platforms, and everything she'd learned at the Library.

"Agnes, I'm so sorry! I've been so busy, I genuinely forgot." Grace pleaded.

"Not me you need to apologise to…" She smirked.

"Can you please tell him I'm sorry? I'll rearrange, I promise." Grace knew this was a lie, but she felt terrible for hurting Harry's feelings.

"I will, next time I see him. But anyway, what can I do for you?"

Grace had to shake off her guilt and focus. "Have you heard of Olympus?"

Agnes tapped her fingers on the desk. "Of course."

"Do you know where it is? I'd like to go there if I can." Grace hesitated in asking.

Agnes rose up, walked around the desk, and headed towards the elevator Grace had just come from.

"Follow me."

Grace caught up and followed closely behind. She was deep in thought if she should share the reason why she was going to Olympus. Maybe Agnes would tell Gladys. Grace hoped she wouldn't, but would Agnes even care? They were hardly chatty, and it didn't seem like they were interested in gossip, unlike Brenda.

Agnes stopped at the elevator door, whipped out an orange card wrapped inside a plastic cover, and pressed on a panel Grace hadn't noticed before. She scanned the card on the reader and the elevator doors opened, machinery prepped for an uncommon journey.

"There you go. *This* elevator will take you to Olympus. Just step in and press the door button." Agnes aloofly commanded.

"Thank you, Agnes." Grace said, careful not to upset her.

"Anything else you need from me? Or can I go back to my break, *uninterrupted*?" Agnes rolled their eyes.

Grace sighed and shook her head. "No."

Agnes sniffed and walked back to her desk.

She pressed the door button, they slid shut, and the elevator whirled into action. Grace felt a weird sensation in her stomach, and realised she couldn't tell which direction she was travelling.

What do I say to him? She thought to herself. She had no idea how to approach Hesiod regarding Pandora's Box. But before she could continue the thought, the elevator came to a slow stop. The doors opened and a dozen excited women got inside, dressed to the nines in multi-coloured cocktail dresses, chatting to each other, unintentionally ignoring Grace until one of them noticed her.

"Is this going to Olympus?" A woman sporting a large beehive hairstyle and a peach-coloured dress asked.

"Yeah, it is." Grace said awkwardly.

"Oh great, exactly where we want to be going!" A half tipsy voice came from the gaggle of bodies.

Grace couldn't concentrate on her own thoughts with all the noise. It was starting to become claustrophobic with so many bodies pushing up against her shoulders.

"I love how good this glitter looks on my eyes! What do you think girls?" One of them dressed in rose gold urged.

"Incredible!" They harmoniously chimed.

"I'm so glad we had some pre-drinks before heading out, I'm already feeling the buzz." Said one dressed in pastel purple.

"I never leave the house without having at least one!" The beehive haired woman said.

A sequined sky-blue dressed body struggled to turn and face everyone in the elevator. "I just realised, girls... we're finally getting to try the 'Cumulus Fortuna' cocktail!" Everyone clucked a squeal of excitement, except Grace who was visibly confused.

"That's the best way to start the night. We've been talking about that cocktail for the past month. My treat!" said one of them dressed in light green.

"Well, if it's your treat, then make mine a double!" A voice joked.

"If I have one too many of them tonight, I'll end up flirting with that nice piano player." There was a resounding support of whistles and cheers for the flirting.

"You deserve a good night. She's always smiling at you!" A voice towered above them all.

"I *know*! but I don't want to flirt with her where she works—"

"— Wait, what?" Grace asked out loud before she realised the question didn't stay in her head. The flock fell silent, and every eye was suddenly on her.

"What?" A woman in a red dress asked.

Grace realised she'd butted in on a conversation. Why were they talking about cocktails and a flirty woman who plays piano in reference to Olympus? It's a mountain, she thought.

"Sorry... Are you all talking about the same Olympus I'm going to? I thought it was a—"

"Honey, have you ever been to Olympus before?" The beehive haired woman asked sweetly.

"No..."

"Oh, sweetie pie. It's not *that* Olympus." She said, as the rest of them gave a small giggle amongst each other. "It's a nightclub!"

"It's a what?!" Grace asked, shocked.

"It's not just *any* nightclub!" The woman dressed in blue said. "It's truly the peak of nightlife. But it is quite exclusive."

Grace suddenly got worried. If it's exclusive she might not get in, and then she'll be right back to square one. She didn't feel like sneaking in. "How exclusive?"

"Well, we're the Jewel Tones, so we're there monthly." The beehive haired woman said proudly.

All twelve voices rung out an "Amen!" in an immaculate harmony, resonating through Grace's ears.

119

"We're the nine-time champions of the 'A-Muse-Us Ball', so we always get in. Do you have a reservation?"

Grace shrugged her shoulders. "I don't have anything…"

"You do now. You're coming with us!" The woman in pastel purple chirped.

"The more the merrier!" Everyone else squealed.

"Are you sure?" Grace was shocked at the instant open invitation.

"Of course!" The woman in red said. "All women, no matter their colour or creed, should stick together!" Everyone raised a hand and snapped their fingers in agreement. "Why were you going to Olympus alone?"

"I, eh…" Grace didn't know what to say. She didn't want to open up to these strangers about her plan, but she had to tell them something they'd believe. "I heard they had a new cocktail and I, eh… I loved cocktails when I was living and thought… I thought they'd help me feel better…?" She managed, hoping it was convincing enough.

"Wait a minute." The woman in sky blue said, pushing her way towards Grace, who was looking highly suspicious. "You've never been to Olympus, but you've heard about the cocktail?"

Grace gulped.

"Then you're in for one *incredible* treat!" She said and everyone squealed. "The 'Cumulus Fortuna' is supposed to be the mother of all cocktails!"

"Oh… yay!" Grace forced out, trying to match the excitement.

A loud ping came from the speakers above and the elevator doors opened. Grace couldn't have been more thankful for the timing. The gaggle of rainbow bodies exited the tightly packed elevator and Grace finally felt like she could breathe. She took a moment to herself before darting out the doors as they automatically shut and became soaked in the incredible sight in front of her.

*　　　*　　　*

A gigantic asymmetrical circus-like tent made from stripy red velvet was directly ahead, several peaks made it look like smaller ones blended together. A mixture of bulbs and arrowed neon lights crudely hammered into the supports, advertising the show inside. Several windows cut out from the fabric gave a peak into the wonders going on, with bodies standing on their tip toes to get a better look. The entrance was decorated by gold branch like beams, holding the plush curtains open, with an elegant sign titled *Olympus* above. A long queue was formed around the circumference of the tent, twisting and twirling until it nearly reached the elevator. Grace stood in awe of the scale; she'd never seen anything like it.

"C'mon you!" The bee-hived woman shouted back to Grace, waving her hand. Grace quickly caught up to them.

"Am I dressed okay for this place?" Grace asked, suddenly uncomfortable in her jumper, leggings, and trainers.

She was looked up and down several times as she paced beside them. "Well, no… but we know the staff, so you'll be fine!"

"Don't worry, you'll get in!" The woman in red winked.

A tall older man in a black suit with slicked back hair was standing at the entrance, his hand placed on a crimson rope with a gold buckle on the other end. "'Allo, 'allo ladies! Has it been a month already?" He asked, unhooking the buckle and holding it away from them.

"Indeed it has, and you're always the highlight of the night. You know that, Jerome!" Said the woman in light green.

"I'm only here at the start and the end for you lot!" Jerome laughed.

"Well, it means our night starts off well, and then you make sure we all get home safe." The woman in red warmly squeezed Jerome's arm.

"Every time — you ladies always know what to say! Enjoy yourselves now."

They all walked passed the front-of-the-queuers, who were unhappy at others skipping ahead. "Hold on, is she with you?" Jerome stopped Grace from going further.

"Yeah, they said I—"

Grace was pulled through the open velvet barrier by her hand. "Oh yes, she is my sweet. We're recruiting a new Jewel!"

"Ha! I hope she can keep up." Jerome called, locking the rope back in place with a smile.

Grace strode through the dimly lit tunnel, hearing music get louder, and met the Jewel Tones standing at a pair of slatted doors, leaking colourful light from the gaps.

"Ready?" They buzzed.

Grace nodded, having no idea what to expect.

Two of the Jewel Tones pushed the slatted doors open and the atmosphere washed over everyone.

Grace stepped inside and immediately fell in love. Tall, scaffolded walls made of marble, framed by pillars, bridged the gallery together. Tasteful Grecian art, hung at uneven angles along with paint splatters, decorated the surrounding marble. Statues of the Gods with a drink in their hand and comfy couches underneath were scattered throughout. Cumulonimbus clouds, suspended from the rafters, glowed in multicoloured lighting. It slowly shifted through the spectrum and lit invisible paint on the floor as it passed between yellows and blues. A steady but airy beat was being kept up by a DJ on a stage high above. The bar ahead was a harp shaped island built directly into the floor, with gold leather stools swimming around it.

A hand rested on Grace's shoulder, and she turned to find out who it belonged to. "I'm Emily, my sweet." The beehive haired woman smiled.

"Oh, yeah, I'm Grace. Sorry." She awkwardly stumbled.

"That's alright, I can tell you're new here. Thought you should at least know mine before we settle in for the night. You might want to speak to Christine behind the bar though — you can see her there in the white blazer — she'll let you know what there is to drink. We'll have a booth near the jazz stage, it's got the best view, and you're more than welcome to join us!" She smiled, squeezing Grace's arm.

"Thank you!" Grace called after her, as she twirled and blew a kiss to join the rest.

Grace felt bad these women went out of their way to help her, and she didn't even ask their names. They may have been a rowdy group, but they were so accepting and unjudgmental of her without question, even lying for her on the spot to Jerome.

Grace found her way through the congregation of bodies, dancing and sipping highballs, to the bar where she slid over a stool and sat with her elbows on the edge. She caught eyes with who she assumed was Christine and flagged her down. The slender young woman put down the glass she was cleaning and skated over to Grace. She was short with wavy brunette hair, large hooped earrings, and thick square glasses.

"Welcome 'o Olympus! Firs' 'ime with us?" A loud Cockney accent came from her.

"Yeah! It's the most amazing place I've ever seen." Grace exclaimed.

Christine grabbed a small glass and a sapphire bottle, poured out the orange liquid inside, and dropped a Bada Bing cherry in the centre.

"What's that?" Grace asked, fascinated by their mixology skills.

"Everybody ge's 'he Olympus Vermouth on their firs' visi'. Can make a non-alcoholic one if you'd prefer?"

"I'll give it a go!"

Grace was excited to have a drink, something she didn't realise she may have needed up until this point. Holding the glass to her nose, she could smell the slight burn of alcohol with a sugary undertone. Instead of a small sip, she downed the drink in a single gulp, which was followed by a fast full-body shiver as she chewed on the cherry.

"Woah! That was so good. I thought it was going to be bitter, but it was sweet."

"Always goes down well! 'ere's 'he menu. Tell me wha' you want, I'll make it. Been 'ere tha' long it should be my name ou'side!" Christine laughed and slid the laminated parchment menu over the bar top.

Grace scanned it completely, letting the pulsing music and gentle laughter from other patrons mellow her into Olympus.

"These are all so fancy… I've never really—"

"Wan' me 'o make wha' you used 'o drink?" Christine asked with a knowing smile.

"I'd normally have a Peach Schnapps with lemonade… is that silly?" She asked.

"No' at all, if any'hing, it's underra'ed! One Peach Schnapps an' lemonade comin' righ' up." Christine said, whirling her arms behind the bar making the drink.

Grace took a moment to appreciate her surroundings, soaking in the ballroom outfits others had on while they loosely danced on the colour changing floor. Christine returned to the bar top and placed down a highball glass with an opaque pink fizzy liquid inside, and a thin straw to accompany.

"Seen you come in wi'h Emily, you a new member of their group?" Christine asked with a smirk in her smile.

"It's a long story, but no." Grace exclaimed, eyeing the concoction in front of her.

"I was goin 'o say — an' please take 'his 'he righ' way — you're no' exac'ly dressed to be part of their singin' group." Christine chuckled, hoping Grace would get the joke.

"I know, I literally met them on the way here! Thank you." Grace laughed and took a quick sip of her drink.

It was perfect. It took her back to a summer's night out with Gabe; they'd both left the club as it was closing and walked for so long, singing songs at the top of their lungs, they woke up in the middle of a park the next morning, hungover. Grace laughed and smiled to herself.

"Like I said, I've been 'ere tha' long." Christine winked and wiped the bar down. "If you're no' 'ere with Emily, wha' brings you to Olympus?"

"I'm actually looking for Hesiod. I was told he would be here?"

Christine rolled her eyes. "Tha' old plonker, yeah, 'e's 'ere alrigh'. Le' me ge' 'im for you." She disappeared behind a curtain at the bar leaving Grace alone with her drink.

She took another sip and used the time to wrap herself in that memory with Gabe. She remembered the song they were singing had a chorus they had to shout at each other while holding hands. Gabe fell over in the park and pulled her down with him; and as they lay down on the grass, they looked up at the stars and just talked. She couldn't remember what about, but she felt a huge smile cross her face as she took another sip.

Grace was brought out of her warm memory by voices coming from behind the curtain. She could only hear every other word until an old man burst through with thick grey hair and a large grey beard joining it. He was tall with a pot belly and small hands. His dress sense was outlandish; a yellow and red stripy suit accompanied by a purple robe, with brown snakeskin shoes.

"Ah, hello, hi! Yes, eh… were you the woman asking for me?" He asked.

"Are you Hesiod?" Grace asked, taken back by his presence.

"I am he. And you are?"

"Grace."

"Whether you're filled with or falling from, you'll always be *Grace*." He lyricised, smiling while his eyes filled with stories. "How are you enjoying Olympus? I think I did rather well with the place!" He asked, nodding feeling proud of his work.

"*You* did this?" Grace slammed her drink down gently.

"Did this? My dear, I built this from the cloud up. Not the easiest thing I've done, but between us, without Christine this place would fall apart!" Hesiod leaned in.

"I heard that." Christine shouted from the other side of the bar, making a drink for another guest.

"It really is stunning, there's nothing like this back home." Grace stared around in awe.

"Back home being… the Land of the Living I imagine?" Hesiod asked.

Grace sharply looked back to him, realising what she'd said, and nodded.

Hesiod chuckled, and loudly clapped his hands together. "Now, what is it I can do for you, Grace? I normally don't come out until show time!"

Grace finished her drink completely. "I didn't know… I was told I could find you here is all… see, I was reading something you wrote and—"

"— Living or dead?" Hesiod interrupted.

"… What?"

"Did I write it when I was alive, or when I was dead?"

It never occurred to Grace that writers, or artists of any sort, would continue doing their passion even in death. It gave her something extra to smile about, next to her newly unlocked memory with Gabe.

"I think you were alive? I'm not sure..." She asked herself.

"Ah! I'll need to see if I can cast my mind back. You may need to go to that big Library—"

"— That's where I just came from. They said I could find you here. See, I was reading something you had written and wanted to clarify something." Grace was being careful, especially with two drinks in her, she didn't want to randomly bring up Ooze or any of her plan. She needed to make a coherent story that excluded both.

"I see, I see... and what was it that you wanted clarification on?" Hesiod asked leaning on the bar.

"Pandora's Box." Grace said in a confident whisper.

Hesiod's eyes widened; his brow furrowed. There was a hesitation and stutter as he answered. "Wha — What about it? I literally made it up." He awkwardly answered, fingers tapping the bar edge in rhythm.

Grace sighed. "Oh, it doesn't exist?"

"No, of course it doesn't."

"At all?" She asked hopefully.

"Exactly." He shook his head.

Grace looked around at the art. "Well, did anything inspire it? Everything comes from somewhere, right?"

"Yes, well... In a way you are right, everything is inspired from somewhere else..."

"So that means something did inspire it?" Grace pressed.

"Well..." Hesiod said taking in a deep breath.

"Hesiod!" A loud voice came from behind Grace, giving her a jump. She turned around to see Mr Morgan beaming. "My old friend!"

"Now this *is* a surprise! It's been too long." Hesiod jumped around the side of the bar. They immediately embraced each other laughing. "What are you doing here? I can't believe my very eyes!"

Mr Morgan put his arm around Hesiod's shoulders and escorted him away from Grace, reminiscing about something she couldn't hear.

"Eh, Mr Morgan?" She asked, finding his actions rude.

"Oh, I'm so sorry Grace, these glasses are so dirty. I thought you were a big smudge!" He laughed.

"I was actually talking to Hesiod about something—"

"— Why don't you just enjoy yourself here?" Hesiod asked, sounding relieved. "Your drinks are on me tonight. Just read the book, it's more reliable than my memory could ever be these days." He smiled at her and snapped his fingers to Christine to get Grace another drink.

"As I was saying —" Mr Morgan said putting his arm round Hesiod's shoulder again as they walked away.

Grace sat there shocked. She didn't know what to do. She was so close to finding out about Pandora's Box and Mr Morgan swooped in at the most inconvenient time. Before Christine could put down her drink, Grace had already stood up and decided she was leaving.

"Oh, Christine?" Grace turned back and leaned over the bar quickly. "My free drinks from Hesiod, can they be put over to Emily's table?"

"Say less." Nodded Christine.

Grace thanked her and exited Olympus, slipping through half-drunk dancers and admirers of the artwork. She was deep in thought about what Hesiod told her. Although he admitted that Pandora's Box wasn't real, she could feel he was withholding information. She passed through the slatted doors, walked through the dimly lit tunnel, and smiled at Jerome, thanking him for letting her inside in the first place.

"Are you not staying with the rest of the ladies?" He asked.

"Not this time, but their table has free drinks all night, so look after them when they leave!" Grace said.

"Oh my goodness, thank you for the heads up. Have a good night!" Jerome said waving her off.

Grace waved back, noticing the queue had disappeared inside. She was starting to feel tipsy and had to concentrate on her sense of direction. She turned towards the elevator when suddenly—

"What did I say?" Gladys asked, their glasses balancing judgementally on the end of their nose, hands on their hips.

*　　　*　　　*

Grace was too stunned to speak.

"What did I say? I said that you were to go straight home!"

Grace couldn't look them in the eye. She felt like she was being given into trouble by the head teacher at school.

"What are you doing in Olympus of all places?"

Grace had to get out of this. Despite having two drinks, she had to keep things concise if she was going to get through this without Gladys hating her.

"I was on the way home but... I met some people. Yeah... I met people on the way who said they were going for some drinks and... well, I thought I could use that."

Gladys stared sceptically through the story Grace was stringing together. It wasn't a complete lie, but it was definitely stretching the truth.

"We got chatting, and they invited me to this place... and we—"

"Grace, hen, I don't believe you. I don't mince my words. Come on. What is *really* going on?" Gladys asked, walking slowly towards her with an arm outstretched to gently grab hold of Grace's hand. "I'm not going to bite your head off. I'd like to think you'd know that by now, my lovely. I'm only looking out for what's best for you, for everyone! I always am." They said and chuckled with their friendly angelic laughter.

Grace couldn't do it, she couldn't lie anymore and had to tell Gladys about the plan. She lowered her head and from the corner of her eye she seen it.

The Shimmer.

She finally saw what Gladys had been talking about; an iridescent glint that fell out of her hair and onto her hands. She suddenly exploded with emotion.

"This. Gladys. This!" Grace shouted. "This is what is going on. Ever since you told me about this gold stuff, I just don't know what is happening, how I'm feeling, where I am... Sometimes I feel like I'm okay and then other times I'm just not. I'm not okay, I can't handle it. I just can't come to terms with being here forever when this sparkle-shimmer-thing is happening. And apparently it means I'm not dead? But I am dead? But I can't go back because it's not a constant shimmer? I just don't get it. I don't get any of this!" Grace let the tears fall down her face, not realising she'd pent up all this emotion.

She looked to Gladys who was taken aback, tears in their own eyes.

"Oh, my lovely..." Gladys came in close for a hug, and despite how Grace was feeling, she needed this from them. "Thank you for opening up to me. It's not easy, I know... But you have to listen to me, and listen really well, alright? Like I said, I'm only here to do what's best for ye. Because your Shimmer wasn't there from the start, and it comes and goes... If I sent you back now, truthfully, it would be an absolute gamble if you were to return to the Land of the Living or if you'd return as a Ghost. That means you'd be Earthbound, lost in a world of your own." Gladys wiped away the tears from Grace's cheeks. "Not able to talk to anyone. No way to return."

No way to save Gabe, Grace thought.

Gladys let out a little whimper as a tear fell down their cheek as well. "Look at that. I knew as soon as you started crying, I was in trouble." They wiped their cheeks with their daisy print sleeve. "Listen, do you fancy coming back to mine and having a proper chat. Get things off your mind, we can really have a heart to heart, order in food, watch a movie and all sorts. What do you say, hen?"

Grace's mind was still ringing with a mixture of her own words and Gladys'. She felt alone anyway, never mind about being a Ghost. Her friend is about to die, and she could have stopped it from happening.

She *can* stop it from happening.

She can.

She had to speak with Ooze. She couldn't do it alone; Ooze *had* to help.

"That actually does sound really nice Gladys, thank you." Grace said, smiling and wiping away her tears.

"Oh, good! I've got plenty of snacks—"

"— But..." Grace added. "I think, I need sleep. I've had a few drinks, I'm not in the right place... What do you think?"

"I'm not going to force you to do something you don't want to do, my lovely! I'll heavily suggest, but never force you." They said with a wink.

Grace smiled as they walked back to the elevator. "Thank you, Gladys."

"What for, my lovely?"

"For listening. I really shouted back there and I'm sorry. I'm sure you've dealt with worse, but you listened to me and... sometimes that's all someone needs. They don't want advice, or a lesson, or an answer... they just want to be listened to."

"And I'm always here for that, my lovely. I won't pretend to be an all-knowing Soul who'll be able to help with everything. But you know what I will be able to do? Be there for you, my lovely. It might not sound like much, but it's the bare minimum we can do for each other."

Gladys swiped their card at the elevator, waited a few moments, and the doors opened with a whirl. Gladys looked behind them at Olympus. "If you're alright to get home yourself, I'll get Mr Morgan away from Hesiod. The moment they get together and drink, it's like a monstrous Stag-Do! You should have seen the chaos they caused a few years back; I still can't look a Garibaldi in the face."

Grace chuckled and stood inside the elevator. "I'll be fine, Hairy Harry showed me the way, I know where I'm going."

"Amazing, hen. And remember—"

"Straight home" Grace said, mimicking Gladys. They chuckled and waved their finger mockingly back at Grace.

"Right you, I'll check in tomorrow at some point. Look after yourself, my lovely!" Gladys said as the elevator doors shut.

Grace was left alone inside, looking back at her own reflection from the mirrored doors. She looked down at the console with all the buttons for the different floors and back at her reflection, not recognising the face staring back at her.

She is dead... But Gabe isn't, the thought lingered.

The elevator clunked into action and threw Grace sideways onto the floor. She looked up to see the DLS button lit up and secretly smiled to herself. It looks like fate made this decision for her. She was going to speak to Ooze.

~ Chapter Thirteen ~

THE INFERNO DEPARTMENT

"Ooze?" Grace beckoned, her voice echoing down the circular pit. She hoped the Hole would feel less lonely this time, but the sightless abyss made her feel more uneasy.

"Ooze!" She said, a little more urgently this time.

It wasn't there. She looked to the walls, remembering it appeared from there before. She carefully stepped over to the outer curve, eyed some of the brick work, and knocked on it twice. "Ooze? I need you!" She said, still in an urgent whisper.

Grace let out a deep sigh, her icy breath hanging in the air. She didn't remember it being this cold before.

From the corner of her eye, she saw something move at the archway. She turned quickly to get a look at what had moved and audibly shuddered.

On one side of the archway was another creature made up of an unidentifiable liquid mass. This one seemed to be more humanoid in shape with shades of red and black in it. Grace could make out symbols written all over but couldn't understand them. She looked at its face, and unlike Ooze, this one seemed to have some visible features: a mouth that was slightly wider than a regular persons, and eyes that were a dark red with black pupils, the opposite of Ooze's creepy milky ones.

"Hey! Don't get scared!" The voice spoke, in a shaky and gargled pattern, as if it were underwater.

"I'm not." Grace said confidently, although her back was pressed up against the wall. "What are you?"

"Ouch. Really? You look at me and think, 'what' is the best thing to call me?"

Grace could see that the creature looked visibly hurt. "Well... I—"

"I'm only joking!" The creature said through laughter. "Although I will say I do prefer 'who' to 'what'". They said, taking squelchy steps towards Grace.

"Okay then, *who* are you?"

The creature held out a dripping appendage. "I'm Mük."

Grace stared at the long arm being outstretched for a handshake and obliged. She grasped its oily hand and gently shook it. Mük howled as the arm fell off, splatting on the floor. Grace yelled loudly before quickly muffling the sound with her free hand.

"What did you do?" Mük cried.

Grace took a couple of steps back, squirming. "I don't know. I'm sorry! What happened?"

"You ripped it off!" Mük shouted.

"I just shook your hand!"

Mük sniffed nonchalantly and shrugged. "Yeah, you did. My bad!"

The gooey puddle at Grace's feet slithered to join onto Mük's leg, absorbing into the body and regrowing the arm. Maybe *what* was right.

"Anyway, who are *you?*" Mük asked.

Grace wondered if she should even answer. "I'm looking for Ooze."

"That's not what I asked" Mük waved a sticky finger.

She scuffed her shoe on the ground, sighing. "Grace."

"Hmm. And you're looking for Ooze?" The creature pivoted the upper half of its body around, keeping the lower half still. "You won't find it here. We alternate shifts at the Hole." Mük shifted to a mocking voice. "For we are the Keepers of the Hole. We make sure everyone who goes down is meant to, and in a timely manner." They said, grinning widely.

"What does that mean?" Grace asked, concerned for her own safety.

"Sometimes we push them." Mük giggled.

Grace gulped hard.

"You want to speak to Ooze though. Why?"

"Oh, well, we—"

"I mean, Ooze isn't great at conversation. You've seen where its mouth can go, right?" Mük pointed behind them on their body. "Whereas I'm filled with all sorts of things to talk about. Why not stay and chat with me for a while? I'm sure you've felt how lonely this place gets. Imagine working here until the end of time, it's not pretty."

Grace nodded and shuddered simultaneously. "Well, I need to speak to Ooze because—"

"Blah blah blah, sure, you can speak to Ooze, but you're not going to like where it is." Mük dramatically lifted their arm and pointed to the Hole. "Tehe."

"I'm not jumping down there!" Grace protested, her heart beating faster at the thought of being pushed.

"Well... this conversation with Ooze can't be *that* important then, can it?"

Grace peered over the edge, breathing in the sulphuric sting in the air, making her cough. "How long is the fall?"

"Long enough for every decision and act that led to that very moment of you falling to flash before your eyes." Mük's eyes shone bright with glee.

"But I'm just visiting."

"Oh. In that case, you can take the stairs!" Mük said, bouncing over to the wall and pushing their arm into the brickwork. A gap opened and a large lever appeared, which Mük pulled down on with a glorious clunk.

The floor below Grace rumbled as the sound of stones grinding against each other revealed a staircase. It was circular, following the circumference of the Hole all the way down into the shadows.

"No railings, they just get in the way." Mük added as he watched the steps form.

The rumbling fell silent, and a few scattered pebbles clanged off the sides as they fell. Grace listened out for their ultimate landing, but it never came. She looked back to Mük.

"So, I just... I just go down?"

"I'm not going to make you ask for permission to go down some stairs, I'm not a monster!" They laughed.

Grace held out her foot over the edge which had one large step on the same level. She slowly applied her weight and felt it supporting her. She kept one hand on the wall with every step as she descended lower, slowly letting the darkness envelop her fear of the unknown below.

Grace stopped. The darkness was so thick she couldn't see the steps ahead of her; one wrong move and it was over. She could hear her heartbeat so loud in her ears, she didn't hear the slithering sound next to her.

Grace looked up, trying to get a better view. "Mük!"

"Yes?"

The voice invaded her ear closest to the wall and Grace yelped. "Where are you?"

"I can travel through stone... You don't expect me to jump or walk all the way down, do you? Now that's just silly." Mük said, unbothered by her situation.

"I don't care, I can't see! What do I do?" Grace panicked, turning to face the wall to press her body against it. As the steps disappeared from view, she gave into the darkness around her. She instantly forgot how many stairs could be ahead of her or how wide they were. She felt herself lose balance.

"Not to be gross, but your face is directly in mine at this point." Mük spurted.

"Just do something!" Grace shouted, closing her eyes.

"Alright, alright, no need to get upset."

Grace could hear the flickers of fire igniting around her.

"You can open your eyes." Mük said.

Grace opened one eye slightly to see blurred candles had lit the staircase all the way down into the abyss.

"Better?"

"Better." Grace said trying to find her breath again.

"Good. I was about to go back up there and pull that lever."

Grace turned to the wall to see Mük's oily face sliding over the brickwork.

"How are you even doing that?" Grace asked as she took a tentative step to begin the descent once again.

"That's a good question. I don't know. I just walk into the wall, and I become a face. Isn't that interesting?" Mük said, bemused. "But I will say it's a much better way to travel."

"I wish I could do the same right now. Some of the steps are missing!"

"Yeah, that's on us. We're supposed to keep it up to standard, but... it's a difficult job. Especially since one of us doesn't care and the other is Ooze!" Mük laughed while sliding next to Grace. "Speaking of, what do want to talk to Ooze about?"

"Nothing." Grace sharply turned her attention away.

"Nothing? Weird conversation. Then again, Ooze is weird. Would you believe I'm the sane one? Neither would I. It does seem a bit odd; you going down the Hole to speak to one of the Keepers when you could have just waited for tomorrow's shift."

"I don't have time to waste." Grace said, getting increasingly annoyed by Mük's ramblings.

"Time-sensitive, is it? Interesting. See, I knew it was something you were wanting to talk about. No one makes a journey like you are over *nothing*."

Grace stopped and took a deep breath.

"Yeah, I forget to breathe sometimes too." Mük said, taking a deeper breath than Grace.

"Mük."

"What?"

"Do you have to talk all the way down? It's really distracting." Grace asked, trying not to hurt Mük's feelings.

They looked down at the steps and back to Grace. "I'm distracting you from walking?"

"It's just... a lot of talking you're doing." She half-joked.

"Well, there is an even faster way down."

"Like an elevator, like Paradise has?" Grace asked, hopeful.

"Sort of." Mük said, biting their oily lips. "But you won't like it."

Grace was confused. "Will the stairs turn into a giant slide or something?"

"Worse."

And in an instant, Grace was surrounded by Mük, being pulled into the staircase wall. She tried to yell but was muffled by the stickiness of the goo. She closed her eyes in fear, but wished she'd went for her ears instead as a howling wind rushed in. The wind turned into screams, getting louder by the second. Screams for help, of begging.

"Make it stop!"
"Please, my children!"
"I can't do it anymore!"
"I didn't mean to!"
"Please! It wasn't me!"

Suddenly the screaming stopped, and Grace hit the ground hard. She opened her eyes and groaned at the rough landing, realising she was lying on a dusty stone floor. She lay there for a moment shuddering, trying to erase what she was subjected to. She sat up and noticed the bottom of the staircase.

"Told you, you wouldn't like it." Mük laughed, sliding out of the wall in their full humanoid form.

"Who were those people screaming?" Grace asked, still shaky.

Mük sniffed. "I don't know. They're always there. You learn to tune them out."

Grace started to get cold feet at the idea about finding Ooze again. If those voices were real people, what could she expect the rest of the Inferno to be like? What terrifying horrors would she have permanently tattooed into her brain? And would she ever truly be able to forget about them?

She took a few deep breaths as she focused on one of the candles on the wall, watching the flame flicker until she felt like herself again.

"You okay? You looked queasy for a minute." Mük asked. "I didn't want to say anything in case you threw up!"

"I'm okay. Just never let me travel that way again." Grace spoke slowly as she stood up, keeping her eye on the candle. "So, where do I go from here?"

*　　　*　　　*

Mük raised one of their dripping arms and pointed down a dark hallway, which was suddenly ignited on either side by wooden torches. The flickering hallway led to a pair of large wooden doors, reinforced by weathered iron grating. The doors were old and rotted, chipped and scratched as if something violently tried to escape. Grace had only seen something this grand in movies that depicted entrances to castles.

"Walk down there, and you'll be at the reception. They'll let you know where to go from there." Mük said, smiling. "This was nice."

"What was?" Grace asked, looking down the hallway.

"I never get to walk or spend time with people like this, unless they're crying or screaming." Mük shrugged a little, and Grace could tell they were being genuine. "And you put up with me, for the most part. So yeah, this was nice."

Grace smiled back at Mük. "Yeah… I mean, I don't get to meet many people like you, but I imagine you're one of the nicer ones."

Mük blushed and backed into the wall at the bottom of the staircase. "You said *people*".

Grace watched as Mük completely disappeared into the stone wall, giggling with glee.

She turned her attention back to the large castle-like doors and started walking. Grace looked for a handle as she got closer, but there was nothing there to push or pull. The doors were so big, she looked up in case there was a knocker above, appropriate for the size of a giant.

The wood of the doors snapped and groaned as it began to slowly open without Grace doing anything. She passed through small billows of dust as it dropped from above and found herself in a long rectangular room with a single desk in the centre. The desk was part of the back wall and jutted out with enough room for someone to sit behind it.

Grace saw a small, round, red-haired woman sitting at the desk, typing extraordinarily fast on her computer. Her orange eye makeup was pointed with very clean black eyeliner, which only emphasised the incredibly large lashes that poked out from their bob hairstyle. She was in an oversized mustard cardigan, with several buttons missing.

Grace approached, seeing how empty the room was, except for an inappropriate number of mugs along the desk. Neat rows of them lined a shelf behind the woman; some had slogans, some just had pictures, but mostly they were being used to hold stationary. The woman slowly turned her gaze from the computer to Grace, blinked slowly, and rolled her eyes.

A thick Brooklyn accent piped up. "Hello and welcome to the Inferno Department; we trust you enjoyed your trip here. Or if you took the stairs, congratulations on the cardio. My name is Phyllis. Or if you came via DLS, you may have heard certain people refer to me as 'Mug-Stealing-Phyllis'. These are allegations and cannot be proved." Grace looked at the mugs surrounding Phyllis at her desk. "I bought every single one of these." Grace nodded but could clearly see one that said, 'Gladys' Mug, Back Off!'.

Phyllis lifted a small red tray, took each item out one at a time, and slammed them on the desk in front of Grace. "Here is your brochure, your complimentary pencil topper, and your cupcake. Don't get too happy; it's red velvet. Now, what's your name, and we'll get you your Personal Serial Number?"

"I'm just visiting." Grace said.

Phyllis leaned heavily on the desk with her elbows and looked Grace up and down. "Where's your Visitors Pass?"

"My what?" Grace asked.

"Round your neck. You should have a Visitors Pass." Phyllis turned back to her computer and began typing.

"Someone in DLS or Paradise would have given you a Visitors Pass if you were here as a visitor, and right now I don't see a Visitors Pass, which means you are *not* a visitor." She said matter-of-factly.

"I don't have one." Grace said, touching the area around her neck.

"I just said that." Phyllis said, sharply.

"I came by myself. I'm looking to speak to someone I know called—"

"Listen, I'm not here to listen. I have a million things to do." Phyllis picked up the phone on her desk, dialled a single number, and held the phone to her ear. "With you not giving me your name to register you for your Personal Serial Number, and your lack of Visitor Pass, I'm left with no choice but to call Security."

Grace felt speechless for a moment, trying to find words to stop Phyllis from saying anything to Security, when she saw the phone glow with a dark purple aura. It floated from Phyllis' hand and slammed back down onto its holder. Phyllis stood up and glared at Grace.

"Who are you?" She said, curiously furious, holding her gaze, until a voice came out from behind Grace, and Phyllis instantly sat down.

"We should be worrying about people trying to leave rather than coming in, Phyllis." The familiar voice said. Grace turned quickly to see it was Lucy, carrying a stack of five books in one hand, tied neatly together. "Don't you think?" She asked Phyllis, lowering her hand.

Phyllis nodded, and Grace saw that she was visibly panicking, her hands slightly trembling and her eyes wide open. Lucy stood next to Grace, giving her a bombastic side eye. "We met earlier, didn't we?"

"That's right, back in the library." Grace confirmed.

"'The Historical and Biographical Library'." Lucy corrected with a little smirk. "If it has a title, you should use the correct one." She looked over to Phyllis. "Grace is my personal guest. She won't need a Visitors Pass. Anyone who likes a good read is fine in my books." She said, and began striding slowly towards a door on the far-right wall of Phyllis' desk. "Walk with me."

Grace jumped a little at the assertive tone, feeling like she would never be able to relax around Lucy. As she sped over, she distinctly heard Phyllis let out a large sigh of relief.

"Why, of all places, are you visiting the Inferno Department?" Lucy asked as they walked through the door into a large stone hallway. This hallway felt as cold and alone as the Hole was, and as they walked, candles lit up the area.

"I'm visiting a friend." Grace said.

She had no idea who Lucy was or who she knew, but in the back of her mind, she felt she was untrustworthy. As unintentionally helpful as Lucy had been, there was just something she couldn't put her finger on, which meant there was no way she was going to open up about her plan. If she couldn't do it to Gladys, then there was no way she could do it to Lucy.

"A friend?" Lucy said, raising an immaculate eyebrow as they walked. "That ended up here? I didn't expect a nice girl like you to be friends with people that would end up here."

Grace didn't necessarily agree with that. You can be friends with people from all walks of life, but that doesn't mean you know absolutely everything about them. What gets them to the Inferno is their choices. "Well, I only met them in the After —" Grace caught the word before she finished it. It still didn't feel right to say. "— Afterlife."

"I see! They're probably one of the probationers then." She said, tilting her head down to Grace, her updo staying firm. "It's good to see them making progress positively." Grace had no idea what Lucy was talking about, she just hoped she wouldn't press for any further information. "They may be coming from the Inferno, but we do a lot of Rehabilitation and Probationary Programs. There are more intense and stringent ones, but for those people — well, let's just say they'll never make it through them." Lucy slowed her pace down until she had stopped outside an archway leading to darkness. Grace wondered how anyone knew where to go.

"I have some important work to attend to down this way, but if you keep going straight, you'll come to another set of doors that will lead you to the Inferno Courtyard. I trust you'll know your way to your friend from there."

"Oh, yeah. I mean, I should be able to find them." Grace lied.

She had no idea how she was going to find Ooze when she got there. Mük said to ask Reception, but Phyllis didn't seem to be the helpful type. And although Lucy helped her get into the Inferno, she wasn't going to mention Ooze's name in case there was a reaction like Gladys had.

"Be sure and look after yourself." Lucy said, patting off the dust from Grace's shoulders. "If anyone gives you any bother, just say you know me. They'll shake worse than Phyllis did." She chuckled, with a sharp smile. Grace laughed with her and waved Lucy goodbye as she disappeared into the shadows of one of the hallways.

Grace took a deep breath, feeling the air in the room return to normal, regardless of how cold it felt. With Lucy gone, Grace felt like she could relax a little more. She turned to face the darkness of the hall ahead, and as she walked forward, the candles lit the way, and she saw the slight outline of the doors Lucy spoke about ahead.

She felt herself speeding towards them and saw that the doors were more human sized compared to the grandiosity of the Reception to the Inferno. They were metal doors with rounded tops, but they had no handles. Grace was confused again. Why did none of the doors here have any handles or methods to open them? She decided to place her hands on the hairline crack and pushed hard.

They squeaked loudly as they opened, and Grace recoiled as she instantly felt the cacophonous noise and the searing heat hit her.

~ Chapter Fourteen ~

THE OUBLIETTE

Grace looked all around to see a thriving underground world. She could see faces carved into the far-off mountains, with some in the middle of construction; metal scaffolding and machinery all around them. A little closer were large rock towers, with crudely cut out gaps to represent windows, with no pane. There were people walking everywhere through the stone city ahead of her; it was overpopulated and thick with noise and smoke. As she stared down over the rocks and people, she could see a deep pit filled with darkness and at the very bottom an ominous glow of red. Fire was down in the depths, surrounding the city of rock along each side. Above her was a colossal, cavernous roof with huge, sharp rocks dangling down, an ever looming and impaling threat.

Grace couldn't tell if everyone here was a person. It was clear some of them were, but there were bigger creatures that stood dozens of feet above; long curling horns, thick slimy tentacles, large misshapen eyes, even the flying creatures were clearly not birds.

"This is hell." She said out loud, and took a doubtful step forward into the hazardous heat, joining a pathway that led into the city of stone.

Walking through, it was initially shops and stalls that greeted her; she didn't recognise any of the items, but she knew they came from other creatures — claws, hoofs, horns — all on sale for, apparently, a good deal. The people bustling around her were dirty and looked lost. Covered in soot and dirt, with torn clothes, their facial expressions were fixed in fear, anger, and trauma. Grace felt like she would stick out like a sore thumb, and all eyes would be on her, but they all seemed to be in their own thoughts, shouting at each other to get passed.

She managed to find her way to a large circular opening in the busy town square. Most people were avoiding the centre, but there were a few that were sitting on or near the stone carving in the middle. It depicted the Inferno with the nine circles of hell. It had a large base that matched the size of the top circle, a cone shape that progressively got thinner and smaller with each circle until it joined the base. The detail made Grace's mouth drop in awe. Intricately placed throughout were small people and creatures carved into it, down to the finest facial features. Each circle had a complete story to tell, which Grace noticed as she slowly made her way around it.

"Sometimes I cry thinking about all those Souls who don't get to experience the Inferno." Ooze shouted above the busy atmosphere; its slimy voice creeping around Grace's ears, making her jump.

"Ooze!" Grace exclaimed, leaning against the base of the hellish depiction. "I've been looking for you. Where have you been?"

"Even Demons get a day off." It said with an eery smile.

Grace shuddered. "Listen, we need to find another way."

Ooze raised a huge, dripping arm up to its mouth and zipped it shut, keeping its wide, milky eyes fixed on Grace.

"I've not told anyone. But every time I tried to get close, I got pushed back." She continued.

Ooze slid closer to Grace. "You just need to try harder." It grimaced.

"No, I tried!" Grace said in a hushed whisper. "We need to find another way for me to get home."

"No. This is it. This is the *only* way." Ooze said forcefully.

"What do you suggest? Because when I tried to find out more about..." Grace looked around to see if anyone was within earshot. "Pandora's Box," she mouthed to Ooze, "I was told to just read a book. Even from the author, that Hesiod guy."

"Hesiod has always been tricky." Ooze said with a hint of anger. "Kidnap Hesiod and bring him to me. I can make him talk."

"I swear, Gladys, I've never seen her use her power like that. It was so out of the ordinary, you know?" Grace overheard the distinct voice of Phyllis speaking over the crowd, obnoxiously loud.

Grace panicked and darted around, trying to see her among the crowd, but couldn't pinpoint her. "Ooze, we have to go. She's talking to Gladys!"

Grace watched Ooze's milky eyes widen; knowing how problematic it would be for Gladys to get involved, let alone be caught together.

"This way." It said and slithered its hulking mass around the stone carving, pushing its way through the crowd, and hid behind a cart filled with brown vases. Grace was quick to keep up and peaked around the cart to see Phyllis slowly approach where she'd just been.

"No, it was just this random girl. I swear, I've never seen her before in my life, just appeared out of nowhere. 'Visiting' she claimed, but I didn't see a pass on her. And then

Lucy said that this girl was her personal guest. Personal guest! I know! Gladys, she left me speechless. Well, you know her. She never does that. Never. Remember when you-know-who came down and she pretended not to know them? She's very private." Phyllis took a seat on the base of the stone carving. "Oh no, I couldn't. I'm awful with faces. I didn't recognise my husband's till I pulled the plug." Grace watched intently as Phyllis just nodded and affirmed things Gladys was asking on the phone. "Yeah! That's her! Do you know her?"

Grace felt the breath being taken out of her; Gladys knew where she was. Gladys *knew* Grace had lied to them.

"Wait, why are you coming down? It's not happy hour at The Blazing Hoof. Gladys—"

Grace turned back to Ooze. "If Gladys finds me, I'm going to wish I belonged down here. We need to hide so we can figure something out!"

Ooze looked around, its milky eyes floating all over its body, until they relaxed back into their usual spot. "Keep up and follow me." It said, and with loud squelches, began to move its body through the crowd. Grace found it easy to keep up as the crowd was slowing Ooze down, but she was getting odd stares from the sunken faces around her. They turned down alleyways, through streets, crawled through a stall, and even went through the back door of someone's stone house, until they reached a dead end with a pile of skulls in the corner.

"Now what?" Grace asked, breathless.

Ooze chuckled. "Oh, you're really not going to like this."

"Wait, no!" Grace screamed, but it was too late. Ooze already had its large, grimy hands around her and was pulling her downward into the ground.

The screams came back as the darkness consumed Grace as she closed her eyes again, too scared to witness the torture.

"I don't deserve this!"

"It was him, not me!"

"I didn't know!"

"My baby, please! Please!"

"It hurts!"

The pressure around Grace's body began to ease, and she felt solid ground beneath her feet as the voices became horrifying memories.

"You can open your eyes." Ooze said, as it let go of her.

Grace shuddered, trying to let go of the voices she heard. They were completely different, but the pain and anguish were palpably identical.

She opened her eyes slowly and took in the space around her. She was in an underground cavern; sandstone walls with plain white candles strewn throughout, illuminating the space. It was decently large, with a bed in the corner, a table, bookcase, and some boxes filled with all sorts of knick-knacks.

Ooze slid over to the table where a man's ghostly figure was sitting. "Since you're here, you might as well meet the rest of us." It said.

Grace tentatively walked to the small round table, and the ghostly figure slowly turned his head to face her. She saw what looked like a face, with a skull underneath, like it was shining through its grey figure. His hair floated all over, as if he were underwater.

"Hollow." He said, turning a page in a book with a scrawny skeletal finger. His voice was just as ghostly as his figure — breathy and light, but above all, empty.

"What?" Grace asked, holding her breath.

"My name." He turned his head with a snap of a bone, back to the book he was reading.

Hollow wasn't exactly what Grace thought a Ghost would look like.

"He's not a Ghost." Ooze said, reading Grace's mind. "He's a Familiar, like me." It said, pulling out a chair for Grace.

"What does that mean?" She asked, sitting down slowly, keeping her eyes on Hollow who took in a deep, dusty breath and exhaled.

"A Familiar is a being that is chosen to obey. We do as we're told, when we're told." Ooze said, its mass feeling like it was sucking out the candlelight.

"Okay…" Grace said, finally taking her eyes off Hollow. "And who are you a Familiar for?"

"SATAN." Shouted a raspy voice from the corner of the room. Grace jumped and stood up, breathing heavily. The voice belonged to a tall, skeletal woman with long white hair, covering her entire body. She was spider-like with the way she crawled down from the ceiling and slowly made her way over to Grace. "We follow his every command, without will or objections." She said without moving her lips. The voice came from her hands, where Grace could see a mouth nestled into each palm, with grim, painful scars.

As the woman drew herself to complete height, Grace looked up and gave out a little gasp.

"We are forbidden to hurt inside this room." Hollow said, sounding exhaustedly bored. "We are aware of what we look like, child. We are no rose in a garden, but rather a weed. We are not for the faint of heart." Hollow raised his skeletal hands to calm down his hair. "Yet, rest assured, no harm shall befall you in this room that you didn't do to yourself."

Grace looked to Ooze for confirmation, who just smiled with an extra-wide grin. "He speaks the truth, which is no fun at all."

"Seek the fun elsewhere!" Hollow barked, smacking the book shut. "I'll be in the other corner. Still within earshot unfortunately, but out with the distance to smell you." He said as he floated over to a box to sit on.

"He's always like this, don't take it personally. I'm Willow." The tall woman said. "I didn't mean to scare you... I can't help how I move."

"I did. I'm built to terrify." Ooze said gleefully.

Grace felt her knees weaken. This was a lot to take in. The ghostly man, the skeletal woman who speaks from her hands, and Ooze taking her through the ground. She sat down heavily on the chair she jumped up from.

"Where am I?" She asked, closing her eyes and massaging her temples.

"This is the Oubliette." Ooze said sickly.

"The Oubli — what?"

"Oubliette!" Hollow shouted from across the room, which oddly still sounded like a whisper. "It's French."

"It's lonely." Willow said, her eyes glowing with sorrow. "Until we're called upon by Satan for any job he has for us, we stay here."

"Except for Ooze and Mük. They have the extra duty of being Keepers of the Hole." Hollow said, with a slight resentment, as if he thought were more appropriate for the job.

"You just stay here until you're called for?" Grace asked.

They both nodded.

"That's not much of a life though, is it?" She shrugged.

"LIFE?!" Willow screamed, making Grace jump. "None of us have had a life for centuries. We paid an unspeakable price to be what we are now."

"Unforgivable price. All four of us." Hollow moaned over Willow.

"I enjoyed it." Ooze said, its mouth to its side.

"I can't even think of anything that bad." Grace said.

Hollow slowly turned to face her. "Good. Unspeakable and unforgivable for a reason."

Willow sat herself down at the table, her long body not built for such small furniture. "Why did you bring someone here?" She asked Ooze. "We're not supposed to have Souls here. Remember when Mük tried to have a pet?"

"We needed to hide for a bit." It smirked.

"Say less, you wobbly imbecile." Hollow muttered from across the room. "We just want to keep our heads down. You keep causing more problems than we can keep up with!"

"No, it's true!" Grace said, jumping to Ooze's defence. Willow snapped her neck to look at Grace. "I've got a friend who is still living, and I might be able to save them if I go back to help him, and Ooze was just helping me."

Hollow dramatically floated over to Grace. "You think this amalgamation of watery hatred will genuinely help you? You're a fool if you believe that."

"Hollow!" Willow screeched, her hand thrusting into his ghostly face. "You had friends once too. What would you do to take back what you did?"

Hollow stayed floating in the air, his eyes locked with hers, and he began to frown. "For the most learned amongst us, I am so quick to judge." He said. "I apologise."

"It's okay… I just really needed help, and Ooze did." Grace said.

"Not for free, I imagine." Hollow said sceptically.

"There's no need to get into details now." Ooze began.

"I would do anything for my friend." Grace said, looking at Hollow, realising that although a small amount of time had passed since they met, she no longer felt the same fear towards him. Even with Willow, despite them being the most unsettling in the room, knowing that they wouldn't hurt her in the Oubliette really helped. "Apparently, I have this 'Shimmer' thing."

"SHIMMER?!" Willow screeched and came in close to smell Grace, forcing her back against the wall. "You don't smell of life." She took a deep sniff and held it. "There's a hint of life, but that's because you're quite fresh on this side, I imagine... unless?" She looked over at Hollow, who was examining Grace.

"Nothing. There is no trace of life. Just Soul." He said.

Willow backed off and let Grace breathe. "Well, I had it... or have it? I don't know, but it means that I have some sort of chance to get back to my friend. But then I met Ooze, and—"

"You really should speak to Phil." Willow interrupted.

Ooze slid around Willow in a panic. "No need to involve them!"

"No, no... she makes a fair suggestion." Hollow said, his skeletal hand rubbing his bony chin, bemused. "There's no one who knows more about this kind of thing. We could sit here and go back and forth with hypotheticals; we could even visit every department in all Three Realms. But you know that Phil is the only one who could confirm if there is anything to be done."

Ooze's eyes darted between Hollow and Willow. "All of this just for a little friend? An insignificant Soul? We shouldn't bother Phil with something so meaningless. I'm helping her already!"

Grace was taken aback by Ooze's words, but not more than Willow, who had drawn herself to her full height and loomed over Ooze. From her feet, gnarled tree branches came out, covered in thorns, thick and seemingly never-ending, aiming directly for Ooze. Ooze was too slow in reacting, and the branches wrapped around them, capturing it in a grasp it couldn't escape.

"How dare you. You know what Hollow went through." Willow said, their tone beyond deathly serious. "Each of us know what we did to get here. How dare you say something like that in front of Hollow."

Ooze looked over at Hollow, who was floating, simply watching the interaction unfold, but was clearly hurt.

"You know the rules, Ooze." Willow said.

"Yes, but—"

"The rules." Willow threatened, as the branches tightened their grip. "In the Oubliette we respect what we regret."

Hollow raised his hands. "That's enough, Willow. Truly."

The branches engulfing Ooze slithered away with a rattle and returned to Willow.

"Sorry, child... when you're cooped up in here like common roommates, even the smallest things become life-or-death tragedies." Hollow said to Grace.

"I get it." Grace said with a smile. "Some of the arguments I had with my mum when I was living were... well, they were quite pointless. There was no point in the argument, we should just have enjoyed the time together." Grace tried to hold back the tears that were building up, she tried not to think about her mum. "But I get it from Ooze's point of view as well." Ooze whirled its eyes over its head to stare at Grace. "It is just a small Soul, in the grand scheme of things... but they're *my* Soul. *My* friend. They might mean nothing to everyone else, but to me?" The tears came out of Grace. There was no holding back. "To me, they're everything." She said through sobs. "They deserve so much more."

Hollow slowly floated over to Grace at the table and tried to wipe away the tears, but his hand fell through her face. He gave a little laugh. "Despite my terrifying facade, I can sympathise, Grace."

Willow walked over to a wall and drew a haphazard circular door using her long unkept fingernails. She placed her hand in the middle and screeched a word so loudly that Grace couldn't understand what she said.

The sand on the wall began to disintegrate and fall away, as if it were being pulled into a vortex.

A void was now present where Willow had drawn the circular door. "This will take you to Phil. We've not been called, so we cannot leave." Willow said, gesturing with a snap of a limb to Hollow. "But you and Ooze can, so go."

"There are many rules for someone dying, and Phil knows them all." Hollow said joining Willow's side.

Willow shot Ooze a glaring look. "We have jobs to do. We are not inherently evil. Don't destroy this girl." She said.

Grace digested what Willow had just said. They were not inherently evil, but whatever unspeakable and unforgivable thing each of them had done meant they were now prisoners of their own doing. But when they came back to this room, they couldn't hurt a Soul in it, they were no longer forced to be evil.

Grace really felt for these tortured beings. Were they stuck here forever? After spending time with Hollow and Willow, she hoped not. Even Mük had some redeeming qualities. Ooze was unpredictable.

Ooze slithered up to the void. "Ladies first." It said with a forced smile. Grace slowly made her way forward into the void.

"You're right." Grace said to Hollow and Willow. "You might have a job to do, and you might not be inherently evil, but I can see who you are. I hope someday, no matter how many years away it is, that you find some sort of peace or comfort."

Before she could hear or see any response from Hollow or Willow, Ooze had pushed her through the void, and she fell face first on a cold, clean, black marble floor.

~ Chapter Fifteen ~

NOWHERE

"W-why did you push me?" Grace asked, picking herself up from the floor.

Ooze slithered through the void beside her. "You were about to sympathise with them. We're all lost. Kind words would bring them false hope." Ooze turned to face the room. "Besides, you have a job to do."

"False hope isn't that big of a deal." Grace said as she looked around the place she had landed.

A grand room in both scale and decor, covered in varying shades of black and white. It all seemed old-fashioned and mysterious, yet somehow futuristic. Paintings on the walls of distinguished people from eons past with eyes that followed her. Large, broken pillars in the room cast shadows that could be easily hidden in. She looked up and saw objects floating high above her: stones, glass, candles, cushions, and chairs. A grey hue overshadowing the entire atmosphere.

"Ooze, where are we?" She asked.

Ooze's mouth slid onto its back while they both continued to move forward. "This is where Phil lives. Everyone wanted you to meet him so badly. Well, here we are." Ooze said with a bitter tone.

"No, I mean, *where* is this?" Grace pressed. "It feels like we're in another dimension." Ooze halted, sharply turned, and moved swiftly over to a window that was almost as tall as the room.

"Look outside." It said.

Grace swallowed and slowly peered out of the window. There was a white, dusty plain, but beyond that was darkness. No trees or buildings, no light, no life. "Are we… are we on the moon?" Grace felt stupid for asking but felt like anything was possible given everything she'd seen and gone through already.

"Moon?" Ooze let out a wicked cackle, the liquid mass wobbled as its mouth opened and closed. "Silly girl, no… we are Nowhere."

"What?"

"Nowhere." Ooze repeated, finding Grace's confusion delicious.

"You say that as if 'Nowhere' is the name of a place. We can't be nowhere because, well, everywhere is somewhere."

"Not here. We are right in the middle of Nowhere." It's smile getting wider.

Grace looked around again, feeling like she was being watched from a distance.

"This way," Ooze said, "Phil will be in his study. He always is." They both climbed a lengthy set of black stairs that led to rotted oak doors with iodised copper handles. Ooze pointed a large, wet hand towards the door. "You need to knock."

Grace raised a hand but stopped herself. "Wait, why do I have to knock? You do it." She said.

"I'm not the one who wanted to come here. I protested." Ooze said, filled with spite.

Grace rolled her eyes, raised her hand to knock, and stopped again. "Nothing is going to happen, is it? We're not standing on a trap door or something."

"Knock!!" Ooze barked.

Grace jumped and knocked three times on the door. She could hear a little cough coming from behind it and an old voice calling out. "Come in!"

Grace pushed on the door, and Ooze followed her into a large yet cosy-looking room. Velvet, high-backed chairs, piles of books, and a roaring fireplace in the centre-back wall. In the middle of the room was a raised platform with a large, round desk and an old man holding a feather.

"Who is that? Come closer!" He said, annoyed that he couldn't make out the faces. "I may have glasses, but they're useless!" Grace walked up the few steps to reach the desk he was sitting behind. The old man had a large, bushy beard that covered his mouth completely, it grew so long that it twisted around his desk all the way down to his bony feet. His obsidian-coloured suit was sprinkled with dust and ripped on one shoulder. The old man played with his glasses as he squinted at Grace. "Oh, it's a Soul! Hello! It's been an age since a Soul was here." His wispy voice relaxed and filled the room. Ooze slithered up beside Grace, catching the old man's attention. "Oh… and you. Did you mess up again, Ooze?" He asked, annoyed.

"Not this time." Ooze snarled.

"Not yet!" The old man laughed and looked over at Grace. "Why are you here with Ooze, Grace?"

She widened her eyes. "Wait. How do you know my name?"

The old man looked at her sceptically. "Do you know who I am?"

Grace looked over at Ooze, who just grinned knowingly. "You're… Phil? Right?"

"Yes! That's my name, but do you know *who* I am?"
Phil leaned forward, his big, bushy beard bunching up around
his face.

Grace opened her mouth to speak, but nothing came
out.

"I am Death." He said simply.

Grace took this in as she tried not to break eye contact
with Phil. "But... aren't you supposed—"

"Supposed to have a big black cloak and scythe?" Phil
rolled his eyes. "Dramatics. The Land of the Living simply
can't accept the normality of nature. They can't wrap their
heads around the simplest of things, so they create fearsome
beings and divine creations that ultimately render mundane."
Phil picked up a mug and took a sip. "Death. I'm not a tall,
ghostly creature. I'm an old man, older than he looks, who
enjoys bitter coffee and a good puzzle."

"So, what does that mean?" Grace asked. "You don't
appear beside people when they die?"

"Did I appear beside you?" Phil teased with a smile.

Grace thought back to her passing moment and
scanned through it quickly. "No..."

"Another illusion made up for either comfort or fear."
He said. "Sometimes, I don't know where I stand with the
Living. Yes, most of them fear me — loathe me, in fact! They
hate my very existence. But then there are those who take
comfort in knowing that one day I will be there. One day I
will appear by their side, take them by the hand, and walk
with them."

Grace opened her mouth to ask a question, but Phil
jumped in. "What is it I do? Contrary to popular belief, I
don't decide when, why, or how people pass. None of that is
my decision. You must believe that Grace, sincerely. I would
have granted mercy upon many innocent people who
deserved better... and done swiftly the opposite to those who
earned a worser fate." He took a deep inhale to smell the
coffee in his mug and then proceeded to take another sip.

"The most terrifying thing about passing? It's truly in the hands of the Living Soul. Or in some vile situations... another's hands."

He took off his glasses and wiped the thick lenses on his beard. "What is it I do? In its simplest form Grace, I'm a bookkeeper. I record everyone, no matter how sinister or auspicious, they must be recorded. *That's* what I do."

"You're an over-exaggerated librarian." Ooze snapped.

Phil glanced his gaze over to Ooze. "Don't forget who you're speaking to. I know *your* name too." Ooze's mouth withered in size; its eyes dropping to the floor.

"I'm good friends with Satan." Phil said to Grace. "I have power over his Familiars much like he does by knowing their names. The only difference is that they obey his word without question. Personally, I don't think one being should have absolute control over another. But, if they step out of line, it's good to know I can stop them."

Grace looked to Ooze, a thought sparking in her mind. Was Ooze once human?

"Look at me, rambling on and on. Once I start, you can't stop me!" Phil chuckled. "So, Grace... why are you here?" His tone shifting. "It's unusual — actually, it's *exceptionally* unusual for a Soul to be here."

Grace swallowed and tried to be as concise as she could. "Well, I want to go back to the Land of the Living. I know it's nearly impossible but listen!" Not wanting to be interrupted with a speech about it being completely impossible. Phil leaned forward to say something but decided to listen to Grace. He picked his mug up and leaned back comfortably.

"*Apparently*, I have 'the Shimmer'. People have witnessed it but it's not always around me, no one can pin it down. I understand the complications of going back as a Ghost. I mean, there's complications with almost everything here." Phil chuckled in agreement. "But my friend." Grace said, clenching her jaw. This may be her final chance of returning to save Gabe. She is speaking to Death, if they couldn't help, then who?

"My friend is in life-or-death danger. You said that *we* get to choose when, why, and how we die. He didn't choose it to be his time. Yeah, he made the decisions that led him there, but it's someone else that is going to take his life, and that isn't fair. He deserves the world!" Grace's eyes were filled with tears, making them glisten. "Look at how far I've come to save him. I'm *literally* speaking to Death. And yes, I know there are countless people that need saving, and you can't save them all. But I'm just asking for one."

Phil looked deep into Grace's eyes, she could feel him reading her Soul, understanding who she is, what she's done, and her friendship with Gabe.

"Just one person." She said it again. "Just one."

"Grace…" Phil began.

"No." She interrupted. His sympathetic tone told her everything she needed to know. He was going to explain how impossible it was to do it. "It *is* possible. I know it is."

"Grace… You're an incredible friend, I can see that. I won't lie to you… it is indeed possible."

Grace gasped at Phil's words.

"What?" Ooze asked, shocked.

"It is possible, but the butterfly effect of it could alter things severely, if it is indeed his time to pass."

Grace blinked. Someone finally just admitted it can be done, it felt like a weight lifted from her shoulders. Her swelling tears felt more like happiness than pain or hope.

"However, I think you already know what I'm going to ask." Phil said.

"I can't… I don't know if he will." Grace said. "I went to the Viewing Platforms, and he wasn't immediately about to die."

"Yes?" Phil said, urging her to continue the trail of thought.

"He might stand a chance of getting out of it." Grace said with an empty sorrow. Something like that should fill her with hope, but the fear of the Shadow Man returning to Gabe to finish what they started... it filled her with dread.

"The cost of saving a life is so great. The energy needed for Divine Intervention — I don't even... no one would ever do it. There are Souls I have grown incredibly fond of over the course of time, and even I wouldn't contemplate the cost. There are some moments that *must* happen, Grace."

"No..." She said in a whisper.

"There are several stages to life and death, even beyond human comprehension. Only the greatest of Souls understand and fully grasp them. That's why there is the Academy for Angels. The Academy instructs and teaches the rules and regulations of life and death; the balance, upkeep, everything before, during, and after."

Ooze and Grace looked up to Phil. "After?" They both asked.

"Oh, yes." He said putting down his mug and stroking his beard back into place. "We call it 'the Fade.' Only powerful Ancient Tools can be used to invoke the Fade, but they've been known to do more." He got up from his velvet chair and walked around to a bookshelf. He laid his fingers over the books, muttering to himself as the dust was wiped away under his fingers. "Where is it? Where is it? Ah! There it is!" He pulled out a thick purple book, returned to his seat, flipped through its pages, and slammed it down at an open page covered in cryptic language and decaying illustrations.

"There we are. This chapter discusses the Ancient Tools that hold the power to invoke the Fade. It even advises that powerful beings can as well." He lifted his eyes from the book and nodded at Grace. "Yes, I'm one of those beings."

Grace looked at the open pages of the book and saw items she didn't recognise in the drawings. "What do you mean Ancient Tools?" She asked.

"Oh, this book merely touches on a handful of the Ancient Tools, but there are hundreds of them. People call them relics, but really, they're Tools created by the Divine."

"Like what?" Grace asked.

Phil picked up the book from the table and flipped forward a few pages, some dust flying into the air. "Like this, for example. The Shroud of Turin." He said, pointing at a drawing of it in the book.

"I've heard of that." Grace said, inspecting the image. "I've never seen it before, though."

"Most haven't! Ancient Tools aren't just lying around for anyone to pick up." Phil flipped to the next page of the book, and Grace saw something she instantly recognised.

"The Crown of Thorns." She said.

"Yes, quite right. The Crown of Thorns. That truly is a powerful piece of work. I've seen Souls…" He winced. "You don't want to know."

Grace looked at the images again. 'Powerful Ancient Tools that can invoke the Fade… and more'. That's what Phil said. One of these could potentially get her back. She just needed to fully understand everything regarding them. Do they all carry individual powers, or does it not matter which Tool you use?

Grace lifted her head from the book, a thought sparking in her mind. She turned to face Ooze, who was slowly sliding its eyes to look at her. Ooze had come to the same idea that she had.

"These Ancient Tools could really be anything?" Grace asked, trying not to raise suspicion.

"Within reason, yes." Phil said, turning to the books around him. "I can get you all the books on them if you're interested. It'd just take time to sift through these piles."

"What about something like Pandora's Box?" She said quickly. Phil turned back around. "Or is that made up? I can never remember." She said trying to sound unbothered by whatever the answer was, looking back down at the book and pretending to read what was on the page.

"Oh, that old thing?" Phil said, chuckling to himself as he sat back down behind his desk. "It is the most confusing Tool with the most mundane answer." He took a large gulp from his mug.

"What is it?" She asked, not looking up from the book but listening intently.

"It's a cup." He said.

"What?" Grace whipped her head up.

"Well, more formally, it is better known as... the Holy Grail." He said and smiled.

Grace couldn't stop her jaw from dropping. She turned to face Ooze, whose milky eyes were fixed on Phil. She couldn't believe all this time she wasn't really looking for Pandora's Box, it was the Holy Grail. It exists. She thought about all the steps she took looking for Pandora's Box and wondered how much simpler it would have been if she had just asked for the Holy Grail. Did Ooze know they were the same thing?

"No, it can't be the Holy Grail." Grace said thinking it through. "It's Pandora's *Box*. It's a box."

Phil smiled playfully. "I assure you, it's nothing more than a glorified mug. It's beautiful, but it's nothing more than a cup — a chalice — if you're fancy. People think of the word 'box' and think of something square or cuboid in nature. But think of it more as a vessel. Although it never did have a lid, that bit was made up."

Grace's heart began to pound in her chest. All she could think of was all the wasted time spent looking for the wrong thing. "Where is it? Have you seen it?" She asked. She couldn't control the urgency in her voice.

"Of course I have. I witnessed it being created." He said and began to take the book off the table and return it to its original spot. "It's up with JC, and it's one of his most prized possessions. Right next to his glitter collection, if my memory serves me right. He has a fascination with all things that sparkle."

Grace felt her mind melting for a moment. Who was JC? A thought of something Big Mandy said from The Department for Domestic Hauntings popped into her head. "They're all real." She spoke out loud.

There was no way she would ever be able to get close to the Holy Grail if it's one of JC's most prized possessions. It would probably be under lock and key, with laser surveillance and security guards everywhere.

"If you ever want to see it, there are tours all the time in Paradise. Just ask… oh, who is it that is working there now? Agnes! She'll know how to get on one of the tours. Only if you're interested, of course!"

Grace and Ooze looked at each other and nodded gently with determination.

"Yeah, I might be interested." Grace said continuing to try and remain as nonchalant as she could over the information.

"Do you want to take one of these books with you?" Phil asked, pointing at the books around him. "You never know when the information will be helpful to you."

Grace shook her head. "No, thank you. I think we should go now. We've taken up so much of your time, and you've answered more than enough of my questions."

"I'm sorry I couldn't be of more help to you, Grace. I know I didn't give you the information you were hoping to hear."

"It's okay. Honestly, you told me exactly what I needed to hear. Thank you!" She said, signalling at Ooze it was time to go.

As they began to leave, they could hear Phil's wispy voice getting further away. "You're welcome! I'm glad to hear it. You're a bright-minded individual, don't lose that." He said, smiling as Ooze and Grace closed the door behind them.

~ Chapter Sixteen ~

ON A MISSION

"Where is she?" Gladys asked Phyllis, their cheeks red after speed walking down the spiral staircase of the Hole.

Phyllis received an early warning that Gladys was on their way down from Mük and had enough time to hide a particular mug that Gladys had been missing for months. "I don't know!" She said, shrugging. "She walked down that way with Lucy." Phyllis pointed.

Gladys sighed in frustration. "Who was on Hole duty?"

"I don't know."

"What *do* ye know, apart from the diameter of every mug within a three-mile radius?" Gladys snapped and held their finger and thumb to the bridge of their nose. "It's on the chart, Phyllis, check it!"

Phyllis spun around on her chair and looked for a chart. "Why are you so snappy over her coming down?" She asked while sifting through paperwork. "Even Lucy said it was fine, she made Grace her personal guest."

"That's not good, Phyllis. Personal guest of Lucy? Not good at all." Gladys muttered.

"Ah, here's the chart, it was..." Phyllis slid her finger down the clipboard and tapped on it when she found the name. "Mük. It was Mük."

"Of course it was. It's always Mük." Gladys said, adjusting the glasses on the end of their nose.

"He tries his best, Gladys."

"Did Grace say anything about why she was down here? Anything at all?" Gladys asked impatiently. Phyllis was about to respond when she noticed Mük appear from the large door that led to the bottom of the Hole.

"I didn't get much out of her before Lucy came in, but you can talk to Mük." She said and nodded towards him.

"Gladys, always a pleasure, my daisy-wearing-darling!" Mük said and wandered over towards Gladys, red and black dripping arms outstretched for a hug.

"You're overly touchy with me as usual." They said, taking a step back. "I told you, the last time we hugged, I had to throw out the daisy shirt because of your residue. I'm sorry, my lovely."

Mük lowered his arms until they fell off his shoulders and lay on the floor. He looked over to Gladys and Phyllis, who were just staring back at him. "Oh, nothing? I went for full on dramatics!"

"I haven't seen that before; I'm a little impressed!" Gladys said.

"Thank you!" He curtsied. "I felt my name being said several times, so I left a shell of myself up at the entrance of the Hole to come investigate the gossip." His red eyes darting from Phyllis to Gladys as his arms reabsorbed into his body.

"Mük, my lovely, that girl you escorted down earlier." Gladys said, after taking a deep breath.

"Which one?" He laughed.

"You know the one I mean. Her name is Grace."

"Grace, hmmm yes... She did not like the Wall Melding." Mük giggled.

"You do remember!" Gladys said, taking a step forward. "Now, do you remember why she was coming down to the Inferno? Why was she at the Hole in the first place?"

"She said that she wanted to meet Ooze."

"Ooze!" Gladys sighed. "Its worse than you. What else did she say, Mük? Anything at all."

Mük put a gloopy hand under his chin in thought. "Nope." He said after a few moments. "That was it. I didn't get much out of her, she was very secretive." Gladys and Phyllis shared a glance at each other. "But Lucy did say she had met Grace before. Something about liking her because she was reading?"

"Lucy did say that. I heard it too!" Phyllis chimed in.

"Aye and I know exactly what she's been reading." Gladys muttered.

"What was it?" Phyllis asked.

Gladys' eyes widened as they realised they hadn't muttered quietly enough. "Oh, nothing, nothing at all. She's just going to get herself hurt!" Gladys knew they weren't getting any more information from Phyllis or Mük. "Right, with all that being said, I'm going to look for her!" They said, storming towards the entrance of the Inferno.

"Gladys, no! You can't!" Phyllis cried out.

Gladys screeched to a halt and sharply turned to face Phyllis. "... And why not?"

"Y — you don't have a Visitors Pass!"

Gladys blinked slowly and took in a deep breath. "Phyllis my lovely, tell you what... you fill out all the forms to confirm that I maybe did or didn't break the rules, and once you've done that and you need my signature? Give me a shout. I'll come running right back to sign them." Gladys was already through the door before Phyllis could say anything else.

Mük slowly turned to face Phyllis. "Now that we're alone..."

"Never in your dizziest of daydreams." Phyllis said and continued to type on her keyboard.

*   *   *

Gladys made their way through the candlelit hallways until they reached the Inferno entrance. They pushed hard on the doors and sped walked their way down into the crowded city of stone and rock, passed the merchants, and houses. They kept seeing people and creatures that recognised them, all too delighted at their visit.

"Gladys, it's been so long!"

"You don't come down here often enough!"

"We need to catch up!"

They had to apologise to everyone as they walked by, making excuses to not stop and chat for longer as they made their way to the circles of hell stone carving. Gladys knew everyone, and everyone knew them; this was a well-known fact about the Three Realms. Even in the Inferno, Gladys knew that certain choices and decisions didn't ultimately make you a bad person, that's why they never judged a Soul before truly getting to know them upon first meeting.

Now that they were out of the hustle and bustle of the streets, they looked around. This area was always a little quieter and gave them a chance to observe their surroundings.

"Now, if I were looking for Ooze, where would I go? Normally, Ooze ends up finding you." Gladys muttered, looking around to see if anything would give them a clue where to go.

Nothing.

"Oh, this is useless, I need to call him." They pulled out their mobile phone, began scrolling, and then tapped the name they were looking for, and the phone began to ring.

It kept ringing.

It continued to ring.

"I swear if this goes to the answering machine, I'm going to — Hiya, Hot Stuff! It's just me, G-Doll. I'm leaving you a wee message because ye never answer yer phone these days. I'm beginning to think I'm the problem!" Gladys chuckled. "No, no, I know that's impossible! I'm actually looking for—"

A slight buzzing noise suddenly began to ring in the air behind Gladys and they turned to face the large stone carving. As Gladys recognised the buzzing sound, a Dimensional Doorway opened in front of them. They closed over the phone, stopping the voicemail, and watched as Grace and Ooze stepped out of the circular void.

Grace dusted herself off and turned to Ooze. "This is perfect, at least we have a better idea now!"

"Grace!" Gladys shouted.

Her stomach dropped recognising the voice. She turned nervously to face Gladys.

"Did you come out of that Dimensional Doorway, my lovely? What are you doing down here? Why are you with Ooze? You get away from her!"

Ooze grabbed Grace's shoulders and spun her back around. "Get to Paradise. Get the Grail." It commanded, as Gladys was getting closer.

"Ooze, we're too late!" She pleaded.

"Get. The Grail!" It said through gritted teeth and pushed her away.

As Grace stumbled, she heard Gladys shouting. "Oh, no, don't you be pushing her! I'll have more than a few words for you!"

Ooze turned to face Gladys as they approached and built itself up to a taller height. It pushed itself down, and part of its body slithered out and created a slimy wall right in front of Gladys, blocking their every movement. Gladys ran over and jumped on the base of the stone carving. Looking over the wall, Gladys saw Grace slowly making her way through the crowd back to the doors of the Inferno. "Stop!" They shouted. "Grace, stop! You really don't know what ye're doing! You're going to get hurt!"

Grace looked over her shoulder to see Gladys jumping and waving their arms to get her attention. Grace turned to face the door, then back at Gladys.

Was she doing the right thing?

Her eyes wandered over to Ooze, who had turned one of its large arms into a sharp point and kept pushing it towards the doors of the Inferno, insisting Grace leave.

She had the choice to stop and turn back around, face the wrath of Gladys, hoping with enough apologies, she would get back into their good books again. Or she could leave, find the Holy Grail, and find a way to use its power and save Gabe.

Grace dropped her head and looked down at her feet. She hated herself for getting into this situation. She hated herself even more for the decision she was about to make. It will always be Gabe. When Phil said it was possible, the hope that filled her was enough to make her fly. "I'm sorry. I have to!" She cried and ran as fast as she could through the crowd of bodies to the doors leading out of the Inferno.

Ooze smiled and cackled loudly.

Gladys slowly lost the enthusiasm in their arms as what Grace shouted at them began to register. They furrowed their brow in anguish, all they were trying to do was help Grace. Gladys stepped down from the base of the stone carving as the wall reabsorbed back into Ooze. Its gleeful smugness turned into shock as Gladys was revealed to be glaring straight into the milky pools of its eyes.

"Now, you listen to me." Gladys said defiantly. "I may not know everything that's going on here, but I know you're to blame." Gladys began to walk slowly towards Ooze. "There's a lot more to this story that I need to know."

"You're right." Ooze hissed. "You don't know everything, and you never will. Until it's too late!"

"Is that right?" Gladys said, coming to a stop a few feet from Ooze, folding their arms. "I may not have the miniscule powers that you've been given, but you know what I do have?"

"What?" It sneered.

"A lifetime and an *after*-lifetime of being a nosey bugger!" Gladys said, their wonky eyebrow becoming even more arched. "And if there is one thing I know, it's that no one has enough Divine Power or Omnipotent Valour to keep their lips sealed around me. Especially when I'm trying to protect someone; someone you're trying to hurt. And I don't know why. So, you can either tell me and save the hassle, or—"

"You talk too much." Ooze said, pretending to yawn.

Gladys' eyes scrunched hard for a moment, then widened. The audacity sent a wave of rage through their body that they had never felt before.

Gladys pursed their lips and gritted their teeth.

"Right. Sit doon!"

~ Chapter Seventeen ~

THE HOLY GRAIL

"It has to be the right thing to do. It *has* to be!" Grace was muttering to herself out loud. "I'm doing the right thing. Gladys will be okay. They'll understand. They'll understand!" She tried to convince herself.

Grace was fidgeting in the elevator, tapping on the handrail as she made her way up to Paradise. She couldn't even remember how she got here; she just remembered the lies flowing out of her mouth.

"I haven't seen them, no!" Stretching the truth to Phyllis.

"Everything is fine, I just need to get up to the top of the Hole!" Fibbing to Mük.

"No, I never saw them. But I'm heading home now!" Lying to Brenda.

Is this who I really am? Why am I not in the Inferno? She questioned. She couldn't believe how easy it was to just lie to keep people quiet and get where she needed to be. And Agnes was next.

What was Agnes going to ask her? Whatever it was, she had to be prepared. The lies seemed to flow out of her easily enough for everyone else, as if she was just saying words automatically without being fully conscious. But now she felt like she was present, and the anxiety of Agnes' questions were looming.

"Welcome to the Paradise Department." The friendly elevator voice said, jolting Grace out of her own thoughts. She slowly walked forwards, trying to delay the moment, hoping her subconscious would take over. It didn't.

Agnes slammed down a folder. "What is this? I don't have time to reorganise files for every person who works here. Who was the last one with this?" She flipped through the file and glanced up to see Grace walking towards her. "What can I do for you now?" She asked, flipping through the pages as if it were a month-old magazine.

"Tours! I mean—" Grace coughed and regained herself. "I was told they do tours about... things? Like things people want to see on tours?"

Agnes rolled her eyes. "The Paradise Relics Tours? Yeah, they're every hour on the hour. Are you wanting to go to one?"

"Yes." Grace said flatly.

"Well, they're normally all booked up, Souls wait months and months for a ticket." She placed the file down and turned to her computer, where she began typing. "But — and it's a big but — there are sometimes, on the odd and rare occasion, 'on hand' tickets are available if people cancel."

Grace couldn't believe there were no other questions. Agnes didn't have the patience for all the hassle, she assumed. She let her eyes wander to the computer screen Agnes was looking at.

"Well, aren't you lucky?" A low humming noise was in the air for a few moments before Agnes ripped a piece of paper from the side of the computer screen and held it out to

Grace. "There was one available. Someone must have cancelled."

Grace took the ticket out of Agnes' hand and read it.

THE PARADISE RELICS TOUR!
Every hour, day and night!
We can't sleep with this much to show you!
Food and drinks are provided!
Our guides are your guides to what you thought didn't exist!

ADMISSION: ONE

"I've asked Knitting Moira to show you the way there." She moaned, getting back to the paperwork.

A light pinged above a doorway behind Agnes, and a short mousy woman appeared. Her flowy trousers, cardigan, and shoes were all knitted and slightly ill-fitting. The colours throughout ranged from pastel to neon, earth tones to rainbows. It did look comfy though, Grace thought.

"I know." Agnes said, catching Grace stare at Moira in amazement.

"Hello, I'm Moira!" She said with an excited wave that moved the two messy buns of hair on either side of her head. "I'll take you to the Paradise Relics Tours!"

As Grace walked towards Moira, she could hear Agnes chuckle under her breath. "Good luck."

*   *   *

"— And then Michelle stood up and said, 'You're *knit*-picking!'". Moira wheezed out a laugh as Grace let out an exhausted giggle.

The walk from Agnes' desk to the Paradise Relics Tours was short, but it felt like eons with Moira's insistent chatter. She wouldn't stop talking, not even to breathe, and even when Grace tried to jump in and divert the conversation, Moira just kept going on about knitting.

Deep sapphire curtains adorned with a sign in gold lettering that read '*Relics Tours*' came into view, and a wave of relief washed over Grace.

"— And that was only my thirteenth scarf as well!" Moira continued but stopped laughing as she saw the curtains ahead. "Oh dear, here we are. Just as we were getting the conversation going as well. You were so kind to let me do all that talking. Everyone says I talk too much, but I just enjoy a good chat! What does Gladys call it? A 'blether!' That's it. Oh, look at me, nearly went on another tangent. You'll want to know about the Relics Tours. Well, they're simple enough. Just go through that curtain, show your ticket, and wait for the next tour. Simple and easy, right?"

"Right." Grace said, unsure if Moira was ever going to let her speak.

"Thanks for letting me *blether* away. My co-workers tell me to be quiet all the time, but I don't mind. They enjoy the homemade gifts I bring in. They're like my extended family, they get cakes and biscuits, socks and jumpers — everything!" Grace pointed to the curtain. "They never say thank you, but that's family! Oh, yes, you just go through there and show your ticket! I hope to see you again soon. You're so easy to talk to!" She said and walked the other way, humming to herself.

Grace let out a sigh and walked towards the curtains. As she walked through, she saw a slender person with short rose-gold curly hair standing at a door. They were wearing a pastel pink and teal-coloured robe, but instead of simply drooping down, it wrapped around each of their legs, creating a fully wrapped jumpsuit with white heeled stilettos to match.

She approached and held out her ticket as the person turned around to see her.

"Oh!" They said as they jumped a little. "Sorry, I didn't see you there! Well, I see you have a ticket." They took the ticket from Grace and pocketed it. "Admission one and one admitted!" They said with a shining smile that made Grace blush. "I'm Alex. I'm your guide for the Relics Tours. My pronouns are They/Them, and I'll happily answer any questions you have once the tour starts. Can I ask your name?" Alex raised their eyebrows to get Grace to answer.

"Oh — Grace!" She said, cheeks still blushing.

"Beautiful!" They said smiling and turned to face a hallway that Grace had completely missed. Inside, she could see at least twenty people buying drinks and snacks. "You actually arrived just in time." Alex said. "We're just about to begin the tour. They all got the big speech at the start, but I'll make it brief for you: There is a tour every hour, but each tour lasts four hours, and there will be breaks along the way. It is an interactive tour, so we all decide where we go. If you need a snack, now is the time."

"I'm all good!" Grace said, trying to not lose herself in Alex's dark brown eyes as their steady voice floated in the air.

"Thirsty?" They asked.

"No — I — Sorry. What?" Grace asked, blushing red.

Alex laughed sweetly. "If you're thirsty, you can get a drink before we go." They pointed to the other people behind them.

"Oh... I'm good, thanks. Sorry!" Grace wanted the ground to swallow her up.

"Okay, everyone, if I can have your attention!" Alex said facing the group, holding out their hands. "If we're all fully stocked, I'm more than happy to begin the tour!"

There was a rumble of noise and movement as everyone gathered around Alex.

"Great! Now, if you'll all do me a few favours; please do not litter and don't touch anything. If you have any questions, just ask. But most importantly, let's have a great time!" They said smiling at everyone, and when their eyes landed on Grace, they winked. Grace looked down, suddenly fascinated by her shoes. Everyone let out a sound of excitement as they were all ready for the tour to start. "In which case, follow me and let the tour begin!"

Alex turned around and pushed open the door they were standing beside. Everyone shuffled through excitedly, while Grace stayed at the back of the group.

Walking into the next room, Grace was blinded by the bright, pulsing white light.

"Your eyes will adjust momentarily!" Alex called out.

Grace squinted to see large buildings that reminded her of colosseums from the outside. They were all relatively the same circular shape and colossal size.

"Now, here is where you all get involved. You get to decide which of these Exhibitions we visit first." Alex said with a glint in their eye. Grace looked at each building in the distance and noticed a sign ahead giving directions: Mythology, Artifacts, Creatures, and Recreation, she read as Alex pointed to each individual building.

"Mythology will give you a deeper look into fabulous stories that have changed and transformed through the ages. It's quite an educational one. You won't believe the truth to some of the things you were taught!" Alex said knowingly.

"Artifacts are... well, it is what it is. However, there are no copies or duplications in any way. These are the genuine pieces of history. A lot of them are lost to time and forgotten in any recent memory, but thankfully, we have placards telling us exactly what everything is." Alex said, turning to the next building.

"Creatures are more—"

"Artifacts!" Grace shouted without realising it.

Alex homed in and found Grace at the back of the group. "Oh, you seem really excited about going there!"

"It's just — well, I'm sure they're all interesting, but I think we should start with the least interesting one." She looked at the Souls around her, slurping on drinks and already eating their snacks. "It means we finish with the *most* interesting!" Some of the Souls began to nod their heads in agreement. Alex caught this and smirked.

"Well, if that's the idea for your tour today, then I would suggest we finish with Recreation. Your minds will be blown away by the spectacle!" There was a theatrical buzz of anticipation from the group. "The first place to visit will be Artifacts!" Grace let out a sigh of relief. "Exciting nonetheless, but... just not *as* exciting!" Alex raised their arms and pointed towards the second building. "This way!"

*   *   *

"— And lastly, I just want to apologise before we head inside for the misinformation going around. So, please let me clarify; JC does *not* guide these tours. To this day, we have no idea who started this rumour." Alex said, and they clapped their hands together as everyone gathered around at the door of the Exhibition. "When we go inside, it is important that you stay close to me and not wander off. However, if you do get lost at all, touch a wall with your hand and keep walking. You'll come to an exit eventually!" They giggled as they turned around, pushed the large white stone doors open, and proceeded to walk in.

As everyone made their way inside, Grace looked behind. Gladys might be coming up the Paradise elevator right now. Gladys could be speeding through corridors. Gladys could be here any second, and the anxiety of that thought made Grace walk forward and begin to push passed people to get inside faster.

As she reached the front of the group, directly behind Alex, she finally looked around and saw a large room, which went on for an eternity. Pale honey-coloured pillars scattered

181

throughout, with items of sorts at the base of each one. "Oh, we'll be here for hours." She sighed.

"Not at all, only an hour per Exhibition, really." Alex said before addressing everyone else. "Now, if you'll follow me, I want to start the tour off with something every single one of you has heard of at least once in your life; the Holy Grail." The audience gasped. "*Yes*, it's real!"

Grace looked at Alex in suspicion; it was awfully convenient for it to be the first Artifact to go to, but she wasn't going to complain. It saved her the time and effort of trying to find it, especially with Gladys hot on her tail.

Alex led them by all sorts of Artifacts which were heavy with their own stories to tell: gloves, swords, masks, guns, flags, flowers, and crowns, until they reached a podium. Sitting at the front of it, was the Holy Grail.

"And there it is, in all its glory!" Alex said, letting everyone take in its grandeur. He walked a little closer to the podium, began pointing, and continued. "The Holy Grail was actually a lot smaller than it is now. But as time went on and, of course, the original creator got more inspired, they added to it."

Grace was surprised that the Holy Grail wasn't what she was led to believe. She imagined it was going to be a large, bejewelled cup made out of gold, crystals, and multicoloured gems. But sitting on the podium was a large chalice, made from dark-coloured wood. Deep engravings decorated the entire framework, scorch marks along the warped handles where centuries of hands swapping ownership left their imprint. This wasn't just *any* old chalice. Something she didn't even consider was if it had handles, but there was one on each side of the Grail that blended in with the body of the cup.

"It originally did *not* have handles." Alex said, pointing at them now. "The handles were actually a gift from Satan himself to JC as a piece offering between the Inferno and Paradise. This is something to remember for later, as we'll see this moment in the Recreations Exhibition!" They said and began to walk towards another pillar, the group slowly dispersing behind Grace to follow him.

What Alex said sparked something in Grace's curiosity. The handles on either side of the Grail were drawing her in. Twisted, gnarled, small spikes all over — something she thought would be very uncomfortable to hold.

The Holy Grail was right in front of her, and she realised she hadn't been told what to do with it.

All this searching, and she had no idea. Grace's thoughts were all piling on top of one another.

Ooze thought it was a box.

The horns will be inside it.

Gladys will be here any second.

How do you get the Grail?

Grab it!

Run!

People will find you.

Angel Police.

Grab it!

Run!

As Grace made her way to one of the walls to collect her thoughts away from the group, she thought to herself how crazy everything was getting. She's running away from a wonky-browed secretary, being told what to do by a slimy creature, and just stole the Holy Grail.

~ Chapter Eighteen ~

GOOD INTENTIONS

Ooze wiped away the droplets of sweat dripping down its face. Gladys had worn it down so much that Ooze had almost become a puddle on the ground.

"Are you joking me?" Gladys asked rhetorically. "This is beyond crazy. This is beyond you and me. Ooze, you're messing with powers that shouldn't be touched, even by Souls who know what they're doing!"

All Ooze could do was groan a little as Gladys paced around it. "Too right, you've nothing to say. You're nothing but a big numpty!" Gladys stopped pacing and began chewing on one of their nails. "What to do next?" They thought out loud.

Ooze began to pull itself together. "How did you do that?"

"Do what?" Gladys asked, annoyed.

"Get me to talk."

"It's called 'the gift of the gab' and you don't have it." Gladys said, rolling their eyes. "Right, once I've found Grace and spoken to her and explained everything, she'll understand. She'll have no choice! Oh, when did I become the bad guy for trying to help and protect someone?" Gladys exclaimed.

"You'll never find her." Ooze said, between wheezing breaths.

Gladys turned around. "I know where she's gone, thanks to you. She's gone to check out the Holy Grail, and then she'll come looking for you. I'll get my best people looking for her. She's way out of her depth! And once I've got her in safe hands, I'm going to find you and rip through you like a midnight chocolate bar!"

"You'll do no such thing." Lucy said, appearing behind Gladys in an ominous purple cloud of smoke. Gladys turned to face her, their glasses dropping to the tip of their nose.

"Lucy? Are you part of this?" They asked, shocked. "Do you know what you're doing?"

"I'm not part of it." Lucy said, raising a calming hand to silence Gladys.

"Oh, thank goodness for that." Gladys let out a sigh of relief. "Well then, I might need your help to stop the madness that this wee eejit's brewing!"

Lucy stared at Gladys with a glint in her eye and a sharp smirk growing on her lips. The smirk grew into a smile until Lucy began to gently laugh.

"I'm not a part of it." Lucy repeated and leaned in until she could see her own reflection in Gladys' glasses. "I'm the cause of it."

In an instant, Gladys' eyes widened, and they let out a cry for help as Lucy swung her hand around in one swift movement. Her hand was coated in a purple aura, and before Gladys could do anything else, they were sinking into the ground in the centre of a circular purple void. Gladys reached for the edges, but they were too far away, and began to sink faster. They scrambled looking around for someone to help, but there was nothing anyone could do, especially against Lucy.

Gladys locked eyes with Lucy, who gently waved as they disappeared completely. The purple void closed with a gentle breeze of smoke, and as it cleared, Ooze saw Gladys' glasses sitting where the void once was.

"All that's left of her!" It said.

"Them. All that's left of *them*." Lucy said, irritated.

"Where did you send he— I mean, them?"

Lucy smirked as she picked up Gladys' glasses and walked away. "To the Oubliette."

~ Chapter Nineteen ~

HIS SLEEPING CHAMBERS

There were no alarms, lasers, security, and guards. It was almost as if people in Paradise just trusted you to be good. The weight of the Grail surprised Grace as she sat with her back against a wall, holding it in her hands, hidden behind the shadow of a pillar. She was right about the uncomfortable handles, and they weren't the same material that made up the body of the Grail.

She felt glued to the spot. Alex could notice she was missing, someone in the tour group might spot the empty podium, or Gladys could come bounding through the door of the exhibition. This was one of JC's most prized possessions; if he came after her, there would be no explanation for this.

She sat in the shadow of the pillar, her heart pounding, terrified of the consequences. Everything had a weird air of magic in the Afterlife, so how terrifying were the consequences? She'd already briefly visited the Inferno, and it was bad enough. She didn't know how much more there was to it, but she was sure she had only scratched the surface.

Grace swallowed hard, trying not to think about the endless possibilities of the Inferno.

She put the Grail down on the floor between her legs and took deep breaths. She needed to rethink her entire situation. She wasn't thinking straight. She wasn't in control. She took a deep final breath and let it out slowly.

Grace let the noise of the Exhibition fade into the background. Her eyes were transfixed upon the Grail, her mind whirling trying to predict every outcome to this impossible situation.

What if my gut is wrong?

It's possible.

What if everyone is right, and I'm making a huge mountain out of nothing?

What if I can't get back?

I should give up.

Put it back.

Go home.

Go home and do what Hairy Harry done and just cry.

Grace looked around to see if Alex was nearby, she could hear them with the tour group a distance away explaining something about a sword. She looked back down at the Grail and picked it up by one of its odd handles as if it were nothing.

Grace could hear her heartbeat in her ears, as if her body was being controlled like an automaton, making the choice for her. It had to be put back. Defeated, she trudged back towards the empty podium the Grail had once perched. Holding the Grail in front of her, an intrusive thought made its way into her mind. Grace stopped dead in her tracks.

Walk out.

Leave the building.

Could she *really* leave with the Grail?

Why couldn't she?

Grace slowly turned around on her heel and walked toward the exit of the Artifacts Exhibition.

Am I really going to do this? She thought.

She started to feel eyes on her, like at any moment the pillars were going to come to life and stop her at the door. Her pace started to quicken as if someone was right behind her. Grace was getting closer to the exit, but just before she put all her weight into pushing the doors open, she was yanked into the shadow of another nearby pillar.

"Ow! What was that?" She asked, looking around to find what had pulled her. Grace recognised the asymmetrical white suit in front of her, she'd seen it several times recently. She slowly raised her head and locked eyes with Lucy, who was looking down at her captivatingly. Grace swallowed hard and gripped the Grail in her hands tighter.

"You're just going to steal it?" Lucy smirked. "It really was *that* easy for you?"

"I'm sorry!" Grace said before Lucy had even finished talking. "I'll give it back. Please, I don't want to spend my life in the Inferno." She pushed the Grail into Lucy's hands. "Take it!" She insisted.

Lucy cowered back. "I can't touch it." She hissed. "It's a Divine Tool. That's why I needed you." She turned to the wall and walked through a barely visible circular portal.

"Wait, what?" Grace asked.

"This way." Lucy said, as her body disappeared.

Grace caught a glimpse of Alex and the tour group in the distance. Alex looked puzzled, noticing she was gone. Wait till they find out what else is missing, a thought creeped to the front of her brain.

Grace stepped through the void, her foot setting down onto solid ground. As the rest of her body came through, she felt a biting chill in the air. The portal disappeared behind her, and she was stunned to see a glacial tundra.

Ice surrounded her everywhere. Snow had gathered itself into large mounds as far as the eye could see, massive spikes piercing through them. A pale blue glow refracted light off the icicles high above her. There was no sense of time or history in this place.

"It's rather beautiful if you don't know what happened here." Lucy said, her voice gently reverberating throughout the cavern.

"Where are we?" Grace whispered.

"We call it 'His Sleeping Chambers'. But before that — before everything — it was called 'the Throne Room'".

Grace grew suspicious of Lucy's tone. "Whose throne?"

Lucy chuckled as she walked towards one of the glacial walls ahead, gesturing for Grace to follow. "Oh, you know exactly who... the one you've been told about." She looked at Grace through the side of her eye. "The one you're trying to resurrect so you can go home."

"How do you—"

"Grace, you think Ooze wouldn't tell me? Look at me! I'm terrifying." Her tone was drier than the punchline. "*And* I'm terrifyingly powerful. Ooze would do anything I say."

Grace hated being proved right, especially about Ooze. "So, where is he then?" Grace asked calmly. Lucy knew about the plan, there was no need to hide any of it. "Where is Beelzebub?"

"He's right there on his throne, under centuries of ice." Lucy said pointing at the glacial wall they were walking towards. Grace couldn't see anything inside the ice. "Trust, he's there alright. I was here when he was frozen. And you'll be here when he wakes up."

Grace looked down at the Holy Grail in her hands and lifted it towards Lucy. "Well, how does the Holy Grail wake him up? Ooze told me he needed horns, which were inside Pandoras Box, which turns out to be this!" She said, waving the Grail slightly. "I thought he needed his horns back, not a big cup."

"The Holy Grail *is* his horns." Lucy said passively, noticing the slight confusion on Grace's face. "Oh, you haven't worked it out? All this time you were just following what you were told blindly. Grace, you're a smart girl." As they reached the glacial wall they faced each other. "Look closely at the handles of the Holy Grail."

Grace raised the Grail up so she could get a better look at it. She knew the handles didn't quite match the rest of the design, and Alex had said that the handles were a gift from Satan. She scanned repeatedly, noticing smaller details each time. Grace's eyes stopped darting over the Grail. How could she have been so blind? The handles were thicker at the bottom and came to a point the closer they got to the top.

Her blood ran cold down her spine in realisation.

The handles were Beelzebub's horns.

"My brother Satan pried them from Beelzebub and gifted them to Paradise. And they attached them to the Holy Grail, imagine! Like a jewel being soldered to cheap metal." Lucy winced as she described the horrific act. "Suddenly, I couldn't touch them. We couldn't touch them." She gestured around to an invisible audience. "The horns were now a Divine Tool. The greatest security. In full view on display at that pathetic Exhibition, but they couldn't be touched by anyone who belongs to the Inferno."

Lucy sighed. "For centuries I've tried to get my hands on them but I didn't know how. Familiars can't enter Paradise, but when an Inferno Soul does, they have restrictions and rules to follow. Ridiculous limitations if you ask me! Even Redeemed Souls cannot touch the Divine Tools." She slowly pointed at Grace. "The only people that can enter Paradise are those who belong there. *I* can enter Paradise of course, but I can't touch them."

"Why can you enter Paradi—"

"No matter what I did to convince someone in Paradise to help me, they simply refused. And who would blame them? Who would willingly help someone known to be evil, chaotic, and quite unpredictable throughout most of their life? Who would help… Lucifer?"

"Lucifer?" Grace asked slowly, staring into Lucy's eyes now feeling unfamiliar. "Luci… Lucy…"

"The penny dropped I see." Lucy said.

Grace was left speechless realising she had been speaking with Lucifer all this time. "You're… not what I expected." Is all she could manage.

"You're not what *I* expected." Lucy said with a sharp smile. "A Paradise Soul willing to help the Inferno? Perhaps there *has* been a mistake where you belong after all."

"Maybe." Grace said, feeling herself become more like a statue as Lucy spoke. "I just want to get back…"

"And you can." Lucy smiled.

"To save my friend…"

"And you will." Lucy put her hands around Grace's wrists, careful not to touch the Grail. "Break off the handles! I'll melt the ice, you place the horns back onto his head… and then we just…" Lucy closed her eyes and took in a deep breath. "Then we watch!"

This felt wrong. Grace was brought up with books, movies, and TV shows with the knowledge that Lucifer was a bad person, the connotations of evil had been imprinted in her mind long before meeting Lucy. How could she trust Lucy when every part of her body was screaming at her to say no.

Grace took a small step away from Lucy, but before she could make any other move, a familiar voice came from behind her.

"You've come this far." It was Ooze, sliding its way towards them both. "This will benefit you too, remember?"

"Ooze is right. You'll go back to the Land of the Living and you can save your friend."

Grace looked between the two, her brain wasn't working as fast as it needed to. She felt stuck, like a pawn in a horrible game of chess. She couldn't see the moves that Lucy and Ooze had planned ahead, and there she was, moments away from having her King check mated. "But what will happen here when *he* returns?" She asked.

"Oh, there will be teething issues, but they're nothing I can't sort. I was always able to communicate with him better than Satan, make him see reason and such. I've done it once and I'll certainly be able to do it again. Don't you worry."

"But I am worried. I'm *really* worried!" Grace said loudly. "I'm talking to Lucifer—

"That is not my name!" Lucy barked.

"I'm sorry… Lucy, a talking pile of goop, and holding the Holy Grail, and you're telling me not to worry?" Grace exclaimed.

"You and I are so alike." Lucy chuckled. "We both know how to get what we want. Two very different approaches, but in the grand scheme of things, I can learn something from your way, and you could learn from my… methods." Lucy blinked slowly, not breaking eye contact with Grace. "You didn't tell anyone about the plan you had with Ooze?"

Grace shook her head slightly. "No, I didn't."

"Not telling anyone might have just saved your life." Ooze said, through a gritted smile.

Grace's blood ran colder than the room she was in. Her spine chilled and her skin goose bumped. Turning her head slowly to look at Ooze, she couldn't work out why that sentence seemed so familiar. The tone… the words…. it sparked a faint and distant memory. Grace couldn't piece it together. Was it a quote from a scary movie she used to watch with her mum, or something more sinister? She couldn't rid the sinking feeling in her stomach.

"Ooze is right." Lucy said bringing Grace back to the room. "You've worked your way through everything to get to this very moment. I'll be able to work this through with him." Lucy nodded her head to the glacier imprisoning Beelzebub.

"We'll bind the Three Realms together, rather than leaving them unfairly divided."

Grace noticed the sadness in Lucy's face. "This isn't living for a lot of Souls. This is *surviving*. The Afterlife is supposed to be where we all truly thrive from the life choices we made while living… and right now, the smallest portion of all known Souls are reaping that benefit. That's an injustice! That's…" Lucy turned away from Grace and lowered her head. "That's just not fair."

Those words resonated with Grace. Ever since she remembered about Gabe and found out she may have a chance to save his life, she felt like everyone was against her. It was the simplest thing. Phil said it was possible. But even then, it wasn't fair. Nothing was fair. Except, this seemed fair. She returns the horns to Beelzebub, saves Gabe, and corrects an injustice Lucy was so determined to right. It seemed like a fair trade, a terrifying, but fair trade. They'd both get what they wanted though. Right?

Grace nodded to herself and made her way closer to the glacial wall. Ooze smiled eerily at her as she walked by, she couldn't get what it said out of her head.

Lucy turned and smiled, hearing Grace's footsteps walking towards the base of the glacier. Without a single word spoken, Lucy lunged towards the wall and raised her hands. A purple aura emanated from her hands and the ice began to melt. A crystal-clear river appeared and flowed from the base of Beelzebub's prison through to a bottomless stretch of the cavern.

Within minutes there was a generous hole carved into the wall that looked like a smaller cave, still dripping from the residue heat of Lucy's Divine Power. Grace peered inside and seen a singular black rock embedded into the back of the icy cave. Lucy gestured for Grace to go inside.

As she delved deeper, she approached the black rock and could see more clearly through the ice. Blurred and refracted, she could make out a large black and silver chair with a dramatically high back to it. Grace had to squint a little more, there was a body sitting on the seat.

Grace froze on the spot.

It wasn't a rock at all. It was the head of Beelzebub, peaking out through the melted ice. His scalp reminded her of cooled lava, a cracked but smooth surface. She could see exactly where the horns had been removed from, splintered circles spiking out from either side. She wished she could see his face, but he was hunched over. Grace had expected a huge demonic beast. Maybe he was and her eyes were playing tricks on her, it was so difficult to trust anything in this moment.

Grace turned back to Lucy, only to see her standing directly beside her.

"Am I... am I doing the right thing?" Grace asked, feeling like literal hell was about to break loose.

Lucy put a gentle hand on her shoulder. "Only you know that." She said softly.

Grace held the Grail in her hands and thought about Gabe. "He's going to end up here."

"Who is?" Lucy asked.

"Gabe. My friend. The one I want to help." Lucy nodded understanding, as Grace snapped one of the horns off the Grail. As sturdy as it was, it was surprisingly easy to break off. "He'll most likely go to Paradise. He's that person. He is the ultimate human. Selfless, loving, and generous. And while he thrives in Paradise, I'll be in the Inferno. After everything I've done, I deserve it." Grace snapped off the other horn and let the body of the Grail fall to the ground with a hollow thud as it rolled to the side of the cavern.

"He would move mountains for me... no. He *has* moved mountains for me. It's my turn. I'm going to move this mountain and come back to life to save his."

Grace raised her hands with one horn in each and put them gently near the splintered circles on the exposed scalp.

Nothing happened.

Grace looked to Lucy, desperately hoping she would tell her what she'd done wrong.

"Keep them there for a moment. It's been... oh, it's been too long. He won't recognise his —" Lucy and Grace both gasped as they watched intense, red-hot light appear and begin to weld the horns to the head. Grace let them go in panic, but it didn't matter, they were fixed in place.

The light and heat dissipated.

"Now what?" Ooze asked from outside the melting cavern.

Grace could see a hint of red light begin to glow from within the ice. It was pulsing. It worked its way from Beelzebub's legs to the tip of his horns. Lucy and Grace stared as the cycle repeated multiple times.

"Now it's time to teethe." Lucy said with a glint in her eye. She pushed Grace outside the melting cave, keeping her eyes locked on Beelzebub completely. "Ooze, make sure she's quite a distance away. Centuries of planning, let's do this right."

Ooze pointed one of its dripping arms to a small ledge that would give a good view of everything about to happen. As Grace walked up the small slope, she couldn't help but hear the words Ooze said earlier go round in her head, again and again. Of all the things to be happening right now, she'd just resurrected Beelzebub!

A sharp thunderous *snap* echoed around the monstrous cave. Grace turned to see that there was a huge crack in the glacial wall and in that moment, she knew exactly where she had heard Ooze's words before.

Grace's mind fell silent. Her heart was beating so fast, literally forcing her body to do or say something. She had to act fast and ignore the overwhelming regret quickly filling her up.

"What...what you said before." Grace said, letting the words fall out of her. "I — I need to hear it again. I think I really screwed up."

"What did I say?" Ooze asked inquisitively.

"About… not telling anyone saving my life?" She said numbly.

Ooze let a grandiose smile creep along its face. "Not telling anyone *might* have just saved your life."

Those were the exact words she'd heard before. He had said the exact same thing. The Shadow Man.

Grace's eyes widened and her stomach hit the floor.

"It was you!"

~ Chapter Twenty ~

THE THRONE ROOM FALLS

Grace stared at Ooze with wide, determined eyes. How had she not realised Ooze had the same voice as the Shadow Man? Her blood ran cold through her veins as the hot rage built up in her chest.

"You did all of this to me!" She yelled. "I'm dead because of you!" She began pacing towards Ooze, who slithered back to keep a distance. "What big plan was this? You abducted my friend, killed me, then used and manipulated me time and time again. And I fell for it all!" Grace stopped and took a deep breath. "Say something!" She shouted as Ooze simply shrugged.

"Ooze... please... at least tell me, why?" She begged, running her hands through her hair. Ooze just frowned, raising its heavy brow.

Another large *crack* came from the glacial wall. Grace turned to see that it was now splintered and partially shattered as Lucy walked out of the melting cave backwards, keeping an eye on Beelzebub.

"*You!*" Grace snarled. Lucy spun around, stunned that such a tone was used against her. "Was I just part of a plan? Did you just use me?" Lucy's mouth curled to the side maliciously.

"Did you figure something out?" She said just loud enough for Grace to hear.

"Was I just a pawn in whatever plan you had?" Grace pleaded, falling to her knees. "Was there ever a way back?"

Lucy strut towards Grace with confidence. "You have no idea how many people we had to manipulate over and over, but they were all infected with moral righteousness." Lucy said through gritted teeth. "Every single one!"

Lucy stopped in front of Grace, towering over her.

"But why? I don't understand. Why did you pick me?" Grace began to sob. "What's so special about me?"

Lucy stooped down, lifted Grace's chin with a finger, looked deep into her eyes, and opened her mouth slowly. "Nothing."

Grace felt like she had been kicked in the gut hearing such raw honesty from the simplest of words.

"You aren't special. Right before the horns were snapped off, you nearly had that moment of moral righteousness. You're just like everyone else we used." Lucy rose back to her full height, letting Grace's head fall. "You're not some chosen hero to save the day; but you will forever go down in time as the one who helped release—"

"WHAT HAVE YOU DONE?" Boomed a voice across the cavern, so loud that it was impossible to pinpoint where it came from. As Grace cleared tears from her eyes, she saw a man standing behind Lucy.

"Ah, I was wondering if you'd ever show up. It looks like this will be just a little more difficult than I anticipated." Lucy said, turning her back on Grace as if she were never there.

"Lucy, I'm being calm in a situation that I shouldn't be, so count your blessings. *What* have you done?" The man asked again, raising a slender hand towards the melting cave. Grace looked at him more closely through her watery vision and saw that he was wearing an elegant red and black suit with lots of beaded embellishments. He had a clean trimmed beard, showing off the pointed bone structure in his face. But what surprised Grace the most was his dark, burgundy skin.

"Oh Satan, you know exactly what I've done."

Satan? I've really screwed up, Grace thought. If Satan were here alongside Lucy, hell was literally about to break loose.

"Lucy, I told you time and again why he must stay there!" Satan growled.

"And I heard you every time." Lucy said in a playful tone. "But I couldn't help and think something was wrong with that.

"I am not wrong." Satan snarled, defiantly. "You saw what he was doing before we trapped him here. You know what he is capable of, have you forgotten?"

Ice fell from the glacial wall and shattered across the floor. "I remember. But I also remember that he would listen to me. Take my counsel. He never had that relationship with you." Lucy walked towards the melting cave that held Beelzebub. "It must have been a decade or two after we trapped him here that I began to remember the days he was here with us."

"Chaotic." Satan confirmed loudly.

"Yes! But who was the one that helped stop the chaos and brought order to things?" Lucy turned to Satan. "Me."

"You can't seriously think you can reason with him at this point? Do you really believe he is just going to wake up and thank you?" Satan asked, bewildered.

Lucy laughed. "I know that's exactly what he'll do once I've told him everything I've done to get to this very moment. You and I both know how much he rewards loyalty. And what shows loyalty more than getting you out of prison?"

"He won't do that, Lucy. He won't reward you! He is complete and utter chaos, you know this!" Satan walked towards Lucy.

"Chaos that I could control!" Lucy spat at him, stopping Satan in his tracks. "I remember how much he would listen, and heed my words of wisdom and warning, then, I began to think differently about our initial plan."

Satan clenched his jaw. "We spoke for months about that plan! Months! Every single little detail!"

Lucy smirked. "I have spent a millennia advancing my Divine Power to focus on controlling him."

"What?" Satan said, furrowing his brow.

"Every single book, subject, and experiment... I honed my Divine Power. He doesn't stand a chance. And if you're not careful, neither will you."

"This is why I insisted we should've demolished this place permanently, in case someone crazy broke in with an idea like this... I never thought—" Satan heard the faint sound of someone crying and spun around to see Grace slumped on the icy ground. "Who is that?" He asked Lucy, who just laughed. Satan walked closer to Grace and kneeled in front of her, laying a gentle hand on her shoulder. "Who are you, child?"

Grace didn't move her body or lift her head. "No one special." She sniffed.

"Lucy!" Satan shouted as he stood up. "Explain who this is and why they're here!"

Lucy flinched at the tone. "*That* is Grace. She is the Soul who found the horns that you hid, and all by herself, restored them to their rightful owner."

"Herself? You expect me to believe she did all of that with her own free will?"

"I couldn't touch the horns, Satan. You made sure of that."

Larger shards of ice fell from the roof of the cavern as the melting cave entrance grew.

"I don't have time for this!" Satan said, raising a hand with a dark red aura around it, which also appeared around Lucy. He pushed her to the side with the flick of a finger and walked towards the cave. "Those horns are coming off, and we are sealing this place up." Satan's legs lifted from beneath him, and he fell on his back.

"You'll do nothing of the sort." Lucy said, lowering her hand with its purple aura.

"Now? You want to do this now?" Satan asked, lifting himself up.

Lucy jumped towards Satan, launching into an attack. Grace could only make out red and purple shapes, while grunts and shrieks filled the air.

Grace couldn't have cared less about what was happening in front of her. Her mind was numbing itself, and it had nothing to do with the ice around her. Part of her brain knew that this was a crazy situation to be in, and if she were able to tell her living self in the past where she'd find herself today, she would never believe it. She couldn't help but feel defeated. All this effort, the fighting, lying, hiding, and running around — it was all for nothing. There was never going to be a situation where she found herself able to go back and save Gabe.

Grace slowly turned her head around to see Ooze watching the purple and red showdown with a monstrous glee in its eyes, a vainglorious smile crossing its entire head.

"Is Gabe okay?" She asked. Ooze looked down at her slowly. "You were the last one to see him. You did all of this to us both. Is he at least, okay? Or is he—"

"More than a few people have died over the years trying to bring him back." Ooze said through its slimy mouth. "I don't know, and I don't care if he is alive or dead. Once we had you, I left him."

"You just left him there?" Grace asked with the faintest glimmer of hope. Her mind quickly whirled knowing what this meant. There was the smallest of chances Gabe got free, and he was safe. Grace brought herself back to the reality of what she had been put through. How did she let so many people manipulate and make a mockery of her?

Grace slumped forward and cried into her hands as they covered her face. She let out a frustrated scream and wiped away the tears. Standing up, she took in the mess she had created: the ice cavern falling apart, the fight between Lucy and Satan, and Beelzebub about to burst out of the ice any second. She turned her back on it all and saw a familiar black shirt with a daisy print on it emerge from a cavern nearby.

"Gladys!" Grace shouted.

The ice stopped falling and cracking, and Lucy and Satan stopped fighting as the name echoed around the cavern.

Gladys looked at each one of them slowly in turn.

Lucy rolled her eyes dramatically.

Satan breathed through his teeth, feigning a smile.

Ooze whimpered and turned a lighter shade of purple.

Grace stood there and prepared herself to accept the wrath.

Gladys simply dusted some debris off their sleeves and stood with their hands on their hips. "Not a single word from any of you."

*   *   *

"I'm about to flip my lid." Gladys said calmly, dramatically holding out their hands. "And don't you lie to my face and say you're busy, Lucy. You've not filled out as much as one report since Lot's Wife. You and I have to have a chat." Gladys walked over the ice, slightly slipping every so often as they approached her.

Grace felt a wave of both relief and fear as she saw Gladys. Fighting the urge to run over and hug them, knowing they would scold her.

"You're completely unhinged if you think this situation is in any way a logical decision." Gladys said, drawing themselves up to their full height in front of Lucy, who was biting her lip anxiously being stared down. "Yeah, you might as well say nothing. I never thought I'd see imbecilic actions like these from a Deity like you."

Gladys turned and locked eyes with Grace, and their face lit up with joy. "Aw, my lovely, I've never been so relieved to see you!" Gladys made their way over to Grace and tightly embraced her in a warm hug. "Are you okay, my lovely?" Grace couldn't speak through the tears, resorting to just nodding her head. "I didn't want you to be caught up in anything like this." Gladys said, wiping away tears from Grace's eyes. "As soon as I knew *exactly* what was going on, I was trying to stop you."

Grace lifted her head from Gladys' shoulder and swallowed her tears. "I should have listened to you Gladys, you were right. I wish I hadn't been so stupid."

"You weren't to know, my lovely. I don't blame you for trying. Well, maybe you went to the extreme end of things. But I don't blame you at all." Gladys hugged Grace again and held her tightly. As Gladys wiped away a tear from their own eye, the ice wall cracked thunderously. "What in the world is happening here?"

"*She* woke him up." Satan said, nodding his head towards Lucy, irritated.

"Oh, I forgot you were here." Gladys said, raising themselves back to their full height. "Do you never have your phone on ye? No? I've been trying to reach you for days!" Satan looked down at his feet and scuffed them on the ground, mumbling something. "What's that? Say it louder for everyone." Satan glanced up to look at Gladys and then back down again. "That's what I thought, you've got no excuse this time for ghosting me. I thought we had something y'know? But it looks like you were just using me whenever you were bored. I needed you. I needed help, and you were nowhere to be seen. Yet here you are fighting with your sister instead of solving the issue at hand!"

As they walked towards the melting cave, Gladys pushed passed Satan, delved into Lucy's breast pocket of her blazer and yanked their glasses out. "Much better, I can see again!" They looked inside the cave and saw the insidious glow of red coming from Beelzebub's horns. "Right, you." They said, tapping the slippery ice with their hand gently. "How are we going to deal with you?"

"I'll be dealing with him when he wakes up completely." Lucy said, strolling forward, feigning confidence.

"You'll do no such thing." Gladys scoffed. "You handled me back there because you thought you were in the right, but now look at ye. Faking this confidence in front of me, pretending like you're still in the right. But you and I both know there is a part of you that's doubting, isn't there?" Lucy pursed her lips slightly. "It's okay to be wrong. Even I'm wrong sometimes. Hardly ever. Rarely. But this isn't for you to sort. You've already messed this up, magnificently."

"This is really uncalled for, Gladys." Lucy said. "You have no Divine Power. You're not a Deity, a part of the Angel Tiers, or the Demon Cycles, you're not even part of the High Spirit Council. *You* are a receptionist."

"Now, you hold your tone there, my lovely."

"I could send you back to any number of Oubliettes until the end of time." Retorted Lucy.

"Do it." Gladys said, smiling, their raised eyebrow mocking Lucy. "You know I'd get out of each one within minutes. There's not a Demon, Beast, nor Creature that wouldn't help me, and I'll always return that favour." Gladys held a finger up to Lucy's mouth to pause the conversation. "Which reminds me — Grace? Get me to return the favour to Willow and Hollow!" Grace smiled hearing both of their names again. Gladys turned back to Lucy. "You may be in a position of power and read thirty books a night, but you've got no brains to back up anything you do. Case in point; the situation behind me." Gladys nodded their head at the melting cave.

A faint hiss could be heard coming from inside the cave, peaking both Gladys and Lucy's curiosity. They both leaned inside to see that the ice holding Beelzebub in place was melting at an alarming pace. They looked at each other and understood, without saying a word, they had to get away as fast as they could.

Running back to safety they picked up Grace from the icy ground, Satan joining them quickly after. Steam began to roll out of the melting cave, alongside the small river of water. Ooze saw everyone stumbling away from the steaming cave entrance and knew something bad was about to happen and animatedly waved to Grace and slithered away into the shadows, disappearing.

Grace saw the wave and it lit a fire inside her. She wanted to tell Gladys everything she had found out, especially that Ooze was the Shadow Man that got her here in the first place. But Grace understood it wasn't the time or place, and most likely, Gladys already knew.

Everyone piled behind a large set of stalagmites, catching their breath. They all looked over the ice they were hiding behind to see the final chunks of the glacial wall completely fall and shatter, shaking the ground. Ice dust flew into the air, water splashing everywhere, and smaller chunks like projectiles darting themselves into the walls of the cave. Grace couldn't see through the thick of it but as the dust slowly settled, there was an eerie silence and a shadowy figure appeared standing where the glacial wall used to be.

Beelzebub stood tall and powerful among the ice. His skin was black like coal, cracked all over, and within, Grace could make out a faint red glow, as if fire itself was fuelling his body. A huge chain adorned his left arm, wrapped around it tightly. Grace widened her eyes as the ice dust settled some more; she could make out from the waist down Beelzebub had the legs of a goat with black matted fur and giant hooves. He wasn't the great hulking creature that she had imagined, probably the same size as Lucy or Satan, but more threatening.

Beelzebub took long, deep breaths as he stumbled finding his footing. The sound of his hooves made Grace's stomach sink. He slowly sniffed the air, cracked his neck, and turned to face the stalagmite that everyone was hiding behind.

Gladys gasped. "Holy shi—"

~ Chapter Twenty-One ~

BEELZEBUB

"— ny windows!" Gladys held their breath and grabbed Grace's hand. "He knows. There's nowhere else to hide."

Beelzebub signalled for his adversaries to come out of hiding and scanned each of them as they revealed themselves. His skin cracked when Lucy and Satan appeared side by side.

"You." He said in a deep growl, gravel spitting out of his mouth. "The betrayal from my own family — you lied and destroyed everything I built." His brow furrowed as the cracks in his arms lit up. "How long has it been?"

"Nearly two thousand years." Satan said flatly. Beelzebub's skin flared.

"Too long!" Lucy said, stepping forward.

"Who are you?" Beelzebub asked, confused at her confidence as she approached him.

"You know me as Lucifer." She said with a bad taste in her mouth. "But I go by Lu—" Beelzebub blasted fire from his hands over her. Engulfed in flame Lucy began shrieking in pain, Grace wanted to shout and tell him to stop. As the flames died down, Grace could see Lucy laying on the ground, scorched and restrained in endless knots of searing magma, twisted to resemble rope. She was alive and breathing, but powerless.

"Weak. That's what you go by now." Beelzebub said, his eyes ablaze.

Satan nervously etched forward; his hands raised high in submission. "Brother listen, we should talk." He gestured to Lucy. "None of this will come of anything. Let's go back to your chamber and discuss things, rationally." Grace could feel every word was picked with great precision, as to not suffer the same fate as Lucy.

Beelzebub stared Satan down in a heated silence until he slowly began to relax his brow. He rolled his shoulders back and sighed heavily. Grace squeezed Gladys' hand and they looked at each other, their eyes full of hope.

"No." He said, maliciously; and in the snap of a finger, boiling magma formed a liquid cage around Satan, its top high above him. Gladys gasped and sprung forward to intervene, but Grace stopped them. As the cage rapidly cooled and solidified, Satan disappeared from view, and became a prisoner in stone. Muffled banging and yelling could be heard as he tried to free himself, but with no success.

Beelzebub smirked and slowly turned his head to lock eyes with Grace. Gladys knew she was next and, thinking fast, jumped in front of Grace to protect her.

"Who are you?" He asked with a growl.

Gladys gave Grace's hand one more tight squeeze before letting go and walking forward. "Hi, son. We wouldn't have met. You were *way* before my time. My name's Gladys. From the Department for Lost Souls, or DLS, whatever you want to call it, no one is really that fussed." Grace was so confused at how casual Gladys was talking to Beelzebub, especially after what they had witnessed him do. "But listen, you've been through it all and a half, haven't you? Your brother and sister tricking you, locking you in this ice cavern, which wouldn't be my ideal place to have been locked up either — not so much as a carpet to be seen anywhere! All because you wanted to... what was it again?"

Beelzebub raised an eyebrow. "Rule the Three Realms."

"Right. Well, if there's one thing I am it's honest and I won't lie to ye, that's a bit dramatic." Gladys could see the flame in his eyes growing. "But so was their idea of locking you up here, snapping your fabulous horns off, and goodness knows what else. Talk about unfair!" Gladys adjusted the glasses on their nose and smiled warmly at Beelzebub. "How about you and I have a nice cup of tea together and come up with a better plan? I just got new biscuits I've been dying to try, and this is the perfect excuse! Even a big, strong fella like yerself likes a good cup of tea. What do ye say, eh?" Gladys could see that Beelzebub wasn't biting into their offer. "A nice wee gab? After years of not being able to say anything, you must be champing at the bit to get some stuff off yer chest. I mean, looking at what you just did to your own family, you've got something to say. And I'm one hell of a listener."

The silence was so loud Grace wanted to shout to make it stop. Gladys had run out of things to say, and Beelzebub wasn't moving. It was clear that one wrong word could be disastrous.

Beelzebub snickered. Gladys swallowed hard, not knowing what was about to happen.

Smirking deeply, Beelzebub unravelled the large, heavy chain from around his arm. It hit the ground with a clang.

"I know I can talk for all of the Afterlife, but over a cuppa, I can listen to anyone, and more importantly, I can help." Gladys pressed again.

Beelzebub let out a roar as he raised his arm and whipped the chain down until it smashed into the ground in front of Gladys. Grace let out a gasp of horror, but she noticed

Gladys didn't move. They didn't even flinch. Beelzebub brought the chain back in and began to whip it in a slow rhythm on either side of his body. The noise was so loud that it echoed above and beyond the ice cavern.

As the chain hit the ground for the final time, he raised a finger to his lips and slowly cupped his hand around his ear to signify that everyone should be listening for something.

Grace couldn't hear anything at first, until there was a quiet and distant drumming. Slowly, it got louder, trembling the room. There was a thunderous roar and the wall behind Beelzebub exploded and a monstrous claw was pushing itself through the hole created. Lucy tried to shout but was gagged by her restraint. Satan furiously smashed his cage, hoping it would soon give in.

The claw pulled itself back into the hole, and a huge face appeared, looking into the ice cavern. A colossal red face with flesh hanging from its cheeks, empty yellow eyes, and uneven sharp teeth. It pulled its whole body through, and Grace was frozen in fear. Its torso was kept together by rotting and decaying flesh. Grace could see through holes in the skin and witness its organs barely staying in place. She wanted to be sick, she'd never seen something so putrid. Its legs resembled those of Beelzebub's, but instead of fur, it had exposed bare bone. As it stood up to its full height, snarling and panting heavily, Beelzebub let out a sinister laugh.

"The Beast." He said.

"The Devil." Gladys corrected him, and his eyes widened. "Right, well, listen, I tried reasoning with you Bebe son. I did try. So, I do apologise in advance for this." Gladys brought out their phone and pressed a single button on the device, held it to their ear, and smiled at Beelzebub. "Thank goodness I've got a signal down here, otherwise this would have been embarrassing."

"What are you doing?" Beelzebub asked, fascinated and confused by the device they were holding.

"Shush." Gladys said, putting their finger to their mouth and turning a shoulder towards him. "Do you mind? I'm making a quick call — Oh, hiya, my lovely, how are you? Aw, that's grand, so good to hear it! Listen, do you remember that favour you owe me? Aye, you do. I made you a full sticky toffee pudding, and you never returned the dish. That's a favour owed in anyone's books. Well, I need to call it in now." There was a tense silence as Gladys nodded, licked their lips, and adjusted their glasses. "Aye. All of you. Oh, and bring that extra wee flare — you know the one, yeah? Perfect! I'll see you soon, my lovely! Cheery-bye now!" Gladys pressed a button on their phone and put it in their pocket, smiling.

Beelzebub slammed the chain back onto the ground, finally reaching the end of his patience. "Enough. You're as weak as them!"

"Wrong. I'm the weakest!" Gladys said simply. "I know I've talked your ear off, but listen to me, my lovely. I'm just a wee ant compared to you. You could blow me into a thousand pieces until I became nothing but mince. For all the power you have, I have even less. You might as well just pat me on the back and send me on my way. Doing anything to me would be pointless, my lovely. You'd just upset everyone at the book club, the bakery, and my wee office bestie Brenda. I've got no Divine Power, no fancy weapons, no brightly coloured pet, and I certainly don't have a revenge agenda. But do you know what I do have?" Gladys asked him.

There was no response.

"No, really, go on and guess!" They pressed once more.

Beelzebub almost shrugged and loosened his grip on the chain. "What?" He asked irritated.

"I have one *incredibly* delicious sticky toffee pudding recipe…"

The ceiling of the cavern began to *crack*, and everyone looked up slowly to see it splinter. Rock and ice began to fall as a hole was created, and a glowing white light pierced through it. Beelzebub waved his hand and all the debris from the ceiling was pushed to the side, hitting a wall instead.

Through the white light Grace could make out blurred shapes slowly descending towards Gladys. As her eyes adjusted, she could see there were seven figures altogether, each wearing a white robe fashioned individually and adorned with silver and gold jewellery. What made Grace's jaw truly drop were the large white wings attached to each of their backs, allowing them to descend safely.

As they landed, one of the figures strode towards Gladys and embraced them. "Gladys, my dear love, I hope we're not too late."

"Gabriel! Not at all. I stalled as long as I could before you made your grand entrance. And not a moment too soon! I gave a banger of a last line, and I would have been bright red if you hadn't come through just in time!"

A deep and maniacal laughter pulled Gladys and Gabriel from their conversation to turn and face Beelzebub.

"The Archangels. This was your big plan." He shook his head gently. "This will be interesting. You're in my territory and I will not hold back!" He shouted, raising the chain once more and slamming it down in front of him.

A huge crack began to form, almost spanning the entire length of the cavern. It grew until it became a small chasm, separating Beelzebub and the Devil from the rest. Grace could hear small clicking noises coming from it, getting louder and closer, until it became a wall of noise.

A plethora of mutated creatures crawled from the chasm. Some of them Grace could identify through their horrible, fleshy mutations. Human bodies with the legs of a spider, snakes with the head of a lion, two-headed crocodiles on the body of a rhino... others she would only see in her nightmares. Amalgamations of red, raw flesh covered in sharp gnarly teeth, large veiny eyes eating creatures next to it with its pupils, and giant magnified insects with matted hair and a slimy coating.

Feeling the surge of victory nearing, Beelzebub smirked. "The Onslaught."

Gladys pulled Gabriel hurriedly towards them. "Did you bring it?" They whispered. Gabriel gently reached into their sleeve and pulled out what looked like a small bird's nest. "Will it work?" Gladys asked urgently.

Gabriel looked over to Beelzebub and recoiled. "There's only one way to find out."

~ Chapter Twenty-Two ~

FALLEN FROM GRACE

Grace stood far back from the carnage she was witnessing. Beelzebub's hordes of creatures were fighting the Archangels, neither side holding back. A stampede of valiant stallions was conjured by one of the Angels to storm through the horde, flattening as many of the vile creatures as possible. Another flew high above and created slow-falling snow and when it encountered the creatures below, it froze them solid. On the ground a singular Angel with long red hair stood silently with a long staff in their arms in a meditative state before launching their body into a flurry of frenzied attacks as the horde approached.

Beelzebub's creatures were less creative in their methods of attack, choosing instead to simply charge, bite, scratch, and claw everything in their way. This played in the Archangels favour, but they were outnumbered by the never-ending horde pouring out of the chasm.

"There are too many of them!" One shouted.

"We only call for help when we are in dire need. We've done this before!" Another called back.

Gladys ran over to Grace, avoiding holes in the ice and flying limbs along the way. "Grace! Stay away!" They shouted over the noise. Grace held her arms out to embrace Gladys noticing they were carrying something, but before they reached each other, Gladys was hunched over trying to catch their breath. "You were a lot further away than I thought." They gasped.

"Gladys, what do we do? What do *I* do? I did this!" Grace said helplessly.

"This wasn't your doing, my lovely. You were manipulated, and that is no fault on you at all!" Gladys outstretched their arms and hugged her. "Now, listen, it's very important you do as I say. You have a habit of doing the opposite, so please listen to me now." Grace nodded, apologising with her eyes. Gladys revealed what was in their hand. "*This* is the Crown of Thorns. It's a Divine Tool that diminishes all power and will render Beelzebub helpless. Then, we can get those horns off him safely and deal with him appropriately."

Grace blinked, looking down at the Crown. "O — okay. What can I do to help?"

"Help? Oh, no, my lovely, this is out of the depths of a Soul like yourself." Gladys said.

"No, I have to help! I *need* to help."

"Not on your Auntie Nelly!" Gladys said sternly. "You need to find a corner in this chamber to hide until he's taken down. End of discussion."

Grace stared into Gladys' eyes, pleading. Gladys just raised their arched brow even higher.

"And what if he isn't taken down?" Grace asked.

Gladys looked over at the battle still raging on and grabbed Grace's hand. "Then you run. You run, and you don't look back, alert everyone, make as much noise as possible. You do what needs to be done. He can't take the

Three Realms." Gladys turned to face Grace again and smiled. "But it won't get to that. Go hide! I need to get this on his head."

Grace watched Gladys run back to the battle, detouring to Satan, still caged in stone. She found a small crack in the ice cavern wall and decided it would be the best place to hide. She had to listen to Gladys this time, not listening led her to this very moment.

As Gladys approached the cage Satan was trapped inside, they could hear him furiously punching the walls, becoming more exhausted with each strike, determined to break free.

"Hot Stuff, are you alright in there?"

"Get out of here Gladys! You're no match for even the smallest of these creatures!" He said through each punch.

"I have a plan! It's fool proof, just trust me! Can you not get out of there at all?"

"If I could've, I would've by now!" He snapped.

"Alright, alright, no need to bite my heed aff!" Gladys turned to face the battle to try and find Gabriel. A sea of black and red bodies piling over each other made it impossible until a blast of white light burst from a large swarm, desperately trying to overthrow its prey. "Gabriel!" Gladys shouted at the top of their lungs.

Gabriel turned to see Gladys waving frantically. He twirled himself into the air and gracefully flew over, blinding the creatures along the way with prismatic light emanating from a bejewelled lantern.

"Gabriel, son, I need you to get Satan out of here. You know he's on our side of this, that won't be questioned here." They said looking over their glasses.

Gabriel nodded and swiftly turned to the stone prison holding Satan. "Cover your eyes!" He said as the lantern focused a beam of brilliant white light through the stone, turning it into rubble.

Satan stood up feeling his Divine Power returning to his body and nodded in thanks to Gabriel. "Time to even these odds." He said, raising his hands with a deep red aura twisting between his fingers.

Gladys piped up quickly. "No, no, no. Not yet! Gabriel, you get back in there! Hot Stuff, you need to get Lucy out of those binds and convince her to join our side in this fight." Satan began to protest. "Not a word from you, you know I'm right! We need you *and* her in this fight!" Gladys looked down at the Crown of Thorns in their hands and back up at Satan, who'd just done the same.

"Good plan." He nodded. "Be safe, we've got you." Satan sprinted towards Lucy, wriggling on the ground trying to free herself. Snapping the now solidified magma at her feet, he stopped to look her in the eye. "I know this hurts Lucy, but I can't free you unless you help us stop him. Have you seen reason?" Lucy rolled her eyes, and with her hands, gestured towards her binds. "I don't know what you're saying. Hang on." Satan crumbled the gag around Lucy's mouth, and she gasped for breath.

"He let that wonky-browed partner of yours speak nonsensical drivel! I had an incredible speech planned! I was going to use my powers and lure him in, but no!" She shouted. "He let that daisy-shirt-wearing fool ramble on about sticky toffee pudding!"

"We're not partners." Satan dismissed.

"I'm on nobody's side, and I *am* going to get out of this with your help or not. But when I do, I'm going to use him as a puppet!"

"You're not thinking right, Lucy." Satan raised his hand and Lucy was lifted gently into the air to see the surrounding chaos. "*Look* at this. He brought the Onslaught. The Beast! Look at him, closely. Do you see it?"

Lucy tried to home in on the battle in front of her. She had heard it all happening, but her vulnerable state left her vision weakened. She saw the Archangels fending off the creatures clawing and biting at them, only to cause little damage to the powerful beings. The horde's numbers took Lucy's breath away. In the distance beyond the chasm was the pyrrhic Beelzebub standing tall, launching molten projectiles towards the Archangels, desperate for victory.

"Do you see it?" Satan asked calmly.

"I see it." Lucy replied annoyed.

Beelzebub had covered himself in a black aura, making him unsusceptible to any Divine Power in this state.

"Until he's taken down, he will never drop his guard and you know that! No matter how much you talk and try to convince him, without your Divine Power being used at the same time as your words, he's never going to be your puppet."

A single tear fell from Lucy's eyes. "Centuries Satan... centuries. I was so close."

Satan lowered Lucy from above. "It was a good plan I'll admit that. But the opportunity is gone."

"I'll have to go up against the High Spirit Council for this, won't I?" She asked, defeated.

"Probably worse. But if you help me now, I'll help you then. Deal?"

Lucy glanced over in Beelzebub's direction one last time. "Get me out of this and we can stop this now!" Through her binds she grabbed Satan's hand. "Just, don't let them Fade me!"

"Despite all this, I'd never let them." He said and freed her.

Satan slowly helped her up to full height and Lucy gasped staring at the scorch marks on her pristine white suit and let out a small whine.

*   *   *

From a safe distance Grace watched every move made. The swift evasions by the Archangels, the erratic attacks from the Onslaught, Gabriel freeing Satan, and now Satan freeing Lucy. Grace prepared herself for another fight between the two but instead smiled to herself when she saw them join hands and use their Divine Power to decimate a wave of the Onslaught with a swirling blast of crimson and violet. As the tide began to turn, Grace thought this was the only chance for Gladys to get the Crown of Thorns on Beelzebub. However, the Beast was the most unpredictable creature of them all. It had been sent to destroy the Archangels, unbiasedly crushing and eating anything in front of it. Grace peered to see if Beelzebub was angry at the Beast, but his concentration was on the Archangels and simultaneously defending himself from Satan and Lucy's co-ordinated attacks.

Blasting fire from one arm to singe the Angels' wings and molten lava from the other to force the pair back, he took a moment to stop, look around, and calculate the next move. He did this again. And a third time.

Grace furrowed her brow in thought.

"He's still weak." She said aloud. "He needs to recover every time he uses too much..." Her eyes widened as she gripped the rock in front of her. "That's it!"

Only after he attacked and was regaining his strength, *that* was the moment to force the Crown of Thorns on his head and weaken him. Satan and Lucy were attacking him randomly, using all their abilities to try and outsmart him, so no one could have seen this pattern. Not even Gladys.

"Gladys!" She gasped. Looking out over the wriggling mass of the Onslaught, she found Gladys trying to cross the very edge of the chasm. Going against Gladys' word, Grace decided to throw caution to the wind and help. This was essential information that she *had* to give Gladys, as it could turn the whole situation in their favour. Pushing the worry in her gut to the side, Grace leapt out of the crack in the wall and ran at full speed towards Gladys.

A shrill shriek from behind Gladys forced a sharp turn to reveal three creatures charging in their direction. Gladys jumped a small gap of the chasm and gave themselves a mental pat on the back for such a large amount of exercise in one day. As Gladys pushed forward, something was caught in their periphery. High above on the wall next to them, a long centipede-like creature using claws to move its body around, was making its way down the wall. Gladys turned back to see the three creatures had already crossed the chasm. They didn't know what to do. Watching the centipede ready itself for a jump, Gladys raised their arms for the impact but instead heard a noise of something falling. They opened their eyes to see the creature curled up, just a few feet ahead of them. Gladys looked up and saw Lucy standing on a large levitating rock with a purple mist around it, high above them. Lucy pushed a hand forward, and from nowhere an enchanted boulder slammed down onto the three creatures behind Gladys, crushing them.

Lucy lowered herself to the ground. "Well, you know what they say? The enemy of my enemy is a friend."

"Do people say that? Well, I have no idea which one I am to you hen but thank you!" Gladys said, smiling gratefully. "I'm nearly there. Can you keep them distracted?" Showing Lucy the Crown of Thorns.

Lucy immediately nodded and ascended well above the creatures in Gladys' path. Lucy whispered a short incantation and five amethyst silhouettes pulled themselves from her body. In tandem, they proceeded to attack and pull the focus away, leaving Gladys free to sneak around and get closer to Beelzebub.

Using his own Divine Power, Satan generated crimson bolts of electricity to paralyse the creatures below, carefully avoiding the Archangels. He had stayed in the air for too long and had caught the attention of the Beast, who lifted one of its huge claws and grabbed him, slowly crushing him. An Archangel nearby acted immediately and flew straight for the closed fist of the Beast but was met by the other claw coming up and swiping them. The Beast roared in victory and slammed them both down into the ground.

"NO!" Gabriel commanded, rising into the centre of the cavern, grabbing the Beast's attention. From a seemingly small pouch on his crystalline belt, he took out a verdant jasper mirror and aimed its back at the Beast. "Look at me!" He shouted as the creature roared, letting its prize free and swiping for Gabriel. Everything around the Beast slowed down, like time itself was being manipulated and within an instant, Gabriel turned the mirror to face the Beast and its eyes shattered like glass. The Beast swatted for Gabriel in a fit of rage unable to see, screaming and panicking for its own existence.

Beelzebub pursed his lips in irritation. He gathered himself and took a deep breath before raising his leg up and slamming his foot down on the ground, a cloud of thick black smog instantly surrounded him. Releasing the breath, he blew the smoke over the Beast, now covering them both. With smoke swirling into the Beast's sockets, it formed dark mustard eyes granting it vision once again.

Still sneaking, Gladys thought if they made a run for the dark cloud, it would be the perfect time to get the Crown on Beelzebub's head while he's distracted having to share his power with the Beast. Grace, however, was hot on Gladys' bootsteps. She had jumped over the small end of the chasm, passed the creatures crushed by a boulder, and walked by a curled-up insect with way too many legs. She could see Gladys in the distance when a blinding light caught her eye, and saw Gabriel continue to take on the Beast. She kept pushing forward to reach Gladys until she saw them run for the dark cloud where Beelzebub once stood. Grace shouted after Gladys, but there was no way they would have heard her. The cloud began to expand in size, surrounding everything in sight. She didn't feel in control of her feet anymore as they lunged forward into the dark after Gladys.

*   *   *

Grace couldn't see her own hand in front of her face. The smoke stung her eyes and every breath hurt as she chewed down on the thick smog, wondering how long it would be before she needed to inhale again. Walking slowly and in deadly silence, there was a flash of orange in the distance. Grace squinted and figured that was Beelzebub, which meant Gladys saw it too. Determined she was right, Grace marched forward assuming Gladys would do the same. Taking a risk, she whispered Gladys' name, hoping they would hear. The name had only just left her lips when the smoke around her cleared, and she could see Beelzebub directly ahead. A diamond bubble with infinite edges had been formed around the two of them by Beelzebub. It was just her and him. Where was Gladys?

"Who are you?" He asked menacingly.

"I'm Grace. I'm not supposed to be here." Her body was shaking in fear, she couldn't really piece the right answer together quick enough in her head.

"Fallen from Grace." Beelzebub smirked.

"Yeah, you could say that." Grace nervously laughed.

"And whose side are you on?" He asked, his voice deep and hollow.

Grace opened her mouth to answer but noticed movement behind Beelzebub. That unmistakable daisy shirt pierced through the black smoke behind him, and Gladys stopped in their tracks. Their eyes locked as Beelzebub tilted his head, Gladys overly gestured to Grace to keep him talking.

Grace looked back at Beelzebub. "No side, really... I mean... I just want to go home. I'm not supposed to be here."

"If you're not with me, you're against me!" He bellowed and raised a pulsing red arm.

"Wait!" She screamed. "I'm the one who brought you back!"

Beelzebub stopped and blinked with a loud clicking noise. Grace saw the glow in his arm die down.

"I went through so much to bring you back!"

"You?" He said with a deep chuckle. "An insignificant Soul like *you* brought me back?" He leaned towards Grace. "...Why?"

Grace remembered every time she was told that it was impossible to return to the Land of the Living. But there was still one way... through Beelzebub, who was now standing right in front of her and listening intently.

She had one last chance.

"I was promised you could do something. I just want to know if you *could* do it. That's all." Grace let her eyes flicker to the side to see Gladys slowly closing in on Beelzebub.

"What is that?" He asked slowly.

"I'm dead, obviously. But I was told that you could make me live again. I was taken before my natural time, and I want to go back. Can you do that?" Grace asked, hanging everything she had on such a simple and yet absurd question.

Beelzebub's smile deepened, his cracked skin snapping around his mouth. "Yes. I *could*."

Right behind him, Gladys made their move and jumped to put the Crown on his head. Grace ran to help, but before she even had the chance to take a step forward, Beelzebub had spun around, grabbed Gladys and wrapped his steel chain around them tightly.

"But for your untactful game of distraction? I won't!" Beelzebub cackled.

The chain around Gladys gave out a dark hue and Gladys let out a small gasp. "Grace! Look away! Look away now, my lovely!" They shouted. Grace watched in horror as the hue turned to thorns and latched itself onto Gladys. "Look away! You don't need to see this!" Their glasses fell from their face as tears filled Gladys' eyes.

"What are you doing? What's happening? Stop it!" Grace begged.

Beelzebub let out a hearty, maniacal laugh. "The Fade!"

Grace watched helplessly as Gladys began to flake away into dust very slowly.

"I'm in no pain, my lovely." Gladys said through stammering breaths. "Look after yourself!"

A single tear escaped in fear and trickled down Grace's cheek as Gladys faded away and the chain holding them aloft fell to the ground with a loud clang.

Gladys was gone.

~ Chapter Twenty-Three ~

A LIVING SOUL

The entire cavern came to a halt as the black smoke cleared and everyone could see what had happened. The Archangels slowed their flight until they hovered in the air silently. The Onslaught below murmured restlessly amongst itself. Lucy and Satan stopped, eyes wide in disbelief. The Beast turned to Beelzebub and watched, emotionless.

Lucy reached out to Satan's hand and held onto it tightly. "No…" He whispered.

Grace stood paralysed, tears breaking their banks, streaming down her face. Was there something she could have done differently? She ran through Gladys' final moments in her head and calculated no matter what, she couldn't have saved Gladys. Grace fell to her knees and let out a loud cry of pain.

"Oh, you really cared for her." Beelzebub laughed.

"*Them!*" Grace shouted back.

Satan threw himself at Beelzebub who sensed the attack coming and connected his molten fist with Satan's jaw,

Satan yanked the chain from his arm before being thrown backwards along the ground, leaving it gouged from Beelzebub's limb. Satan reared himself up onto his side, rubbing his face. "You have... no idea what you've done. Gladys—" Satan choked on his words.

"Gladys was the essence of life in the Three Realms." Lucy said, gliding down elegantly behind Beelzebub. "There will never be someone like them again. Gladys and I never saw eye to eye, but even I knew better than to *kill* them."

"I didn't kill her." Beelzebub chuckled, locking eyes with Satan. "I *annihilated* her!"

Laughing in delicious glee, he soaked up the pain in Satan's face.

"Them!" Lucy screeched, and with all the power in her body, sent a violet wave crashing into Beelzebub. He was caught off guard and fell to the ground. A gothic show of light from the siblings' combined power could be seen for miles around the cavern. Hues of purple, red, and black swirling and cancelling each other out as they fought for supremacy. The Beast stood aimlessly while the restless Onslaught fought and ate each other. The Archangels held their hands clasped to their chest and silently prayed.

Grace, still hunched over in tears, was flooded by her memories of Gladys. From the very first moment she walked into DLS terrified and lost, Gladys welcomed her with open arms, comforted her, and went way beyond her station. They always made time for her no matter how busy or unexpectedly she just appeared at reception. They dropped everything to talk, making sure she was okay, and answered every question, even taking her to the Meditation and Self-Care Halls personally. Gladys tried to protect her from the truth regarding the Shimmer, even about the dangers of Ooze. Gladys made her feel wanted, and all Grace did was return the favour by causing chaos. Gladys forgave and protected her, right to the very end.

Through her tears Grace noticed the Crown of Thorns kicked to the side, dismissed as powerless and of no consequence to Beelzebub. Crawling over to it and holding it tightly in her hands, she looked up at Satan and Lucy desperately attempting to take down their brother.

"I'll do it." Grace said defiantly. "I'm not going to listen to you one more time, Gladys. I'm *not* going to run."

"Is this all you've got? This'll be over sooner than you think." Beelzebub said, looking to the Beast. Without his chain to control it, the Beast stared blankly at the walls of the cavern like a stringless puppet. "Argh! Bring me their heads!" He commanded to the Onslaught. The Archangels whirled back into action to fend the horde back from Lucy, Satan, and Grace.

Grace was determined to get the Crown of Thorns onto Beelzebub's head, but she didn't want to meet the same fate as Gladys. What would he not expect? Grace's eyes fell upon something she wished she hadn't, and the idea made the bile in her stomach churn uncomfortably.

The Beast.

It stood with its huge mouth slacked open, and she knew she could climb it. She sprung to her feet and ran for its hulking body. Looking up to the Archangels for help, she tried to find Gabriel, but they were struggling to hold back the Onslaught.

Grace hooped the Crown of Thorns on her arm as she jumped for the shin of the Beast's bony leg. She tried not to notice the stench, but every breath coated her lungs in a thicker layer of rot. As she reached the hips, the struggle of the climb became real as she started to become breathless.

"I'll... get this... on his head... if it's... the last thing... I do!" She said fighting through the pain of the climb.

A glint of gold caught Lucy's eye as she defended herself from Beelzebub's attacks. She furrowed her brow, confused why the shoulder of the Beast was glinting, until she homed her eyesight and saw Grace pulling herself up with an impossibly bright sparkle around her. Lucy brought up a wall to protect herself as she stared at Grace who looked like she was going to jump with the Crown of Thorns in her hands. "She's crazy."

"Lucy!" Satan cried as he was pummelled by black, smoky hands. She snapped back to the moment and opened a void below and above Beelzebub. He fell through the bottom and down from the top, in a never-ending loop.

"Satan, when I stop the voids, you need to hold him down with everything you have. *Everything!*" She said sharply. Satan affirmed and got himself ready, his fiery aura glowing.

*   *   *

Lucy closed the void and Beelzebub hit the ground hard, leaving him disoriented. Satan roared and unleashed a nest of snakes from his body. Writhing in the air towards Beelzebub, they wrapped themselves tightly around his hooves, wrists, and neck, anchoring him on his knees. Now knowing her plan, Lucy turned and raised her arm towards Grace. Smoke swirled from Lucy and wrapped itself around Grace's body. Grace knew it was now or never and had mentally prepared for this to be her final moment, something she didn't have the luxury of doing before.

"Do it now!" Lucy barked, and Grace leapt from the Beast's shoulder, and everything stopped around her.

Grace was met with a wave of nostalgia, the smell of popcorn as she and Gabe watched an old action movie with her mum, hoping the good guy would make the heroic leap off the burning building. If only they both could see her now.

She felt the chill in the air creep in, bringing her back to reality, and the chaos surrounding her animated once again. As she fell, she witnessed Beelzebub break free from his ophidian ties and rise to meet her. Without a moment to pause or breathe, she slammed the Crown on his head and fell to the ground, cushioned by Lucy's protection.

Beelzebub let out a roar unlike anything Grace had ever heard, it was so loud she covered her ears and thought the bones inside her would crumble. Grace looked up from Beelzebub to see the creatures of the Onslaught and the Beast had turned to face her.

"The horns! Grace, the horns!" Lucy cried over the piercing roar, as she ran towards the oncoming attack. The Archangels descended beside her, separating themselves evenly across the chasm. With a raise of their arms in unison an impenetrable wall was created, blocking the horde's path. "The horns!" Lucy cried again.

Satan leapt at Beelzebub to keep him restrained, singeing his skin from the impossible heat. "Now's the time, Grace. Do it now!" He beckoned, wrestling to keep Beelzebub under control. Putting all feeling of pain and consequence aside, she wrapped her hands around the horns, scolding them.

"You don't have the strength!" Beelzebub said, fighting to look at her. "You're a powerless Soul. I am endless. I am eternal. You are nothing!" He laughed, overpowering Satan and pushing him aside. Grace panicked and pulled as hard as she could thinking of her mum, Gabe, and Gladys... she wasn't doing this for her, but for them.

"What is that?!" Beelzebub yelled, his eyes squinting shut. Grace looked down at her body to see it glowing in an ivory white gold.

The Shimmer!

It was so much more than just a drop of golden glitter. But now... Now she understood exactly *what* it was. It was undeniable. All of a sudden, she felt stronger and more powerful than anyone in the Afterlife. Grunting loudly, Grace pulled on the horns with every ounce of strength that she had.

Beelzebub roared in pain, feeling his life force quickly drain.

Satan conjured more snakes, charming them to restrain Beelzebub once more.

Grace felt a crack form in the horns, and she saw a tear falling from the side of Beelzebub's face. "You're... a living Soul?" He pleaded.

Grace gave one last pull and screamed as the horns buckled and gave way from Beelzebub, falling to the ground splintered. Carmine smoke poured from the cracked stumps and Beelzebub collapsed.

"A living Soul... living... Soul..." He repeated silently, exhausted.

The ferocious horde on the other side of the barrier calmed; the buzz of battle slowly dying. The Beast fell to the ground, inanimate.

Satan leaned into Beelzebub breathing heavily and put a hand over his face. "Sleep." He whispered.

~ Chapter Twenty-Four ~

THE FADE

Grace let out a deep sigh, relieved that her plan somehow worked. The Onslaught retreated into the chasm, scrambling over each other in panic sensing Beelzebub was no longer conscious. Watching them regress, the Archangels lowered the impenetrable wall, leaving no trace or mark on the ground. Lucy fashioned a large chain around the Beast's neck and grabbed onto it tight.

"I'll take care of this one." She said, tugging on the chain.

Grace was hunched over Beelzebub's body, hearing it crackle as it cooled. The horns in her hands slowly pulsed as she finally allowed her shoulders to relax after being so tense.

"Is it done? Did I do it?" She asked, not looking away from Beelzebub.

Satan loosened the vipers wrapped around Beelzebub, returning them to his body, vanishing as they slid up his leg. "You did it. You're very brave. Gla— they would have been proud." Satan caught a lump in his throat and turned away.

Grace couldn't think about Gladys, the moment was too much. She just wanted to collapse and sleep for an eternity, completely drained after everything.

Gabriel glided to Grace and knelt to meet her eye level. "Grace, isn't it?"

She nodded silently.

"We've not met. I'm Gabriel. Gladys spoke so fondly of you." Gabriel noticed Grace close her eyes. "Sorry... but they also spoke about you and the Shimmer." He reached out to touch her hand. "You have the Shimmer, Grace."

"I... what?" Grace said, shell shocked.

"Grace, look!" Gabriel said, smiling.

Grace opened her eyes slowly, catching a glittered refraction from her fingers. Pure essence flowed through her veins and emanated from her skin in a warm glow. She felt powerful taking on Beelzebub, but she put that down to anger and fear, thinking it would pass. Now, it was permanent radiance, like something had been missing this whole time and had been found.

"Am I..." Grace looked up to Gabriel, holding back the hope in her smile. "Am I alive?"

Gabriel nodded slowly as the other Archangels and Lucy came over to join them. "A living soul in the Inferno... I thought I'd see it snow here first." He chuckled. Everyone bustled into conversation about Grace and the Shimmer shining from her.

"I've only ever read about such things, it's truly beautiful to behold."

"Wonders never cease to amaze."

"There are few words that could describe the simple joy of light."

Satan lifted Beelzebub. "I'll put him back on his throne. He might have just tried to destroy us, but he deserves a proper resting place." He said and walked back to the ice-covered throne, his sibling hanging over his shoulder.

Grace smiled as she watched him walk away and looked down at her hands again, fascinated with the Shimmer. "Hang on." She said and turned to the Archangels. "If I'm alive, does that mean I can go back?" She gasped.

Collectively they nodded and Gabriel stood up, combing his fingers through his hair. "Yes. If that is your decision, you can return."

"A word of caution before you do." Lucy said, stepping forward. "If you do return, this means you'll pick up from where you departed and live with the consequences of what brought you here. Any pain will also return to you. Understand?"

A sudden flash of bright light came towards Grace as she was driven through the memory of the car crash. She nodded slowly with a faded smile.

"I survived. But, what about Gladys?" She asked urgently.

"They Faded." Gabriel said solemnly. "They're gone."

"Forever?" Grace asked, refusing to believe it.

"Forever." He confirmed slowly.

The Archangels muttered amongst themselves, uncomfortably swallowing the truth. "Sometimes the hardest truths are never the easy ones, and even more so, they are the truths that we wish to never hear." Gabriel hymned.

"No, there has to be a way to bring them back!" She cried.

Gabriel shook his head sympathetically. "I hate having to be the bearer of this news, but once someone has Faded, you cannot bring them back."

"You're wrong!" She interrupted.

"Grace, listen to Gabriel. He is speaking the truth." Lucy said calmly, her eyes welling up. Gladys Fading hurt her just as much as everyone else.

"No!" Grace defied. "Phil said something about Ancient Tools or something. What was it?"

"Phil? You mean, Death?" Lucy asked.

"Yes! He said something like: 'powerful Ancient Tools can create the Fade and more!'" Grace said, hoping someone would know what she was talking about.

Gabriel shook his head with a slight frown. "I know what you're trying to say Grace, but it's never been done because it's not possible to do. As heartbreaking as it is to hear—"

"Everyone needs to stop telling me things are impossible, because I've been told that since the moment I stepped foot here. Yet here I am: fighting alongside Satan and Lucy, and jumping from the Beast to save the Three Realms... I'm the proof that anything is possible!" Grace paused, trying to recall what Phil had said. "Have any of you been to the Academy for Angels?" She asked calmly this time.

Lucy smiled slightly, entertained by Grace's thought process.

They all shook their heads in confusion. "— Strictly speaking, the Academy for Angels is for Angels of Death only." said Gabriel.

"And you are the Archangels. Are you Angels of Death?" She asked.

"Well, no, but—"

"Then you *don't* know!" Grace exclaimed loudly.

"I think there's only one way to *really* answer Grace's question." Lucy said, opening a portal next to her. "Let's talk to him. I think we can all agree that he'll know more about it than any of us." Gabriel began to protest, but simply raised his hand to his chest and smiled graciously.

Holding a mug of coffee in one hand and stroking his long beard with the other, Phil appeared through the portal, smiling when he saw Lucy. "Ah, my dear Lucy it's *you* who called me. I couldn't remember whose aura's whose — they all blend into one!" He adjusted his glasses, smiling and waving when he recognised the Archangels, and paused when he saw Grace. "Now... *you've* changed since we last met." He said smiling deeply.

"She has the Shimmer." Lucy stated.

"Officially?" Phil asked, leaning sideways to Lucy.

"Officially."

"Oh, well yes, I mean, as changes go that, eh... that's quite the change." He said adjusting his glasses, taking in Grace's glow. "Now, I take it I haven't been brought here for a chat about your Shimmer."

"Can you bring someone back from the Fade?" Grace asked quickly, not realising how fast the words came out of her mouth.

"Oh yes." Phil said, taking a sip of coffee from his mug. Grace laughed and simply gestured to Phil while looking at everyone else to prove she was right. "...But it's impossible." He added.

"W — What do you mean?" Grace asked, confused.

"Well, it's a little delicate and one of those never-ending-circle-paradox things, you see." He took his glasses off and wiped them on his long grey beard. "A living Soul must willingly give their life to bring back the Faded Soul. However, no living Soul is *aware* of the Fade when alive. Once they pass on and find out about the Fade, it is too late. It's a weird one, I grant you."

Everyone slowly turned to look at Grace. She didn't fully understand as everyone gave her expressions of hope and sympathy.

"What are you all — Oh yes, I see." Phil said, placing his glasses on his face and tipping his head.

Satan walked up from behind Grace and laid a large, gentle hand on her shoulder. "No one is asking you to give up your life, Grace. This is your decision. Whatever it is, we understand and will *all* respect it." He said with a glint of water in his eyes.

Grace laughed, and everyone looked at her confused. "I'm an idiot." She said. "Gabe will be fine. He was always going to be okay. He wasn't *really* in danger; it was all to just get me here, right?" She asked Lucy.

"I'll ensure that your friend is safe." She said sincerely.

"It was that simple?" Grace laughed louder. "Wow... I feel like I'm about to wake up and point to people who look like you all and say, '...And you were there, and you were there...'" She ran her fingers through her glowing hair and took a deep breath. "Okay... If I decide to do it, can I speak to Gabe before I do?"

"Unfortunately, you cannot." Phil said, stroking his beard.

"Please. What about my mum?" Grace pleaded. "Just a minute, a single minute!"

"If this were of my design, I would let you. It would be horrifyingly bittersweet and completely essential. However, we're stuck with the Department of Totems and Mementos, and I don't think they would grasp the urgency of your situation."

"Can't you break the rules?" Grace asked everyone individually. "You're Angels, Satan, Lucy! You're literally Death, for crying out loud!"

They all looked to Phil to see if there was something they could do together, but he shook his head slowly. "Grace, if I could, I would let you. I'm not just being mean for the sake of it."

Grace nodded, turned away from everyone, and took a moment to collect her thoughts. This small glimmer of hope meant she could survive the crash, see her mum and Gabe again, and return home. But she couldn't shake the overwhelming feeling that doing that would be the wrong choice.

Gladys.

She sniffed the tears away, knowing exactly what she was doing next. She turned back to Phil and smiled at him. "Okay... I'll do it."

Satan gasped, not believing what she said. "Are you sure?"

"No!" She said faking a laugh. "I've never been less sure. But all I know is that Gladys made me, a stranger, feel special. I'm not, but please, someone look me in the eye and tell me I'm the only person they ever made feel that way." Grace said, begging for an answer as complete silence fell among them all.

"See? Gladys made *everyone* feel special. And let's face it, I'm a bad person, so... I might as well finish my time bringing back someone everyone can't be without." Grace sighed.

Satan leant in and hugged Grace. Gabriel followed suit, as did Lucy.

"This is where I hope you all tell me this was just a test and there's a happier ending." Everyone awkwardly laughed at Grace's joke. Grace took a deep breath and smiled acceptingly at Phil, closed her eyes tightly, and braced. "Okay. I'm ready. Do it."

"Do what?" He asked, finishing his coffee.

"...Th— the thing..."

"What thing?" He asked, looking around.

"Whatever it is that you do to make me get Gladys back."

Phil chuckled. "Oh no, that's not something I do. You do it. I'm going straight back to Nowhere while you do. I'll often think of you!"

"What?" Grace asked, even more confused. "What do I do then?"

"You must go into the Fade, find Gladys, and bring them back. It's never been done before so I don't completely know myself, but I'm sure there will be a book about it somewhere!" He gestured back to the portal he had arrived in. "Let me go and find it!"

Grace was speechless, her mouth wide open. Moments ago, she was ready to be forgotten and taken by the Fade. Now she's being told she has to go and find Gladys to bring them back. At least, that's what Phil thinks.

"Hey! S'cuse me!" A husky voice shouted from the cavern's entrance. Everyone turned to see Brenda bustling towards them, waving them down. "Oh, what a journey. I've never been this far down before. It's so cold! Oh…" She took in everyone's dazed expression and pulled down her tight suit jacket, wiping her hands on her skirt to get rid of the remnants of powdered sugar. "Well, hello, Lucy, Satan, and Gabriel. Are *all* the Archangels here? Phil, is that you?" Her eyes fell on Grace. "Oh, sweetheart, just who I'm looking for! Look at you, you're glowing! Oh, you have the Shimmer!" She ran over and gave Grace a tight hug. "I'm so happy for you, I knew it from the start didn't I say?" Brenda said pointing a finger and winking at Grace. Brenda spun on the spot and noticed the melancholy mood amongst everyone. "I need to read rooms better. What's happened?"

"Brenda, let me walk you back to DLS, there's something I need to discuss with you." Gabriel said, acknowledging the news of what had happened to Gladys would be best coming from him.

"Oh no, I can't. I need to speak to Grace!" Brenda remembered.

"Me?" Grace asked, exhausted.

Brenda licked some melted chocolate from the side of her finger. "Well, there's a particularly special someone who's wanting to have a word with you because of something *you've* done. I told them they had the wrong person, and it could never be you, but his messenger was adamant and said you were needed in the Sphere immediately."

Grace watched the Archangels whisper to each other in a serious and hushed tone. She looked to Lucy who had closed her eyes and began to breathe meditatively. As she turned to Satan, he stared at her in worry but kept his mouth closed. She scratched her head trying to figure out who it was that needed to speak to her, and why everyone seemed a little on edge at the mention of the Sphere.

"Who's asking for me?" Grace asked, nervously.

Brenda sighed and pursed her lips. "Apparently, you stole JC's Grail..."

If you made it to the end… congratulations!

Thank you so much, and I sincerely hope you enjoyed my book. If you did enjoy it (even if you didn't) please feel free to tag me in your review of it on Instagram or TikTok @GeezahGobble as I would love to know what you thought.

Once again, thank you for going on this journey with me! Let's get ready for the next one…

Printed in Great Britain
by Amazon